Bake Off
Book Two in the Bake Believe Trilogy

© 2026 Cori Cooper

www.coristories.com

Cover Art by Lenore Stutznegger

www.lenorestutz.com

This book is a work of fiction. Names, characters, businesses, organizations, places, events and incidents either are the product of the author's imagination or are used fictitiously. Any resemblance to actual persons, living or dead, events, or locales is entirely coincidental.

ISBN 978-1-953491-37-4 (Paperback)

ASIN B09X6HV9B3 (Kindle Edition)

To Aimee, Amber, Harrison and Hannah. Four of the most witty, movie quoting, book devouring, goof-ball, awesome-sauce people I know. I love you more than ice cream!

1

Pumpkin Chocolate Chip Cookies

Why am I still in this car?

I blink about a zillion times, then squeeze my eyes shut. The sun is right in my face, burning my eyeballs out. Even when I burrow my head into my pillow, I can still see a purplish blob bouncing behind my eyelids.

My brain drags like a zombie moving through Jello. I didn't just sleep, I crash-napped. I try to remember the last thing I remember but it's like there wasn't a time before I drifted off to sleepy town. It's all a mess of randomness.

I peek my eyes open again; everything comes into focus very, very slowly.

The blur of shapes, scrubby bushes, and a wide field full of cows.

The van engine squeaks like hamsters on a wheel.

Dad pats the steering wheel, urging the van to go faster than the car we're trying to pass.

Mom scrunches down in her seat, reminding Dad we're in no hurry so he needs to chill-ax.

Bubby snores into his pillow behind me. I bet my cupcake-shaped measuring cups he's drooling.

Penny taps her feet to whatever music's traveling through her ear buds.

Oh yeah, and then there's my numb bum and the seatbelt lines etched into my cheek. Proof of what the last forty-eight hours have been like. I suddenly remember exactly what's going on here, right about the time I wish I could forget it again.

I groan and shift. My arms lay heavy on my pillow; my movements are as slow as snails in marshmallow creme.

"Are you awake?" Robyn's hot breath stings my cheek.

I squirm away, mushing my face into the cool glass window.

"Cat?"

Poke, poke, poke into my side.

"Cat?"

Poke, poke, poke.

"Cat!" Robyn shrieks right in my ear this time and shakes my arm like we're in the middle of an earthquake.

I bolt upright, my heart pumping. "What? Yes! I'm awake! I'm awake!"

"Finalmente!" Robyn thuds back into her seat, her hands slapping her legs. "You've been asleep forever and a day and a half!"

I rub my face, trying to smooth out the wrinkles, and look around.

Robyn, my bestest, most favoritest cousin in the whole wide universe—that I want to throw out the window right now—sits beside me.

I send her my best gremlin glare. "Robyn! What the heck?"

"We're here, Bean-up! You're missing everything. Wake up, wake up! This is the Best. Day. Ever!" She bounces all over the place: into the window, into me, ramming Mom's seat, hitting the ceiling, whacking my leg again...

She has had *way* too much sugar. I think it was a bad idea to stop for snacks at that Maverick in Flagstaff, and an even worse idea for Robyn to choose the jumbo pack of Sour Patch Kids.

Is she right though? Are we really here? I was kind of thinking I would spend the rest of eternity in this car. We've been driving so long I'm not sure what life was like before I buckled up, buttercup. I lean into my window again, trying to see something other than thirsty, squatty trees.

"Look! Look! Look!" Robyn thwacks my arms and legs some more in her excitement.

A bunch of old buildings line up along the main street like a row of hunched old men. Our car slows down, so I'm thinking the bakery has to be one of these buildings.

But which one is it?

My heart gets stuck somewhere in my throat, making it hard to swallow. I've waited *months* for this moment, months that felt like *years*.

And now it's here!

I finally get to see the family bakery. I finally get to meet my Great Grammy Ginny, who used to live in fancy pants France, and my mom's little sister, Aunt Jojo! And maybe, just maybe, I can finally figure out why my family is so stinking weird.

Toward the end of the parade of shops is a sunny yellow sign with a turquoise border that says *L'Amour Bakin'*. It waves in the breeze like a hand, welcoming us.

"We're here!" I screech, all sleepiness gone. I am about to burst into the air like a firecracker and explode in hot pinks and lime greens so the world knows how over-the-top excited I am.

Bubby groans, pulling his pillow over his head.

"Wake up, you slug-a-bug!" I wad up my blanket and toss it over the seat behind me.

He snuggles it up to his chin with a sleepy, "Thanks."

Yeah, he's a lost cause.

I fumble with my seatbelt buckle as Dad eases the car into a parking space in front of the bakery. With hulk strength I overpower the motorized sliding door until there is a gap large enough for me to slip through, then I fly around to Robyn's side and do the same to her door.

"We're here, we're here, we're here!" I jump into the air, taking Robyn with me. We aren't quite in sync; her up throws off my down and we both crash into the car.

"You guys are so weird." Penny steps out of the van, then grabs the arch of her foot and pulls her leg straight up next to her face in a stretch that looks completely unnatural.

And painful.

Bubby is limp as licorice, so Dad has no trouble lifting him out of the back of the car. It's when Dad tries to set Bubby on his feet on the pavement that things get dicey. Bubby leans into Dad's leg and blinks with heavy eyelids; his thumb sneaks to his lips.

The kid looks like he's about to timber into the bushes.

Dad rests a hand on Bubby's head and takes a deep breath, letting it out slowly. I copycat him to see what that's all about. The air is crisp and clean, like it is in the mountains around Boise. It's the kind of air you want to fill your lungs with and hold onto. It makes me think of fall and love and happiness and home.

In fact, this whole place feels like coming home after a long, tiring trip.

Which, in a way, I guess we are.

Dad smacks the hood with his palm. "Wow. I forgot how much I love this town. Coming, Bridge?"

Mom slowly steps out of the car, her face pinched. Her eyes dart around, not stopping on anything for more than a couple seconds. She looks like she wants to run screaming down the street with both hands waving in the air.

That would be funny!

But also, supes embarrassing.

I better do something.

I skip over and throw my arms around Mom's waist, squeezing her guts out.

Mom laughs and hugs me back. I don't think she can help it; I'm kind of irresistible, you know.

"We're here!" Robyn reaches for Mom's hand.

The smile that was just starting to climb, falls fifty stories. Mom's arms go stiff at her sides. Her lips flip upside down, the corners stretching to her chin.

I follow her gaze to the door of the bakery, which just swung open. A tiny lady with snow white hair that curls around her ears toddles towards us. She clings to the arm of my mom's clone. Except this version is younger, and her blonde hair is cut in an A-line bob with bright blue tips.

Aunt Jojo.

And the lady with her has to be Great Grammy Ginny.

They wave like they are trying to bring us faster to them with just the power of their arms.

Or bring them faster to us.

Or whatever.

Great Grammy Ginny takes tiny, mincing steps that make it seem like she walks in slow motion, but she covers the ground in no time at all. Once she is within reach, she throws her arms around my mom.

"I can't believe my eyes! Oh, my Bridget, my love. You've come home!" Her voice is a tinkling bell that slips into my soul and quivers.

I love her already!

The top of her cutesy-patootsie head comes to my shoulder, and I am kind of a shrimp. Next to Robyn, Great Grammy Ginny looks like a little kid. She's plumpish, in a cozy way, with brown eyes that look almost black. The weird thing is, even though she has old lady hair, her face is young, with zero wrinkles. When she pulls me down into a tight hug, the scent of vanilla and cinnamon cling to me too.

"Oh, we are so happy to have you here!"

"Me too." I raise my voice, since my mouth is still muffled into her hair. "Thank you for letting us come visit, Great Grammy Ginny."

"Oh no, no no," she tuts, pulling away. "That is too much of a mouthful. You call me GG. That's easy, no?"

"No, I mean yes, GG."

She takes my face between her palms and stares at me with so much focus I start to wonder if I have a booger or something hairy in my teeth. "You are how old? Remind me."

"Fourteen."

"Hmmm." GG's eyes dart across my face a moment longer, then she squishes my cheeks so my lips poof out. "You are the most beautiful girl. I wait my whole life to see you here!"

I try to smile, but my lips won't move upwards with her hands there. They pooch out like I'm eating a lemon. It's okay, though; she's not paying attention to my expression—she's too busy smacking big smooches on each side of my face.

GG pats my cheek and turns to squeeze the life out of Robyn. I watch for half a second before I disappear into a tangle of arms and fringy green kimono.

"Cat, Cat, Cat!" Soft hair tickles my cheek as Jojo gives me an anaconda squeeze. Right when I think she will let go, her arms get tighter. I gulp a breath and disappear into her shoulder again. Even if I could think of something to say right now, there wouldn't be enough air to pull it off.

But that's not a bad thing.

I wouldn't move right now for a whole tray of ooey gooey brownies.

Jojo leans away, keeping her hands on my shoulders. She stares at me the way GG did, like she's trying to find out everything about me at a glance. Tears glisten in the corners of her eyes, but don't fall. When she smiles, cute little wrinkle lines move from her eyes to her hairline.

"I can't tell you how happy I am to see you." She twirls a lock of my hair around her finger. "I started to write you a letter so many times, but couldn't find the words. I am glad, glad, *glad* that you guys are here!"

I try to answer, but there's something stuck in my throat. Even when I clear it, the thing stays put. It's having the weirdest effect on my eyes... They like, sting and stuff.

Prickles.

And now there's a tear sliding down my cheek.

Yeah.

I have no idea.

Jojo plants a noisy kiss on my forehead. "I can't wait to get to know you. I can't wait to find out everything about everything. I only wish you guys were here longer—a week is not enough time to catch up on forever! Robyn, come here, girlfriend!" Jojo stretches one of her arms to enfold Robyn and pull her to us.

Robyn rests her cheek against Jojo's head. "This is, like, my dream come true!"

Jojo laughs. "Seriously, Cat, every year, Robyn says, 'Cat would love this, I wish I could show this to Cat, I'll have to tell Cat about everything'!"

"Really?"

Jojo and Robyn nod together.

It makes me feel all rosy glowy inside.

"Jojo!" Bubby interrupts the love fest, tugging her hand. "GG Grammy G said you have cookies for me."

"Oh shoot!" Jojo slaps her palm against her forehead with a thump that makes Bubby giggle. "I am so silly. I left them inside. Come with me, Mr. Andy-roo. Let's go on a super-secret mission to get some cookies!"

Jojo takes Bubby's hand, and they disappear into the bakery.

I watch them go; part of me wants to see the inside so bad I can't wait another millisecond, but I stay put. I don't know why exactly, except that there are so many feelings I'm feeling. Maybe I just need a few more minutes to feel them all. It's a super good thing I'm not trying to bake right now. If I did, the results would be *Cat*-astrophic, I'm pretty sure.

So, I'm just going to just lolly-gag here for a little while longer and soak it all in.

GG and Dad stand with Penny between them, pointing up and down the street. Knowing my dad, they are probably talking about all the things that have changed in the one hundred and fifty thousand years since he was here last.

Wait, where is my mom?

Oh.

She's back in the car, rooting through her purse. At least, that's what she appears to be doing. For realsies, I think she's hiding. It doesn't take that long to find chapstick or tissues.

It is obvious she needs me.

Before I make my move, Robyn puts her hand on my arm.

"Cat?" She shifts from foot to foot. "I have to talk to you." Her face is so serious, my breath catches.

Did something bad happen while I was taking my car nap? Did Black Gryphon stop making YouTube videos? Or worse! Did they discontinue my favorite shade of nail polish: Bubble Gum Cotton Candy Glitter Pink Happy Dreams?

Robyn takes a deep breath. "GG and Jojo love pumpkin."

"Okay?" I'm still thinking about the nail polish, so it's hard to focus on Robyn's words.

"I mean, they love to bake with pumpkin. A lot. Especially in the fall."

I wrinkle my nose.

"Stop that!" Robyn cuffs my shoulder. "It's Thanksgiving; there's going to be a lot of things made out of pumpkin. It's practically a rule!"

"A dumb rule." I shake my head. "Vegetables do *not* belong in dessert."

"It's not all bad. Like, pumpkin pie, you know you really only taste the whipped cream."

"Yeah, if you put whipped cream on like you do!" I mime swirling to the sky.

Robyn swats my hand away from her face. "Anyway, just please don't hurt their feelings, okay?"

Like I am a complete Neanderthal.

"Okay, I won't. I'll just take a bite and spit it in their faces, slap my tongue, and scream."

Robyn rolls her eyes. "Yeah, okay, you do that."

I cross my eyes and stick out my tongue.

"Super mature, Cat. I'm being serious. You have to promise." Robyn holds out her pinkie.

She really wants me to make a super serious unbreakable pinkie promise?

Over pumpkin?

Why is this such a big deal?

I don't know the answer to that, but it obviously is. I mean, Robyn's stubborn face is no joke. I can't remember a single time in my whole life when I got out of doing something after Robyn looked at me like this. So, I guess I'm going to have to suffer through eating pumpkin.

Seriously though, why do people put vegetables and raisins in things? It's not as if there aren't any other options. Like, right now I can name three things to use instead, without even straining my brain.

Chocolate chips,

Gummy bears,

And

Sprinkles.

Lots and lots of sprinkles.

Now I'm hungry. Where's Jojo with those cookies?

"Fine." I heave a great sigh. "I promise I won't be a stink brain about the pumpkin. Happy?"

"I guess that will work." Robyn grips my pinkie with hers, then looks over my shoulder. "Hey, what's up with your mom?"

"I don't know, I was just on my way over to check. Wanna come?"

Robyn's eyes move to the van and back again. She shakes her head. "I think I'll wait here."

I shrug and skip over to the van. "Hey, Mommy, Mom, Mom." I lean on the open door, resting my cheek against the smooth metal.

"Hey, Kitty Cat."

"You okay?"

Mom sighs and looks up at me. "I'm okay."

I nod like I'm convinced, but I'm not. "Liar."

"Yeah, maybe." Mom scootches over and stretches her arm out to the side so there's room on the seat next to her.

"Okay, tell me everything." I slide into the nice Cat-sized space she created for me and pull her arm tight around my shoulder. "Why are you hiding?"

Mom sighs. "You know why. We talked about this. It's just really hard for me to come back here."

"Because of Jojo?"

"Partly." Mom stares out the windshield at the bakery and shivers. "But also, the whole bakery and baking thing and this place. So many memories."

I'm no Robyn when it comes to figuring people out; but based on Mom's grimace I'm guessing her memories are pretty much the worst.

"Yeah, well..." I twirl a loose string from my shirt. "Thank you for doing this for me, Mom."

"Oh, Cat." Mom snuggles me closer. "I didn't mean to sound like I don't want to be here or I'm a martyr to your cause or something. This is just hard, but"—she takes a deep breath—"I can do hard things, right?"

"Yes," I agree, because it's true. "You can."

"Right." Mom leans back so she can see my face. "And so can you. You know, I have this feeling..."

Uh-oh.

My mom's feelings usually mean I have to clean something.

"You and I, we might need to do some adjusting on this trip. I don't know what's going to happen exactly, but I think it would be good for us if we decide to go along with everything. You know what I mean?"

My blank stare says more than words.

"What I mean is I'm going to let all my expectations go, and I think this will be good for you too. What if we decide right now that we will be super flexible?"

I instantly picture Penny and her impossible ballerina stretches. There's no way I can make my legs do those things. "Flexible?"

"This trip could be uncomfortable; we might have to stretch a little." Mom sounds like she's talking more to herself than to me. "So, what if we made the choice to be good for whatever? I think we could make this trip pretty great if we are just good for whatever. What do you think?"

"I think..." I pause to think about what I think. There's a lot of thoughts in there and I haven't had a chance to sort any of them into piles.

My mom smiles and rubs my back. "Let's just try, okay? Will you try with me?"

The fruity scent of Mom's lotion and the rustling breeze quiet my mind so her words work their way into my brain. Like a worm. But not a bad one. More like a caterpillar. If I let it stay for a while, it might transmogrify into something butterfly level amazing.

I know this is hard for Mom; she doesn't want to be here, but she is.

Because of me.

So that I can learn how to bake responsibly instead of emotionally. If she can do that for me, then I can for sure be good for whatever with her.

Right?

Right!

I nod with so much enthusiasm that some of my hair flies out of my half ponytail. As I brush it back into place, Mom's eyes light up with zeal.

"That's my girl. We can do this. I am ninety-nine percent sure we are going to survive this week."

"Those are pretty good odds."

"Pretty good indeed. Look, there's Jojo. Come on." She tickles me until I squirm out of the car, then she stands up and takes my hand. We walk over to Jojo and Bubby, who are handing out cookies.

Horrible, orangey-brown lumps that look like unspeakable things.

I paste a smile on my face and take a cookie from the plate Bubby offers me, but don't eat it. Instead, I hide it in my hand and lean over to look at the one Robyn has. "What is it?"

"Pumpkin chocolate chip." She takes a huge bite. "My favorite!"

I'm sorry. It does not look good before—or after—the chewing.

No one is paying attention to me, so I discreetly dissect the cookie in my hand. I really don't want to eat it; it looks obscene, and pumpkin is super gross. That pact with my mom is the worst timing. I should have made it *after* the cookies were passed around.

A hand squeezes my shoulder and I look up at my mom. Her eyes widen, then she winks. "Good for whatever," she whispers. Then, with a deep breath, she slips between Robyn and I to stand in front of Jojo.

"Hello, Jolynn." Her voice is really loud.

Jojo startles, almost toppling the plate from her hands to the asphalt. She turns slowly. "Bridget."

Mom presses her lips together, then relaxes into a smile. "Yes, hello. It's been a long time. How have you been?"

It's not the smoothest delivery, but no one can doubt Mom's sincerity.

Tears leak down Jojo's cheeks without warning—not even a lip quiver. It's like when Bubby forgets to turn the nozzle on the bathtub all the way off, and it leaks steadily into the tub. She pushes the plate of cookies into GG's hands and throws her arms around my mom.

"Oh, Bridge! Thank you! I thought you hated my guts. I'm so glad you talked first. I don't think I could have done it; I've been so scared! But now, now it's all okay, right? We can be friends again?"

My mom bursts into noisy tears that make the rest of us find sudden interest in whatever is on the ground. This is a thousand times more awkward than a middle school dance. I peek up at them after a few seconds though, 'cause I have to look. Like when someone has toilet paper stuck to their shoes.

GG clasps her hands at her heart with a smile that could light Batman's cave. Robyn can't stop hopping in place. Dad watches with each arm around Penny and Bubby. Just when I think I'm the only one geeked out by all the feelings, Dad catches my eye.

"Walk," he mouths, jabbing his thumb behind him.

I nod as the three of them turn up the street. Should I go with? That might be better than watching this scene.

Before I decide to do it, Mom's arm shoots out and pulls me to her.

"I can't tell you how relieved I am." Jojo wipes her eyes. "Or how many times I thought about flying to Boise and showing up on your doorstep. It's just hard to get away from the bakery and I thought you'd slam the door in my face. I've been so terrified to see you. Seriously, I hardly slept at all this whole entire week!"

Mom gulps. "I'm so sorry, Jo. I'm sorry I haven't called or written or come home. I'm sorry—"

"No!" Jojo grabs Mom's hands. "I'm sorry! I'm so, so sorry, about everything!"

It is very obvious they are about to start bawling again, and since I'm trapped in my mom's elbow and can't make a getaway, I have to do something.

Quick.

The only problem is I can't think of a single thing to say to change the subject. I mean, nothing that will work outside my head anyway.

'That was fun, now why don't you tell us all the family secrets?'

Or

'Great, now let's talk about my emotional baking problems.'

Or

'What do you think Noah Centineo eats for breakfast?'

Yeah, none of those things make sense in the current moment. The only thing I have to work with is the cookie in my hand. "These are really good cookies," I say before my brain catches up to remind me that I haven't eaten it yet and that, oh yeah, I don't want to.

Thanks a lot, slow poke brain!

"Did you try it?" Robyn blinks in surprise.

"No," I shift from side to side, "But everyone really loves them. You've eaten, like, four."

Robyn looks at the cookie in her hand. "This is number six."

GG laughs and pinches Robyn's cheek before she looks at me. "It is okay if you don't like the cookie, my Cat."

I turn the cookie from one palm to the other. The chocolate is starting to melt and leaves pockmarks on my palms. Even though I know GG means what she says, I can't bring myself to throw the cookie away. Mostly because Robyn's stern eyes warn me she will do something heinous if I do. It's obvious whatever it is she's contemplating is a thousand times worse than eating a vegetable cookie. But what really gets me is my mom. She just spoke to Jojo, even though she's been dreading it for weeks.

If she can do that, I can eat a cookie.

"Just try it, *gata*." Robyn gives a tight laugh. "You're being *ridiculouso*. You can't say you don't like something until you've tried it."

"Oh really?" I stand on tippy toes so I'm closer to Robyn's height. "What about Skittle nachos?"

Robyn's face contorts. "That's different, Cat, and you know it!"

"Is it?"

"It is! Skittle nachos are an abomination."

"What are Skittle nachos?" Jojo asks.

"Believe me, you don't want to know." I look at the cookie again. Maybe I could try it. Maybe it tastes better than it looks. Like those no-bake cookies Tobey and I scooped and plopped in Culinary. They looked like dog doo, but they were delicious.

At least, I think they were. I didn't actually try any before Tobey got all infused with sadness. But since he ate a bunch of them, I know they weren't disgusting.

Ugh, I'm going to eat it. We all know I'm going to eat it. It's just so hard to bring my hand to my mouth. Especially with everyone watching me. This is way more awkward than my mom and Jojo's reunion. I was young and innocent when I thought that was super uncomfortable. Try eating something disgusting in front of a bunch of people who want you to like it!

I bring the cookie to my lips, holding my breath so I don't have to breathe in the pumpkin smell. Just concentrate on the chocolate.

Chocolate, chocolate, chocolate.

I open my mouth and take a tiny nibble.

"Atta girl." Mom smiles.

Okay, but here's the thing, the cookie is actually super delicious. That tiny nibble is not enough. I avoid looking at everyone else as I shove the rest of the cookie into my mouth and lick my fingers and palm. My taste buds jump in delight.

I swallow, super sad it's all gone.

Oh yeah, and also, I'm super sad because Robyn is going to rub this in until the day I die. Maybe longer. I can totally picture her sitting on my crumbling gravestone with a plate of pumpkin cookies, talking about how I thought I would hate them, but I really liked them.

But Robyn has more self-control than I thought. She puts her hand on my shoulder without any rubbing at all. "Not bad, huh?"

I barely hear her words because there's this sudden flutter in my belly like the first time I met Tobey. It spreads through my arms, leaving tingles that fade slowly as parts of my face lift upwards. Mouth, cheeks, then eyebrows. I can't remember any bad things, only good things everywhere I look.

I love this place!

I love these people!

I love this cookie!

I fling my hands out to the sides. "Are you kidding? Not bad? More like fantasticalsome!"

This switcheroo of feelings is so out of nowhere I have to wonder if it is the cookies. Did they bake something into them? I mean, besides pumpkin and chocolate chips?

An emotion?

And if they do bake emotions into the stuff they sell, how do they control it?

I sure can't.

If I made these cookies, we wouldn't just be feeling happy, we'd all be laughing our heads off and running around in circles, bouncing off each other. Is this pumpkin chocolate chip cookie proof that it's possible to bake emotions without people going all cuckoo?

My body fills up like a helium balloon. If it is possible, I'm going to do it. I'm going to figure this out and conquer it.

By the end of this trip, I will know how to bake without making people go bonkers.

I will.

Pumpkin Chocolate Chip Cookies

2 C. Pumpkin
1 C. Sugar
1 C. Butter, softened
2 tsp Vanilla extract
2 Eggs
5 C. Flour
1 tsp Baking Powder
1 tsp Baking Soda
1/2 tsp Salt
2 tsp Cinnamon
1 tsp Pumpkin Pie Spice
1 & 1/2 C. Chocolate Chips

Preheat the oven to 350°F.

Prepare 4-5 cookie sheets with cooking spray, 'cause this recipe makes a butt-ton of cookies! That's not a bad thing, by the way; they freeze super well and are the most deliciousest thing you will ever put in your mouth.

90% sure.

Pro tip for the day: use a stand mixer. This is such a big batch; the dough gets super thick and might burn out your hand mixer. I mean, I assume it might, not that I know that. I mean, I have totally not gone through four hand mixers in the last two years.

That would be ridiculous.

Combine pumpkin, sugar, butter, vanilla, and eggs in the mixer bowl.

Separately mix together flour, baking powder, baking soda, cinnamon, and pumpkin pie spice.

Here's a little tipperoo: I add the chocolate chips here, even though the original recipe says to add them later.

Gasp!

It's true. It's true, I tell ya! I have a good reason, though, hear me out. The flour coats the chocolate chips, making them mix into the batter more evenly. True story! No more sad, depraved, chocolate-less cookies because some cookies have all the luck. Now they can all be friends and dwell together in perfect harmony.

So now, slowly add the dry stuff to the wet stuff in the mixer bowl while it's on low. Any higher than that and you'll get flour to the face.

Despite what naturalists say, flour doesn't do anything for the complexion.

Mix just barely until the wet and dry are combined. It's okay if it's lumpy. You just want to be sure there aren't any rogue dry flour pockets.

Ew.

Use a cookie scoop to measure 15-20 cookies per cookie sheet. They usually expand up instead of out, so you can probably squish 20 on there.

Bake for 12-15 minutes. Let cool completely on the cookie sheet.
Eat them while they're warm.
Trust me on this one.

2

Macarons

When we finally move our keisters from the parking lot into the bakery, the first thing I notice are the smells.

Pumpkin and spices and cinnamon and sugar. I didn't know sugar had a smell, but it totally does. I stop at the entrance and breathe it all in, almost making Mom and GG bump into my back.

They catch themselves just in time.

Which is good, 'cause I can't move right now. I am all frozen in place.

There's that twist in my belly, and my knees feel kind of shaky.

My heart is pounding.

Oh my goshness!

I totally just fell in love.

With a bakery!

"Keep moving, kiddo," Mom prompts and I start walking again, though I can't seem to connect my feet to my brain. I collide with a chair and bounce off a table, finally ending up at the glass bakery counter where I let out a whoosh of air.

Is it even possible to fall in love with a thing?

I can't say for sure, but I do know this is exactly what happened when I first saw Tobey.

Robyn comes over to stand next to me.. She peers into the glass display counter, her lips moving without any sound coming out. I lean over to see for myself what she's looking at.

Most of the shelves are empty, with chalkboard labels to explain what goes where, but the top row is filled with colorful sandwich cookies. Lime green, aqua blue, cotton candy pink, skittles purple, and banana yellow. They look so fun! My fingers dance along the top, wanting to snatch one.

"What are these things?" This is such a whisper moment I can barely hear my own voice.

"Macarons." Robyn whispers too; she totally gets me.

"Huh?" Or should I have said *Gesundheit*?

"Macarons." Robyn gets a dreamy look on her face. "They are French cookies, crunchy but chewy, and *so* yummy. But why are they still here? Didn't they sell?"

We both look around for GG or Jojo. I want to know the answer too.

"Ah." GG taps the side of her nose. "We make them a day ahead. Macarons are like these old bones; they need a rest to be the best."

Everyone giggles, except for me. What she said is cute, and better yet, it rhymes, but I'm too distracted reading all the labels from the empty trays below to get carried away right now.

French Bread,

Cinnamon Rolls,

Scones,

Madeleines,

Pain du Chocolat,

Cream Puffs,

Eclairs,

Sable,

Palmier,

Napoleon...

Isn't that a movie?

I have no idea what I'm reading.

Cream puffs and eclairs, I've had those before. Also, I know scones, French bread, and cinnamon rolls, but other than those things?

Totally clueless.

It is super inconvenient that Mom has my phone in her purse. I mean, I get her point that we're all together and I don't really *need* it, but I do need it. I need to look all this weird stuff up and see what it is, so I don't look like an uncultured swine.

Where is Mom anyway?

Oh, there she is, standing in the doorway with her arms wrapped around herself, as if she is freezing or has the willies.

There's a deep V in the space where her eyebrows are supposed to be, and her lips have totally disappeared into the thin line she's still pressing.

Now is probably not the best time to ask her if I can have my phone. Not when she's already on the edge. While we were driving and she thought I wasn't listening, she told Dad she's all worried about me getting addicted to my cell phone and living in their basement eating fruit loops for the rest of my life.

Like that would happen!

I don't even like fruit loops.

If I want my phone, which I do, I'll have to lighten her up and distract her from her stressful thoughts.

I run over, grab her arm, and pull her to the display. "Lookie, what is all this stuff? If you could have any one of these things right now, which one would you choose?"

My mom gives the labels a bare smidgen of her attention, then shrugs. Her eyes flicker from one corner of the room to the other.

I think she wants to run screaming down the street again.

"Does it look the same?" I try to pull her attention to me with words.

Mom blinks.

"The bakery," I say very slowly. "Does it look how you remember?"

"Mama told me everything is just like when she was a girl except the curtains. They used to be lime green. But, actually"—Robyn tips her head to the side—"those tables look different."

"Good eye, Robyn, my girl!" Jojo flicks a crumb off the counter. "We just replaced the tables a month ago. What do you think?"

"I *love* them!" Robyn grins.

I don't know what tables and chairs they used to have, but I love these too. Each table is small and round with two decorative iron chairs. It's like a chic outdoor cafe in Paris.

Not that I've been there, but sometimes I see pictures of things.

"Yay!" Jojo twirls in place. "I'm so happy you like them! I really agonized over this decision; the poofs were falling apart, and we needed to make a change."

Something like cloud cover moves across Jojo's face. She shakes her head and smiles sunshine-bright again. "What do you think, Bridge?"

"Hm?" Mom runs her fingers along the curved edge of the counter.

GG tuts as she walks across the hardwood floor. "This is hard for you, my Bridget, but it doesn't have to be. The bakery is your blood, it always will welcome you." She slips her arm through Mom's elbow.

"I don't know about that."

"I do," GG says firmly. "Now, blues shoo-shoo. In this place, we 'Bake Happy'!" She swings her arm above the cash register.

I follow the arch and stop at a large sign on a piece of barn wood that says those words, *'Bake Happy'*.

That's right! I almost forgot Marissa and Mom told us that's our family motto.

I squeeze my mom's hand to remind her that we are good for anything. She gives me a small smile and nods. "Yes, the chairs are lovely, good choice."

"Yay!" Jojo claps, then stops abruptly. "Oh! Guess what else is new around here?"

"What?" Robyn and I say at the same time.

"Mr. Bojangles!" Jojo squeals.

I look at Robyn; is that a code word for something?

Robyn shrugs.

Jojo holds out her palms so we can see each long finger as she wiggles them in our faces. "My. New. Mixer!"

Mom covers her mouth, shoulders shaking. I think she's finally starting to thaw out. "Jojo! I can't believe you still name all your stuff!"

Jojo moves her hands to her hips like she's upset, but her face says otherwise. "And why not? Who says our stuff isn't alive? Mom swears her keys wander off on their own all the time."

Mom ducks her head. A very unhuman-like snort leaks from between her fingers. She's not quite herself today, so I swallow my piggie jokes to give her a break. When Robyn catches my eye, I twirl my finger around the side of my head.

"They are super *loco*." Robyn grins, then the corners of her mouth drop. "I wish Mama was here, she would *love* this! She should be here with her sisters and her Grammy, not at home alone while Papa does stinking overtime."

I hug her arm. "Well, I'm glad *you're* here."

Robyn rests her cheek on the top of my head. "Me too, I just wish Papa didn't have to work all the holidays. I wish he got time off like *Tio* Drew. Then we would all be here, and it would be totally perfect."

I lean back to look at Robyn's face.

Interesting.

I spend a super lot of time wishing my family was like Robyn's family, but it never occurred to me that she might do the same thing.

That's something to think about, I think.

GG brushes a lock of hair out of Robyn's eyes. "We always miss those who aren't with us. But maybe they are here in the spirit. No?"

"*Sí.*" Robyn pulls her phone out of her back pocket. "I'm going to go call Mama, so she knows we got here safely."

"Tell her to tell Tonio hi for me."

I seriously love that guy.

Robyn nods and takes her phone a short distance away so I can't eavesdrop.

Because I was totally gonna.

"Hey, wait a second!" I just realized something else. "Where's Granny P?"

"Oh." GG's eyebrows lower, but she smiles. "That Penelope! Off she goes to Jamaica for the holiday."

"What?" Mom blinks. "She's not here? I thought she said she would be here."

"She did." GG shakes her head. But you know your mama, a thought flitters into her brain and she goes to chase it."

Jojo swings herself up to sit on the counter. "She said she couldn't stand the thought of another freezing cold Thanksgiving in the bakery with all that pumpkin." Her voice goes lower with the last words, like she's trying to sound like Granny.

She doesn't, at all, but it was a valiant effort.

Mom frowns. "I was really looking forward to seeing her."

"Never fear, she might get bored and come home early." Jojo chuckles, then leaps off the counter. "In the meantime, I want to show you everything! Let's go on a tour of the bakery! You have to see Mr. Bojangles. He is so dreamy! The dough hook is this long!" She extends her arm to show us. "I should have traded Ringo in a long time ago, but he was such a good old boy I couldn't bring myself to do it!"

Robyn walks back from calling her mom, tucking her phone into her back pocket with a brave smile.

"All better?"

She nods. "I just needed to hear her voice. What are we doing?"

"Touring the bakery."

"And Mr. Bojangles!" Jojo sing-songs.

I lean into Robyn with a giggle. "She talks like the mixers are her boyfriends!"

Jojo looks over her shoulder, as we follow her into the kitchen. "What was that?"

"Cat thinks you need a man!" Robyn says in such a loud voice that it echoes back to us.

GG and Mom belly laugh.

I gasp from the bus Robyn just threw me under, too flabbergasted to defend myself.

Jojo stops and twirls around, her hip jutted out. "I do not need a man! I don't even want to talk about men unless they come in stainless steel with five speeds." She blows me a kiss and then dances over to the mixer.

While Robyn and Mom *ooh* and *ahh* through Jojo's enraptured monologue on the virtues of commercial grade appliances, I look around.

The kitchen is ginormous, for one thing, way bigger than our kitchen at home. I think we could fit ours into this one at least four times. One whole wall is shiny silver cupboards that practically beg me to open them. My fingers get a little tingly so I lace them together as I imagine all the super fun things that might be inside.

Sprinkles.

Lots and lots of sprinkles.

Powdered sugar.

Huge sugar granules for muffins, yum!

Chocolate chips.

Mini, dark, milk, white, butterscotch.

Cookie cutters and icing bags and spatulas.

Oh my!

I wonder if they have fondant, since I finally know what that stuff is. I've been watching a lot of bake-off shows. But I think fondant is like a wedding cake bakery thing, so probably they don't have it in a normal bakery like this one.

Under the cupboards is a long counter, completely clear of clutter and winking in the bright lights. This is my favorite part so far. At school, my kitchen in Culinary barely fits the four people in my group. There is just one tiny counter by the sink and it usually gets loaded with the dirty dishes.

When we made bread a couple weeks ago, Paisley, Brigg, Tobey and I had to take the dough to our table to have room to knead it. A counter like this would be magical.

I turn away with the sigh of a martyr and instantly forget what I was martyring about. There are four, count that, *four* refrigerators! *Mammoth* refrigerators!

I go off in dreamy contemplation at how much butter they could hold.

So much buttery, buttered deliciousness.

Wait a second.

The sink! The sink is *huge*. Holy cow, I could take a bath in that thing! Well, I could if I thought bathing in the kitchen was a good idea—which I don't, by the way.

I move closer to check it out. There's no divider in the middle like other sinks I've seen, just a big rectangle that could fit whole ginormous cookie sheets without having to flip them mid-wash.

Wow.

Just, wow.

And *two* dishwashers—big ones, *gargantuan* ones—the mother and father of all dishwashers. We definitely need those at our house. With two of those babies, I might never have to do the dishes again!

There is also an island in the center of the kitchen with a bin attached to the side that has a plastic lid. My curiosity pulls me over to it. No one pays any attention to me, so I think it's okay for me to tug the lid off. Inside, at the bottom, is a smattering of white flour.

I step back. This whole hugey thing is for *flour*? How much flour do these people use, exactly? This bin is like the size of my whole house.

Okay, not really, but almost.

I could make *so* many brownies with this much flour.

Dozens and dozens of cookies and cinnamon rolls...

"So," Robyn says, breaking my revelry with irresistible words, "Jojo, who are you *dating* these days?"

I drop the lid back over the flour and scoot to where everyone else is standing. This is what I'm talking about—things just got super-duper interesting up in here.

"Who says I'm *dating* anyone?" Jojo runs a hand over the top of Mr. Bojangles' gleaming surface. "Didn't I just get done saying I don't need a man?"

"But..." Robyn purses her lips. "What happened to that one guy?"

Mom perks up, so I know she's interested, but she keeps opening drawers and moving things around inside like she isn't listening.

Jojo grabs a dish towel off the counter and folds it with tight lines into a teeny, tiny square. "What guy?"

Robyn chews her bottom lip. "I think his name was Jake?"

The towel drops to the ground. When Jojo stoops to pick it up, her ears are bright red. "Nope. Definitely not dating anyone."

Robyn opens her mouth to ask why, the word already formed on her lips, but GG flutters her hands across the counter, effectively distracting us.

"We have seen the kitchen; shall we go on a tour of the rest of the house? Your room is just as you left it, Bridget; you'll want to show Cat, of course."

"Hey, wait! Do you still have your list of all the cat names in your room?" I bounce from one foot to the other.

Mom laughs. "What? I forgot all about that! I bet it is in there. I know I don't have it at home. Let's go find Dad and the kids; they will want to see the house, too."

Just as we all get back into the main bakery, my dad walks in with Penny and Bubby close on his heels.

"What is that smell?" Robyn clamps her hands over her nose and mouth.

I do the same; there is a vile stench wafting in neon green waves over the top of my siblings. Seriously, it's so strong I can *see* it!

What? Did they, like, take a bath in a latrine?

Dad shakes his head. "Oh, nothing. It's fine. Just, we're going to go take some showers, right, guys?"

Penny nods miserably, but Bubby looks like he found the toy at the bottom of the cereal box.

"We fell in the water! In the crick! And it was full of cow doodie!" He bounces on his toes, his body too little to contain all that excitement.

"The crick!" Jojo claps her hands. "I love it!"

GG steps forward. "The bathroom is up the stairs, at the end of the hall. You remember, Andrew?"

Dad nods.

"We have cleaned the towels and there should be soap. Please let me know if there is anything else you need."

"Soap should do it." Dad tilts his head towards the stairs. Penny drags her feet while Bubby prances ahead of her. If I was Penny, I'd use my elbows to get to the bathroom before him.

That smell will haunt my nightmares until the end of time.

"When you are done, we'll have supper." GG keeps her smile hidden until Penny's back is to us.

Dad waves without turning around. "We'll be back in a flash."

Mom pulls open one of the front windows, sending a cool breeze into the room.

Thank goodness.
I haven't taken a full breath since those stinkers walked into the bakery.

Macarons

Shells:
1 C. Powdered Sugar
2 C. superfine Almond Flour
5 Egg Whites - room temperature
1/2 tsp Salt
1/2 tsp Vanilla extract
2 drops Gel Food Coloring or ½ C. Cocoa Powder to make them chocolate. Yes Please!
Filling:
1 – 8oz pkg Cream Cheese
2 C. Powdered Sugar
1 tsp Vanilla extract
1 TBSP Heavy Whipping Cream

In a food processor, combine powdered sugar, almond flour, and cocoa powder—if you're using it.

Process until extra fine.

Just to be sure it's the finest of fine, sift into a large bowl.

Beat the whites and the salt with a hand mixer until stiff peaks form. Like, you should be able to tip the bowl over your head and shake it without anything falling out. I'm being a thousand percent serious, but you better be pretty sure you're there before you test that out.

Though, I have heard egg whites are great for your hair.

Add vanilla and food coloring (if using). Gel is important because it's a more vibrant color and because the liquid food coloring will affect the texture of the macarons. Not in a good way, in case you were wondering.

Stir just until combined.

With a spatula now, fold in almond flour mixture a little at a time. The texture you're going for at the end of all this folding is like wet sand. You know it's mixed as much as it should be when you do the figure eight test.

What's that, you say? Thanks for asking. It's when you can dribble batter off the tip of your spatula across the top in a figure eight without the ribbon of batter breaking. If it breaks, it needs more folding. If not, it's ready!

Now, we pipe.

Put the batter in a piping bag, or one of those nifty plastic thing-a-ma-roos with a lever. Use a big round tip. Cover your cookie sheets with parchment paper—just do it, it's fun. Pipe three dots across the narrow part of the cookie sheet and four dots down, including the row you did first. Twelve total.

Good mathing, guys!

Important: Lift the cookie sheet about an inch off the counter and *drop it*! For reals. Do this five or so times. It releases air bubbles to make a smooth macaron.

And everybody *loves* a smooth macaron.

Plus, also, it relieves stress. I recommend dropping cookie sheets whenever you feel squished. It helps, I swear.

Also important: Once all the macarons are piped, let them rest for 30-60 minutes. Before you bake, you should be able to run your finger along the top and they feel dry. No sticking.

There are a lot of important things going down in this recipe. Don't you feel way professional doing all these important things?

Yeah, me too.

Bake at 300°F for 17 minutes. Try to remove a macaron right away, carefully; if it sticks to the parchment paper, they need to bake a little longer. Just a minute or two. Transfer to a wire rack to cool completely.

Make the filling by whipping the cream cheese, gradually adding the powdered sugar, stirring in the vanilla and adding cream just until the consistency is thick and creamy. Put it in a piping bag.

The macarons need to be completely cool before filling. Just dollop icing in the center of the cookie, leaving a little room along the edge for the icing to spread out when you smush the two halves together to make a sandwich.

Smush is my new favorite word.

Let rest for 24 hours in an airtight container before eating. Like so many things, they are totally worth the wait!

3

Brioche

Jojo waits for, like, thirty milliseconds before she jumps up and starts towards the stairs. "I just want to make sure there are enough towels up there."

"I'll come too." Robyn follows, and since I don't want to be left out of *anything*, I go along. Even though moving closer to the stench is not my first choice.

Robyn and I follow Jojo up the stairs, but I pause to look at the black and white photos on the walls. So many people, all related to me. I wonder what their lives were like and if they could bake their feelings too.

"They're gorgeous, aren't they?" Jojo stops to wait for me. "Our family is my very most favorite thing."

"Mine too!" Robyn bounces onto the tips of her toes.

I skip to catch up to them. "Do you know *all* about our family?"

And by that, of course, I mean does she know *all* about our family's baking gift. Like, how it started, and how it really works, and *all* the everything else there is to know.

"I've picked up quite a bit over the years, but I don't know everything." Jojo swings her arms as she starts walking again. "Everything is a lot!"

We pass some closed doors, and then an open one. My curiosity gets the better of me and I peek inside. The room is pale green and lovely. I take a deep breath; it's like being inside a scoop of mint chocolate chip ice cream.

There's one entire wall covered with a painting of a white flower in a frame. I squint at the signature: Georgia something or another.

"Oh! That's Jojo's room." Robyn squishes into the doorway with me. "Do you love it?"

"I love it." I let out a slow breath of air.

"Girls? What are you...?" Jojo comes up behind us. "Oh, shoot, I haven't cleaned in ages." She squeezes between us and starts picking up clothes off the floor.

"No." I wave my hands. "It's perfect! I love *all* of it! Especially that picture."

Jojo follows the direction of my finger. "Yes! It's gorgeous, isn't it? I love Georgia O'Keeffe paintings. Course, it isn't the actual painting." She dumps the load of clothes into a hamper in the closet. "It's just a print. When I went to Chicago, I saw her real paintings at the art museum there. Breathtaking."

"You've been to Chicago?" I tiptoe to the unmade bed and sit on the edge, running my hand over the down comforter. It looks like chocolate and feels like butter.

Jojo shuts the closet door and leans against it. "Oh, sure, Mom loves to travel. I go with her when I can."

"But not to Jamaica?"

"No"—Jojo has a smile in her voice—"not to Jamaica. I wouldn't miss you guys coming here for the world!" A stray piece of hair falls back into her eyes even after she blows it away.

Robyn gasps. "Is that new? I don't remember seeing it when we were here last." She crosses the room to stand in front of a big silver picture of the Eiffel Tower.

"Have you been to France, too?" I can't keep the awe out of my voice.

Jojo shrugs. "A few times."

"To Paris?" The glittering poster makes my eyes water.

"Paris, Marseille, Levaine—"

"What's Leviane?" I've heard of the other places, but not Levaine.

"Oh." Jojo bends to pick up a piece of notebook paper and then puts it on her desk. "It's our village."

Our village.

I breathe in the magic of those words; they make my fingertips tingle.

Jojo rocks back on her heels. "It's not there anymore, not really. Boundaries changed, people moved... I think it's part of Brittany now. Girls, it's *so* beautiful. Crumbling brick buildings, tall, old trees. It's like stepping into a fairy tale."

Robyn and I sigh, leaning into each other.

"Why did we leave, then?" I ask.

Jojo squints her eyes. "The village was tiny to begin with. There wasn't any industry, just family businesses like our bakery. It couldn't self-sustain, I guess. GG said the mill hung on the longest, but even that went under. The family who owned it immigrated to America."

My thoughts swirl a minute at the thought of a fairy tale village aging, overhung with ivy. Sort of like the Sleeping Beauty story, except there's no one there to make the place come alive again.

I hug my arms closer to my body.

"I saw the remains of the mill when I visited, but the bakery, unfortunately, was demoed to build houses."

"Oh." Robyn sucks in a breath.

I know what she's feeling... It's like all the daydreams shatter around us. This is the same thing that happens every time Bubby climbs on the counter to get a glass from the cupboard.

"I wish it was still there, I'd love to see it."

"Oh! You can, sort of, GG has—" Jojo claps a hand over her mouth.

Robyn perks up. "What?"

"Never mind." Jojo waves her hands like she's trying to erase her words. "It's nothing. Forget we had this conversation."

"What?" I slide down from the bed.

"Nothing, nothing." Jojo bolts out of the room before Robyn and I can surround her. "Let's go help out those poor kids. Robyn, will you check the hall closet for extra towels?"

"Jojo!"

"Yes, Cat, you know where the suitcases are. Maybe you can find your brother and sister a change of clothes?" She scrambles away without waiting for me to answer yay or nay.

Robyn and I exchange a look, the kind that says 'Grown-ups are the Worst', and then get to work. It takes me a few tries, but I find the rooms Bubby and Penny are staying in. I'm so deep in thought, I don't notice what clothes I pull out for them. Seriously, I could be holding clown suits and I would have no idea.

After I set the clothes outside the bathroom door, I tap my foot and chew my thumbnail while I wait for Robyn and Jojo to finish up whatever they are doing. When they finally do, Jojo starts babbling about random stuff as soon as she comes into sight.

I know that trick.

I invented that trick!

She's using Distraction Technique Number Four to keep us from asking questions! Worse, there is nothing I can do to stop it because the woman doesn't even stop to breathe—not even once—the whole walk back downstairs!

Seriously, she should be an Olympic swimmer with that lung capacity.

Mom moves towards us as I step off the bottom stair. "Is everything all right? You were gone for a long time."

"Yes, I think they are going to survive, though Penny might need chocolate." Jojo smiles. "Where's Grammy?"

"She went to make some tea and cocoa."

"Perfect!"

"Tea?" I make a gooey gremlin face. I obviously can't see it, but I know it's impressive because Robyn smacks my arm.

"And cocoa. Sheesh, Cat. What's up with your attitude today?"

"I have a great attitude," I say through my clenched teeth.

Jojo slips between us. I stare with frustration at her back. I wish she would at least explain *why* she won't tell us whatever she can't tell us right now. Don't grown-ups know that if they give kids *some* of the why, it is usually enough to keep us from asking more questions?

Also, I thought we were done with secrets. I thought the whole point of this trip was to answer the questions, solve the mysteries, unearth the secrets—not add to them.

Ugh!

I plop into one of the iron chairs; it is not as comfortable as it is cute. A bar jabs into my back, making me fix my posture, but I'm not going to do anything about fixing my attitude.

So there.

Mom sinks onto a chair next to me. "Did you have fun with Aunt Jojo?" She pets my hair in soft, comforting strokes.

I nod.

"Yeah?" Mom doesn't look convinced.

"Yeah, it was fun, I mean, I got to see her room and hear about some of her adventures, but..."

"Go on."

"But I thought we came on this trip to figure out all this stuff and I haven't learned anything about my baking gift, and we've been here for like one whole hour!"

Mom chuckles, drawing her hand down my back in soothing circles. "We have four full days to solve all the mysteries of the universe, Cat. Remember our agreement?"

"Good for anything?"

Mom nods. "Let's add a pinch of patience, okay? I think that it will go a long way."

It might, but how in the frosting am I supposed to get my legs to stop jiggling? I cross one over the other and concentrate on not wiggling my foot.

"It's going to be alright, Kitty Cat. I have a feeling that we're going to leave here a whole lot wiser than when we arrived."

That could mean so many things, I don't even dwell on it. Instead, I fix my sights on the kitchen door. Any minute now, GG will come through the door with tea and cocoa.

Cocoa sounds pretty much amazing right now.

"What do you do with all the leftovers at the end of the day? The stuff you don't sell?" Robyn's voice interrupts my thoughts. She leans on the counter, next to Jojo, tapping her finger on the glass in a spazzy rhythm. "You don't throw it away, do you?"

"Oh, Robyn, you are such a thoughtful kid! I am happy to tell you that since you were here last, we made a deal with the food bank. They come at the end of the day to take whatever is left, for free."

Robyn and I volunteer at the food bank in Boise and, sometimes, when I wake up in the middle of the night, the thought of those little kids that come through the line haunts me. It's pretty cool that GG and Jojo donate what they don't sell. I bet people are super excited to get the food this bakery makes. It probably makes them super happy.

In more ways than one, actually.

"Really?" Robyn has glitter sprinkles in her eyes.

"Yep! Today they took away a few loaves of brioche and some scones."

"What's brioche?" I wonder out loud.

"Um..." Jojo taps her lip. "It's like normal bread, except it's eggy and rich and creamy and delicious. It makes great French toast."

"Oh, here comes Grammy, let me help!" Mom leaps to her feet and takes the tray from GG's arms.

Robyn and I pull another table over and grab an extra chair so we can all sit together. Mom and Jojo pass around napkins and pour us each a steamy cup of deliciousness. It is very silent, but not in a bad way.

In a cozy way.

I lean against Robyn's shoulder. Even though I took that fatty nap in the car, my eyelids getting droopier and droopier as I listen to the others chat.

"The bakery looks beautiful."

"Thank you, Bridget. And how do you like Boise living?"

"We love it. It's been the perfect fit for our family."

"Oh, I'm so happy you are happy."

"It is...very far away though. I...I didn't think so, but I miss it here...sometimes."

Jojo laughs. "Family has a way of getting under your skin, am I right?"

"I suppose that's true," Mom admits.

There's a long silence, which Robyn breaks with a gasp. "I love the cooling racks built into the wall."

"Yes, I noticed those too! Are they helpful with big orders?" Mom chuckles. "I remember Marissa and I trying—and failing—to stack all the cookie sheets on the counters when we were kids."

"I marvel how we lived without them." GG sips her tea.

Jojo grunts and I flutter my eyelids open, sensing something juicy.

Mom stops with her cup halfway to her mouth and looks at Jojo. "You don't like the cooling racks?"

Jojo makes a pile of napkins next to her cup, not looking at any of us with all of her might. "The cooling racks are super. I'm glad we have them."

"Oh?" Is all Mom says.

Maybe that's how you tell the difference between adults and not adults.

If I was Mom, and Robyn was Jojo, I would have grabbed her face in both hands and smooshed her cheeks until she told me everything she wasn't saying out loud.

Self-restraint is not my superpower.

I open my mouth to start a slight interrogation, but GG sets her cup down and fixes her chocolatey eyes on me. "Now, I think, is the perfect time for a story."

Brioche Bread

2 C. Milk
1 C. Sugar
2 TBSP active dry Yeast
6 Eggs
1 TBSP Vanilla extract
1/2 C. Butter
1 tsp Salt
5-6 C. all-purpose Flour

Warm the milk to 110°F, then add sugar, yeast, and 2 C. flour. Mix. This creates a dough sponge—cool, yeah?
Cover and set aside for 30 minutes.
Whisk eggs, vanilla, and melted butter into the dough sponge. Add about 4 C. flour, slowly.
You may need more or you may need less. Adding it slowly tells you the best.
I'm almost a poet, and I almost didn't know it!
Knead until smooth and elastic, 10-15 minutes.
Cover and let rise for an hour.
Remove from the bowl and divide into two pieces, then divide each of those into three pieces. Since we're so fancy, we're going to braid it into a loaf. Just like your little sister's hair.
Except you wouldn't eat that.
I hope.
Pinch each edge to keep the shape, then place in a greased loaf pan or on a cookie sheet. This isn't a major decision, like what flavor of toothpaste to buy, it just affects the shape of the loaf. The cookie sheet will make a flatter loaf; the bread pan will make a taller loaf.
Let rise for 30 minutes.
Bake at 350°F for 30 minutes or until golden brown.

4

Caramel Apple Scones

G G's eyes have mind reading powers just like Marissa's, except that *Tia's* are blue and GG's are brown. Regardless, I am in deep doo-doo. Marissa always makes me spill my guts whether I want to or not.

All my deepest, most classified secrets are spiraling out of that place in the back of my brain where I tucked them away forever and ever.

Like the time I dyed my hair hot pink at Jessi's birthday party, and it wouldn't wash out so I had to re-dye it blonde before I went home and that made my hair frizz up like an electrocuted teddy bear.

Then there was that day I ate paste because one of the kids in my class told me it was squished up marshmallows.

Give me a break, I was three!

Or eight.

Something like that.

So, basically, I am about to word-vomit all over the place.

GG leans towards me. "Cat, why don't you start at the beginning and tell us everything."

"Everything?" Robyn and I ask in unison, then look at each other.

"Like, everything, everything?" I ask, just to clarify. I mean, when it comes down to it, there is a lot to tell. I could probably fit the whole story into at least one full book.

GG holds her cup in front of her mouth with both hands, so the steam makes her face look wavy. If she wore glasses, they would be all foggy by now. "How about you start with the reason you have come to visit us."

Everyone looks at me.

I squirm.

This fancy schmancy chair is getting less and less comfortable by the second. Where do I even start? I mean, a lot has happened, and most of it was really confusing.

The rest was, like, the most embarrassing stuff ever.

But there's no way I can say no to those eyes.

Flapjacks.

"I guess..." I stop to swallow and then take a drink. "I guess the best place to start is with Tobey."

Heat rises to my cheeks at the mention of his name.

Robyn chortles into her cup.

I give her laser death ray eyes until she stops.

"Go on." GG waves the back of her hand at me.

So, I do.

I chatter their ears off for however long it takes us to destroy the entire tray of caramel apple scones Jojo brought from the kitchen. The only break in my monologue is the quick interruption to redirect Dad and the stink-free sibs onto the back porch until we call them in for dinner.

My voice is super scratchy; I sound like Batman.

But I finish what I start and don't even leave out the parts I really don't want to talk about. Like, how Robyn and I tried to make Tobey fall in love with me by baking lovey dovey feelings into cupcakes.

Ugh!

And then, how the cupcakes were intercepted by his little brother Conner.

I even tell them about how Conner got super obsessed with me and kept texting an infinity of lovey dovey emojis until his mommy took her phone back.

Jojo has to cough into a napkin a few times and GG's eyes can't hide a twinkle, but we somehow get through that stuff without anyone exploding.

And by anyone, I mean me.

Retelling my experiences with baking emotions is the same as drying my hands with a microfiber towel. It makes all my nerves tingle, like I have the heebies and the jeebies. I really hate how microfiber sticks to every rough spot on my fingers, and I really hate that I baked my feelings before I understood how it works.

"So that's why we're here." I let out a breath to finish. "I need to learn more about emotional baking so I don't get into any more scrapes. Scrapes are not my favorite."

GG watches me, sipping her tea. Even though I don't have anything else to say, I feel the weirdest urge to keep talking. The words come blathering out of my mouth from nowhere.

"I liked the thought of making people feel things. I liked it a lot. I kind of wanted to...control them. It felt good, in a not good way. You know?" I look at my fingers as I trace the decorative metal. The back of my neck heats up. "But it wasn't as cool as it sounded. I don't really know enough to decide what people need to feel, I mean, I thought I was doing good, but I wasn't. Not really."

GG offers me a tender smile that gives me the oomph I need to finish unraveling my soul.

"I just want to figure this whole thing out, to understand it, so I can bake the world a better place. Like you guys do."

"Oh, my Cat," GG murmurs so softly I almost don't hear her. When I finally get the courage to look up, her eyes are brimming with compassion. "We have all felt that way. No? We want to help the people feel better, happier."

Robyn nods.

Jojo and my mom look at their hands.

GG goes on, "It is one of the temptations we face as extraordinary bakers, we feel so strong, we sometimes go overboard with our zeal. The most important thing is what you learn from your experience, and then what you do next."

I suck in a breath and hold it tight. That's pretty much what *Tia* Marissa told me weeks and weeks ago when my biggest worry was that I might be a super big weirdo.

What matters is the heart.

"Tell us Cat, what did you learn from your baking?"

"I learned..." I chew on my lip as I think; it tastes like buttery caramel. "I learned that I can't really control what happens when I bake with emotions. Sometimes the wrong person gets the treat, or it just doesn't work out how I thought it would."

Jojo taps her fingers on the table. "Isn't that the truth? People are unpredictable at their very best. Baking emotions is like adding baking soda to vinegar." She lifts her hands in the air. "Kaboom!"

Robyn giggles.

"Yeah." I twist one of my bracelets around my wrist.

I agree with Jojo, sort of, but I still really like the thought of using my baking to help people. There has to be a way to do that; I have all my hopes waiting on it.

Even though I haven't done very much good so far, I have to believe there's a way to make this work. I think that's what I want to get from this trip. I don't just want to understand how I do what I do, I want to learn how to do it better. Like, what emotions to bake and what to avoid. How to manage my own emotions so I don't bake quite so powerful. I have to know that there are other options besides never baking again.

But I don't say any of these things out loud.

"You know, it wasn't all bad." I keep my attention on my bracelet, going around and around my wrist. "I really helped Penny calm down for her audition."

"You did what?" Mom's voice grumbles like distant thunder.

"I, uh, baked her calm, so she could dance for her audition." I work up the guts to look at my mom's face. "That's why she got the part."

Mom shakes her head. "Penny is a great dancer, Cat. She got the part because she worked hard."

"Yeah, of course, but I also calmed her nerves, so she didn't stress at the audition. That helped."

"Careful, Cat," Mom says.

I turn to GG, sure she will understand. That time with Penny was the first time I baked on purpose to help someone else, not for selfish reasons. It was different; I think that kind of baking might be okay. GG watches mom and me in a super analytical way, like we are a thousand-piece jigsaw puzzle that's a picture of only peppermint sticks. Red and white everywhere.

GG chuckles, warming the bakery a couple degrees. "Ah there, you see, Cat, this is a slippery slope. We want to do good. We want to help; we think we are helping, but maybe we aren't. Maybe things will happen how they are meant to happen without us. No?"

"No?" I wrinkle my nose. "I mean yes. I mean, I don't know."

I am now super-de-duper-de confused.

My mom takes a deep breath, the kind that is about to launch a huge lecture, but GG puts her cup down and covers both of my mom's hands with hers. "What's done is done." Her voice is soft, but her eyes, as they search my mom's face, are serious and steely, almost black.

Mom leans back in her chair, exhaling her big breath. I think she could power a whole farm of those windmill things we saw on the drive here.

"I get what Cat's saying," Robyn says, slowly. "I mean, I helped her with most of that baking. I love the thought of baking people happy. It's just cool, you know? To change how people feel."

Mom shakes her head, her voice low. "No, Robyn, it is *not* cool. Who are we to decide how people should feel? We barely know what *we* feel half of the time! Everyone needs to be in charge of their own emotions."

Robyn looks conflicted, obviously not wanting to disagree, even though she totally disagrees.

I love it when you know a person so well you can read their mind.

Or their gestures.

Or whatever.

Robyn sits up straighter, laying her hands on the table so we can see her palms. "My mama loves to bake, because it makes people so happy and that makes her happy. I think that's a good thing. Like the other day, she baked a couple pies for no real reason and then felt like she should take one to a lady down the street. When Mrs. Tawni opened the door, she almost burst into tears. She had a really rough day and was just wishing she had some pie because it sounded so good. My mama, like, answered her wish. There's no way she could have known that Mrs. Tawni was thinking about pie all day, but she did the one thing that really made a difference. You know? I just think that is really cool, making someone's day a little brighter by sharing things you bake. This baking power really makes people feel better."

Mom shakes her head some more. "We shouldn't be making people feel anything. But I know for a fact that Marissa only bakes happy and that's not the problem. When this becomes a problem is when you use the things you bake to manipulate another person's feelings, to get what *you* want. That is totally different, that is when baking becomes Grammy's slippery slope." She sighs and turns to GG. "To wrap up Cat's story, we came here because we need help. Cat's ability to bake all of the feelings, and make people feel so strongly, is so different from the way Marissa bakes-"

"What about you?" Jojo tips her head to the side so the blue-tinted parts of her hair dangle by her shoulder.

Mom folds her hands in her lap, taking her sweet time to answer. "What about me?"

"Do you just bake happy like Marissa does?"

"I don't..." Mom interrupts herself with a long breath.

Jojo wrinkles her forehead into deep lines. "So, you bake other emotions? Like Cat?"

My mom turns to stone, her face as smooth as granite, her shoulders jammed almost to her ears.

Jojo holds out a hand. "You're upset. I'm sorry. I'm not trying to upset you, I'm just trying to understand why you came all this way for our help when you're such a good baker, and an even better emotional baker."

Mom shakes her head. "No, no, I'm not. I don't do that anymore. I haven't baked in..." her eyes flicker in my direction. "In a little over fifteen years."

"Really?" Jojo leans back in her chair. "I didn't know that. That's interesting."

"Is it?" Mom says vaguely. "This isn't about me. We're here to help Cat harness her ability to bake with emotions. GG and I talked about this some when I called to ask if we could visit. Marissa and I don't know enough to help Cat figure this out. I mean, I saw the effects of most of her baking. It was... Anyway, I don't know anyone anymore who bakes the way Cat does."

Jojo stares at my mom in a way that is impossible to ignore. I know because all of us are now staring at my mom in the same quizzical way.

"Why are you looking at me like that?" Mom twists the hem of her shirt through her fingers.

"I don't know," Robyn says. "I was just doing it because Cat was!"

"And I was just doing it because Jojo was!" I giggle.

Jojo bites her lip to hide a smile. "Well then, I was just doing it because GG was!"

GG holds up her hands in defense. "I shall not be the scapegoat! Jojo?"

Jojo squelches her smile like she doused a candle. "Okay, I give, it was me who started the staring thing. I'm just confused. Bridget, you know more than any of us do about baking emotions other than happiness." Her voice is soft and not accusing at all, but my mom swells like a helium balloon.

"What are you saying, exactly, Jolynn?"

"Just that you..."

"Hey!" My dad's booming voice echoes through the bakery.

I am so close to the edge of my chair that I slip and almost fall. If it hadn't been for Robyn's ninja-like reflexes catching my arm at the last minute, I would be sitting on the floor right now with a super sore—

Well, you know.

Dad stops behind Mom and rubs her shoulders, which are now scrunched way to the bottoms of her earlobes. "Did you forget about us? The kids are starving out there."

Mom twists her neck to look at Dad. "Just the kids?"

He shrugs, "Yeah, well..."

GG rises from the table. "I hope you are very hungry. Jolynn and I made a big pot of Posse Stew for dinner.

My stomach flip flops. Posse stew, is that like possum or something? They wouldn't put possum in their stew, would they? I wish I could laugh and tell myself that's ridiculous, but I saw a lot of roadkill on the drive here and small towns have reputations.

Don't they?

My dad squeezes Mom's shoulders, bringing them down half an inch. "I love Posse Stew! We haven't had it in ages. What can I do to help you?"

"Come along with me and I will show you." GG gives us a parting smile as Penny slips into her chair. Bubby crawls into Mom's lap, still damp, and chews on the edge of his thumb nail. That's his passive aggressive way of sucking his thumb when he thinks he's too old to do it, but hasn't kicked the habit yet. Mom twirls his curls around her fingers, not noticing what he's doing, her eyes look like she's trying to see through the walls.

The silence is excruciating.

Jojo uncrosses her legs and leans forward, her elbows resting on the table. "Bridge, I didn't mean to…"

"Drop it, Jolynn." Mom's lips are whiter than pink.

A look of surprise crosses Jojo's face. She snaps back in her chair like my mom just smacked her in the face. Her hands, all scrunched together in her lap, get all of her attention for a few minutes, then she looks up with a brave smile. "So, I've been trying to come up with ways to improve our bakery. You girls want to help me brainstorm?"

Robyn purses her lips. "Why? What's wrong with the bakery the way it is?"

"Oh, nothing." Jojo waves a hand airily. "It's great. It's super established with the older folks that have been around here forever, but I want the younger kids to love it too. I think there are quite a few things we can do to keep up with trends. You know, like gluten free, vegan, keto, sugar free, egg free…"

I try to keep my face smooth, but everything she just said sounds really complicated. I mean, can you even bake on a keto diet? I thought that was mostly meat. I have a horrible vision of a cinnamon roll with chicken legs sticking out of the side.

Trends come and go the way I lose my socks. Why does Jojo want to try and keep up with that? And besides, I've tasted this bakery's stuff and I gotta say, like my dad always does, if it ain't broke…

Jojo's smile dims a couple watts. "You don't think it's a good idea?"

"Um, maybe, but…I guess…" Robyn looks at me to confirm and I nod. "We don't understand why the bakery needs to change or update. It's pretty great the way it is."

"It is great." Jojo flicks her nail at a spot on top of the table. "But it's, I mean…"

"What is it, Jojo?" Mom's voice is hesitant, but she looks all determined with that crease between her eyebrows.

Jojo smiles a forgiveness smile. "It's just that, there's a bakery around the corner. It's been open a few years and it's fine. We're fine. But their menu changes constantly, to accommodate allergies and all the things. We haven't done much to our menu in the last twenty years. I don't know, I guess I feel like we need to do something different or we're going to be in trouble."

"Is the bakery struggling?" Mom's eyes widen.

Jojo waves her hands. "No! No, we're okay, really. I'm just thinking ahead, you know, just in case."

Robyn gives Jojo a penetrating stare that makes her sigh.

"Fine, you win. I wasn't going to tell you this yet, since we're trying to help Cat and all, but here's the thing, there's this popular restaurant in town, you know the one that always ends up featured in the travel magazines?"

I nod to keep her going, even though I have no idea what she's talking about.

"Yeah, so, they announced last month that their pastry chef retired. They decided to subcontract their baked goods instead of hiring a new person in house. If *L'Amour Bakin'* got that contract, it wouldn't matter how much we sell every day. We would always have guaranteed income, you know?"

I nod some more; I'm pretty sure I get it now. My heart speeds up as new thoughts bob around my brain like little kids in a bounce house. She's talking about a baking competition! A bake-off!

Jojo pushes her hair behind her ear, but it falls back against her cheek. "I'm just kinda worried Jake is going to win the bake-off."

"Worried?" Mom asks at the same time I squeal, "Bake-off!"

And Robyn jumps out of her seat. "Jake? That guy you dated?"

"It was one date, Robyn. One date, not *dated*. That was enough to help me realize I'd rather die ugly, old, and alone than..." Her nostrils flare. "But yes, it is the same Jake." She turns to my mom. "You know him, Bridge; his family owns the mill in the Valley that's been delivering our flour for years."

My mom snaps her fingers. "Wait, was he that towheaded little guy that charmed all the old women?"

Jojo bursts out laughing but stops herself before it can really get going. "I forgot about that! Yes, the very same little guy. Except now he's in his twenties, living in Lakeside and has a bakery around the corner."

I don't know why we're still talking about some random guy when there's the whole matter of a bake-off that hasn't been explained to me yet.

I lean forward so everyone looks at me. "What is this bake-off? I mean, what do you have to do? And when is it?" I really hope we're still here. A bake-off sounds like the most funnest thing ever! I'm picturing dramatic music, toques and bakery shirts, flour in the air and a countdown with crowds cheering.

Jojo brings me back to reality with a thump. "It's on Friday, the day after Thanksgiving."

"Black Friday," Robyn whispers.

That's not ominous at all.

But the good news is, we aren't leaving until Saturday morning. We can totally help Jojo win the bake-off.

Because of course she's going to win.

Duh.

Jojo smiles, "I didn't make that connection. Black Friday. That's ironic, eh? Anyway, we are one of four local bakeries vying for the contract. They're calling it a bake-off, but really all we have to do is set up a table at the high school auditorium. Judging starts at noon on Friday."

Set up a table? That sounds like an elementary school science fair, or one of those city craft shows. My dreams of glitter and spotlights flutter to the floor.

"What are you going to bake?" Robyn asks. "I mean, what are you supposed to bake for the competition?"

"They want a signature item, just one thing." Jojo wraps her fingers together like they each need some hugs.

"What's our signature item?" I look around, like it's a poster on the wall or written somewhere.

"Scones." Robyn nods. "Has to be scones. Everybody loves the scones, especially the apple caramel."

Jojo lifts one shoulder. "I don't know, scones are just so ordinary, you know? I mean, everyone knows about our scones. Everyone has tried our scones. I feel like we need something new and amazing to stand out from the other bakeries. Anyway, if you guys have any ideas I would love to hear them. GG doesn't want to change anything, but if we come up with something knock-your-socks-off amazing, she might come around."

"You know, "Mom says, "the bakery is charming the way it is, I think that's a lot of appeal for people."

"Yeah," Jojo agrees half-heartedly. "It's charming. For sure."

I see a big, glowing *but* in the air above her head.

"But what?" I ask.

Jojo flips Robyn's hair with one finger and watches it fall back into place. "But people with allergies don't come to our bakery, they go to Jake's. And people who want cinnamon rolls go see Bernice at the food truck. For pies they go to Pie in the Sky. I just feel like we need to step up our game or we aren't going to make it."

"Whatever!" I shake my head. "That's ridiculous. This is the best bakery in the whole world! Even if you don't change anything, or even if you don't get the contract thing-a-ma-doo-hickey people will always come here because we're rocking awesome!!"

Jojo's lips curl into a smile, her eyes take a little longer to join the party, but they do eventually, twinkling as she reaches for my hand. "Cat! You're right. We are rocking awesome! I'll just focus on that and stop all the worries."

"Yay!" Robyn cheers.

"It would be super tricky to modify our recipes," Jojo goes on, "especially this close to the bake-off. We'd have to do a lot of experiment baking..." Her hand goes limp in mine at the same time her face loses all the newfound shine.

"What is it?" My mom asks.

"Oh." Jojo pulls away. "I'm just really glad you guys are here to help GG with the baking.

"Oh, I don't..." Mom shakes her head.

"I know," Jojo gives her a small smile. "But I thought maybe Robyn and Cat could help out in the kitchen."

Robyn laughs so loud it echoes in the quiet room. "You don't want me in the kitchen, I am a terrible baker!"

Jojo blinks. "You are not! Marissa…"

"Yeah, Mom tried to teach me, but I'm no good at baking. I just have to rely on my winning personality to make the world a better place." She pulls her shoulders back and bats her long eyelashes.

I shove her shoulder. "And so humble."

"Well, duh, obviously. I'm the best at being humble!"

I roll my eyes. "Right, anyways, I'll help! I can't wait to help, except…"—and I really hate to say this last part; I am sort of like an elephant in the room—"Do you think it's safe for me to bake for people?"

No one answers for such a long time, that I start to feel super self-conscious.

"Don't worry," Mom says, brushing Bubby's hair away from his face, "we'll figure all of this out as soon as GG gets back."

Caramel Apple Scones

2 & 1/2 C. Flour
1 tsp Baking Powder
1/2 tsp Salt
1/4 C. Sugar
1/2 C. Butter, super cold - frozen even works
1/2 C. Milk
1 C. chopped Apple - I like Gala in this recipe
1/2 C. chopped Pecans
Caramel Sauce

Preheat the oven to 400°F.

In a bowl, mix flour, baking powder, sugar and salt with a whisk to smooth out any large lumps.

Large lumps are the worst.

Now this might get weird for you, but stick with me here: Grate the cold, cold butter into the flour mixture. The reason is, when butter gets warm, it melts. (I hope this isn't news to you, but if it is, then I am proud to be the first person to welcome you to the planet Earth.)

Melted butter will mix into flour like a paste. We do not want pasty scones. I know for some kindergarteners, eating paste seems like a good idea, but it really isn't.

What we want is flakes. Remember this: Flakey is good, pasty is bad. Scones are pretty much sweet biscuits, so think of that texture when you're wrapping your head around this recipe.

Got it? Yay! Let's move on.

Mix the apples and pecans into the flour/butter mixture until it looks pretty evenly combined. Then, make a well in the center.

Basically, jab your fist in there to make a crater.

Pour the milk into the well and then, with wide sweeping stirs that make your elbow stick into the air, fold it all together. At some point, stirring won't work anymore so you wanna dig in with your hands. Just to remove the dry pockets of flour.

Don't overmix.

Now, get flour on your hands—so they don't stick to the dough anymore, silly—and pat the dough into a round circle about 2-3 inches thick on a baking sheet with parchment paper.

To save yourself the headache of trying to cut the crispy/soft masterpiece later, make sure you pre cut the dough. Kinda like you do a pizza, to make 8 triangles.

Bake for 15-20 minutes. The top should be beautifully browned and your kitchen should smell like happy feelings.

Remove from the oven to cool before drizzling on the caramel sauce. (If you do it while they are warm, it will all melt away.)

You can use store bought sauce, but I like to home make caramel sauce. That's kinda advanced for this chapter. We'll talk about it more in chapter eighteen.

Are you so excited?

I'm so excited!

5

French Bread

Before I have a chance to decide if I have the patience to wait for her, or if I'm going to rush the kitchen and pull her out right now, GG appears. She opens the big double doors and holds one of them back so my dad can pass through with an enormous pot.

Really enormous.

Like, I'm thinking of the biggest pot I've ever seen and it's this pot's baby boo.

"I hope you girls are hungry." Dad grunts to lift the pot onto the bakery counter and rubs his biceps with a wink at me. "There is enough stew here to feed a horse, his herd and the neighboring cattle ranch."

"I'm not so good at measuring." GG places napkins and bowls beside the steaming pot. "I always make too much, but it's okay, we can share the leftovers."

Robyn leaps to her feet. "Can I help with anything?"

"There's bread on one of the stoves." Dad jabs his thumb back to the kitchen.

Robyn takes off on those long legs of hers, practically leaving us all a cloud of dust.

Jojo hands a bowl to Penny. "Grab the butter, Robyn, and jam, please!"

"I don't think she heard you," I look at the swinging kitchen door. "I'll go get it."

"Thanks honey, both are in the third fridge."

I scamper after Robyn, trying to slip through the doors without touching them. I almost succeed, but at the last minute, one smacks me in the bum. I give it a dirty look, then count the fridges.

"What are you doing?" Robyn stands upright, potholders in her hands.

"Getting butter and jam." I open the third fridge. "Good thing too, I could tell you didn't hear Jojo."

Robyn makes no move to gather bread loaves. She places the hand with the potholders on her hip and juts it out to the side.

An excellent thinking pose, if I do say so myself.

Which, I do.

"Okay, out with it, what are you thinking?"

"I was wondering about all that, out there." She jabs her free thumb in the direction of the bakery.

I shake my head, turning back to the fridge. I don't know what I think about that yet; I need more time to process. I bend down to peer at the assortment of jars on the shelf.

What the sprinkles is orange marmalade?

I lift the jar and turn it side to side to see if it does anything weird. It doesn't. Looks like normal jam to me. When I unscrew the lid and take a deep whiff, all I smell is oranges.

I guess that means it could be amazing or super gross Honestly, it could go either way. But since oranges on French bread don't compute with me. I'm going to keep looking for real jam.

And also, I'm going to keep avoiding Robyn's question.

"Cat?"

Oh!

Hello there, strawberry jam.

That's what I'm talking about! I grab both jars and shut the fridge door with my foot, since both my hands are now *ocupado* with butter and jam.

"Cat!"

"I'm sorry! I got distracted by the delicious jellies and jams. I'm paying attention now." I put the stuff on the counter and lift up my free hands like that proves something about my attention span.

Robyn shakes her head. "Now I'm wondering other things about you. Like if you've ever heard of multi-tasking when your cousin asks you an important question?"

"Yes," I nod. "Oh wait! I remember! You asked me what I think about what happened just now. Right?"

Robyn lifts a thumb in the air.

"Okay, so, you know how Penny starts to slump into the furniture when she misses a meal or snack?"

"Yeah?"

"That's what I think happened. They all be low blood sugared up."

Robyn squints, staring at something on the ceiling behind me. "I don't think so *gata*, I don't know if you've noticed, but we haven't stopped eating since we got here."

"Too much sugar then." I shrug one shoulder, undeterred. "Their blood feels way too fast, and they are all crazy up in here. I don't really know how that works. I'm not a bloodologist."

Robyn rolls her eyes. "Seriously, can you be serious for three seconds?"

I solemnly step around the counter to stand next to Robyn, then I press my palms together at my heart in Robyn's favorite yoga prayer pose.

Because that's what serious people do.

"You are impossible!" She slaps me with the pot holders. "Aren't you even a little curious? There's all this tension and...and...micro-tension in the room!"

"Micro-tension?" I don't even know what that means, but I do know that super big words used irresponsibly can be, like, way dangerous. "Did you seriously just say micro-tension in a real-life conversation?"

"Stop it, Cat, and listen! Do you really think the bakery is in trouble? And there's the bake-off and...and Jake! I met him last year, Cat, he's a super nice guy. I totally thought him and Jojo... Anyway, it doesn't matter, I guess. And then the whole thing with Jojo and your mom—what's that about? Do you know what happened between them?"

She doesn't wait for my serious, mature, well-thought-out answer, she just keeps jabbering away.

"I've been so curious about it, but it doesn't seem right to ask. It's so nosy. I bet my mom knows, I could ask her. Where's my phone? I left it on the table. What are you doing?" She picks up the bread and steps around me, propping the doors with her foot. "Come on Cat, quit lolly-gagging, everyone is waiting."

Like I was the one monologuing for a million years!

Sheesh.

I roll my eyes and pick up the butter and jam from the counter. When I get everything unloaded next to the bread, and my hands are once again free, I take the opportunity to flick Robyn's arm.

She yelps, "What was that for?"

I just walk away, shaking my head.

GG says grace, and with so much to be thankful for, it goes on for a while. Personally, I'm not all that eager beaver to try possum stew, so I'd be good if she was thankful for more things. Like, the air molecules and whipping cream and tectonic plates. But eventually, she comes to the amen and everyone else makes a rush for the food.

I grab Robyn's arm before she can get in line.

"What is possum stew, exactly?"

Before Robyn can answer, I hear my question echoed across the room.

Penny shrieks, "Are there tomatoes in that? I don't eat cooked tomatoes."

"You eat pizza and spaghetti sauce all the time." Mom sighs.

"That's because it doesn't have chunks." Penny folds her arms so her paper bowl is as far from the ladle as she can get.

Bubby makes an impressive puke face. "Tommy toes, ew, what is this stuff?" He holds his already filled bowl away from his body like he's afraid something in it is going to leap out and attach itself to his face. "What's potty stew?"

Dad gives GG an apologetic face, then bends low to hiss through his teeth in Bubby's face. "Posse stew. It's soup. It's good and you will like it."

Or else.

That's what Dad says next, just not out loud. His eyes make it clear, with enough oomph that I feel it across the room. Like a zombie alien, I find myself nodding.

I will like it.

I will like it.

Even if it really is possum.

My tummy flip flops.

Honestly, I tell myself, it can't be much worse than frozen burritos that look like bloated slugs.

Right?

Mom intervenes before Dad has a chance to explode. "Alright, you two, what's the family dinner rule?"

Bubby and Penny examine the wood floors. "Eat it or beat it."

"That's right, you choose." Mom plops a slice of bread in each of their picky hands. "Why don't you take whatever you decide to eat to the back porch so we can talk in here."

I watch their walk of shame and decide I don't want to be thrown out with the little kids. I will eat this soup or perish in the attempt.

But if I do happen to kick the farm or sell the bucket, I'd like to bequeath my glitter nail polish to Robyn.

The turquoise, not the pink.

I shuffle forward in line, trying not to give Robyn a flat tire. She hands me a bowl which I hug carefully to my chest, not so sure I want to put anything in it.

Dad ladles a generous portion into Robyn's outstretched bowl. The smell of delicious things wafts through the bakery. My tummy flip flops for a different reason now. I am suddenly starving.

Okay, I don't care anymore if it's possum in there, the stew smells amazing. I hold my bowl out for Dad and lean over to breathe it in as I walk to the table where Robyn waits.

She gives me a knowing look, but I ignore her.

Note to self: I might want to start assuming everything tastes great around here, despite the name or main ingredient. Otherwise, I forfeit all bragging rights to Robyn until the end of time, and also contribute to her rapidly inflating ego.

"Aw man"—Dad pauses and inhales deeply—"this smells like my childhood! Remember the Fourth of July rodeo? I used to stand in line for an hour to get a bowl of this stuff."

GG pinches Dad's cheek with a smile, then waves her arm at Mom and Jojo. "Come get food. Everybody eat, eat."

"Is it warm enough out there?" Mom's eyes wander to the back porch as she takes a bowl of stew from Dad. It's obvious now that her irritation is cooling, she's having regrets about banishing the littles. "I remember it gets pretty cold when the sun goes down."

Jojo sits next to me and arranges her napkin, "Oh, no worries! The back porch is in the afternoon sun. It stays insulated. They definitely won't freeze."

I take a bite of dinner and forget everything going on around me. Okay, this stew is delicious. What is it with this place? Everything I eat tastes better than the last thing I ate. I wonder how long I can keep this streak up before I max out at the yummiest thing ever? A couple days? The whole week? It's definitely worth the experiment if you ask me.

Which you should.

Because I would say it's totally worth trying.

I drain my bowl into my hollow leg and watch everyone else eat like civilized human beings. I wonder if I should go get seconds or not. Robyn will gloat for sure, but I can handle that. On the other hand, if they made a yummy, delicious dessert, I want to save room.

Life is full of tough decisions.

GG settles into her chair with a smile that squishes her eyes into oblivion, leaving a multitude of wrinkles behind. "I love to be here with all of you. It makes my heart filled."

"Same!" Robyn reaches for the butter. "Just *en pequeno*."

"Or just a lot!" I twirl my spoon around my fingers. "How do you say a lot in French?"

"*Beaucoup*," GG nods at me.

"How do you say a little?"

Jojo answers this time, "*Un peu*."

"Poo!" Robyn hiccups, almost falling off of her chair. She scoots closer to me, laughing into my shoulder. "She said poo."

I pat the top of her head. Poor Robyn. I think all the sugar, excitement, and probably the higher altitude is getting to her.

"Do you know what your mama would say if you said that when she was here?" I press my lips together to hide a smile, and smack both hands flat on the tabletop. It stings my palms, but Robyn jumps a mile so it's totally worth the pain.

She looks at me wide-eyed.

"Robyn Bethany Carolyn Martinez! You know how I feel about words from *el bano*!" I pause to swallow my giggles. "Then she would go into a long string of Spanish that no one can understand."

Robyn turns strawberry jam red from laughing so hard.

Jojo refills a glass of water and pushes it into her hands. "Oh, well done, Cat! You sound just like her! I miss her *so* much!"

"Can I have some more potty stew?"

I glance over my shoulder and there is Bubby, holding out his bowl to Dad. "It was really good, and I love it, GG Grammy G, even though it doesn't taste like a potty."

"I'm so happy you like it, dear."

Dad gives Bubby another scoop of stew, then looks around. "Where's Pen?"

"Sleeping," Bubby talks around the food in his mouth.

"She fell asleep outside?" Mom stands up.

Bubby slurps, then dabs the corners of his mouth with a napkin. "Inside the porch, on the couch thingy."

"The patio furniture is surprisingly comfortable." Jojo smiles.

Mom tugs on Dad's elbow. "We should probably get these kids to bed. All that driving is exhausting…"

Dad gazes into his empty bowl, then longingly at the pot on the counter. With a martyr's sigh, he drops his napkin in the bowl and stands up. "I'll go get Penny."

"We're right behind you." Mom waits for Bubby to finish the last of his soup and then scoops him up like a big baby. His giggles trail behind them all the way up the stairs.

Jojo pats Robyn's arm. "Why don't you come help me gather spare blankets."

"Sure!" Robyn is on her feet before the word fades away; she gives me a curious look over her shoulder.

I sit up straight, the air around me tingles with possibility. I wait for GG to look at me, positive she has something she wants to say.

Except that she doesn't look at me. Her eyes follow my mom, Jojo and Robyn as they tromp up the stairs. After a long, super boring minute, GG presses her hands into the table and stands up creakily.

"Twilight."

Is that a code word? Like the one Mom says when she's had it with us kids and needs Dad to step in? If so, it's way cooler than Asparagus. Mom should have asked GG for input before choosing a gross vegetable as a super spy word.

She reaches out a hand to me. "It's my favorite time of day. Will you walk with me, Cat?"

So, not a code word.

That's cool too.

I take her hand and follow GG out the front door into the crisp night air. It is kinda chilly for my little jacket, but I know I'll warm up as we get moving. I skip forward to fall in step with GG. Now we're walking side by side instead of me trailing behind her like a little kid pull toy.

It feels nice to stroll along the sidewalk, swinging our hands in time to our steps. Normally I would never do something like this, fourteen is way too old to hold hands with a grown up, but it feels different here. It's like a whole 'nother time era where things play with different rules.

"See that building there?" GG points to a little blue house with a poster on the front window of a lady with a cheeky grin.

I can only see poster because the house happens to be under a streetlight. Otherwise, it would be dark gray, like everything else in the town right now.

"Yeah."

"That's where I grew up."

I look over my shoulder as we pass by. "You lived in a real estate office?"

When GG laughs, it's like hot cocoa in my belly. "No, no! It was not always an office. Once upon a time it was the house where I grew up. My papa bought it from a man who had enough of the ranching. I think of that poor man and feel sad for him. Who can get enough of this?" She sweeps her arm away from her body, like she's trying to draw the whole place in for a hug.

I breathe in deep.

And cough.

It smells like cows.

Whew, those things are pungent.

"All the field"—GG points across the main road—"used to be ours, your Great Grandpa Joe's and mine. We sold the land and cows when he got sick. Did your mama tell you this?"

"About Grandpa Joe? Yeah. I'm sorry," I stammer. Sorry feels like such a lame word when it comes after losing someone you love. I'm no good at talking about stuff like this. Death is banished to the unspeakables. Along with politics, spandex, and having something stuck in your teeth when you talk to people.

"No sorry needed. He lived his best life," she says, "we were very happy."

I try to think of something to say, but all that's in my brain is politics, spandex and having something stuck in my teeth.

I run my tongue over my top front teeth a couple times just in case.

"Yes, well." GG sighs and squeezes my hand. "Let us talk, instead, about beginnings. Your beginnings. I know you are brimming with questions. What would you ask me if you knew I have all the answers to everything you want to know?"

I grasp her question as though it is the last Red Vine in the bucket. What should I ask her? What? What? What? There are so many things I want to know. What is the one question that rules them all?

"I want to know how people in our family can bake emotions into food."

GG's hand flies to her heart. "You go straight for the throat, *ma cherie!*"

"You said to ask you anything." I peek at her from the corners of my eyes.

"I did, this is true. But what of Bridget and the others? Should we not wait for them to talk of this?"

"Yeah, maybe," I shrug. "But, actually, how come they don't already know? I mean my mom and Marissa and Jojo? Didn't you ever explain to them how the baking works, like, when they were younger or something? Did you know my mom used to bake emotions other than happy? Or did she bake without asking?"

GG starts laughing in the middle of my question dump and keeps getting louder and louder the longer I go on. She links her arm through my elbow and hugs me close. "So many, many things you want to know."

"Yeah, well." I purse my lips. "Our family is super weird."

"Yes."

She says this in such a matter-of-fact way, I start to think weird isn't all that weird.

Maybe if there is enough weirdness, it turns normal.

GG tugs me back to earth and away from my philosophically weird thoughts. "There is much to know, and much to explain, but maybe we just scratch the tip, as they say. Ask me that first question again."

I don't have to think hard to remember what it was.

"How do we bake emotions? How does it work? How is any of this possible?" That was more than one question, but the rest rush out before I can check them at the door. It's like the questions are afraid they will get stuck inside me, unanswered forever.

"And by 'we' you mean..."

I falter just a step and skip to make it up. "Um, us. You and me and I guess Aunt Marissa is the only other person who does it. I mean, my mom can, but won't. Robyn can't. Jojo..." I pause to breathe and also take a second to think. "I don't actually know what Jojo can do. Can she bake emotions? How come some of us can do it and some of us can't?"

GG's eyes twinkle. "It is a lot to take in, no?"

"No, I mean, yes. Yes, it is! My brain has been like a tornado ever since I found out about this. I want to understand it so bad!"

"And why is that? Why do you want to understand it?"

I look at her, incredulously. "So I can do it right!"

"Do what?"

"Do what?" I try not to get frustrated, but GG is doing the thing.

That thing where people answer you with questions instead of answers.

I do not love that thing at all.

"Bake! I want to learn how to bake emotions the right way, so I don't mess it up like I did with Tobey and Conner. I want to bake, I mean, make, people happy!"

GG stops walking and moves around until I face her. Her squinted eyes roam my face. "You cannot make people happy; you know this? People decide to be happy on their own."

I shift from foot to foot. "But Marissa does it. She bakes, people eat and they're happy. It worked for me too, when Robyn ate the snickerdoodles I made when I was happy. She was crazy giddy all the way home."

"Oh." GG waves her free hand like my words are pesky flies. "That is not happy. That is enjoyment, or fun, or momentary satisfaction. Happy is a choice Cat. It is always a choice."

I run the toe of my shoe along a crack in the sidewalk.

Is this true?

"Now"—GG lifts a finger—"that is not to say that what we do is not important. That is not to say that what we do does not make a difference. Cat, everything we do matters. What I am trying to discover, as I pepper you with questions, is your reason. Why do you want to learn how to bake emotions?"

"Why?" I chew my bottom lip, afraid I'll say the wrong thing.

GG's face softens as she rubs my arm. "Your mama does not. Jojo does not. They cannot control their feelings. What will it be for you, I wonder...?"

"Wait, so Jojo can do it?" If she lumped Jojo in with my mom and me, that's a natural conclusion, isn't it? That Jojo bakes the same way we do?

"Tell me what you mean, 'Jojo can do it'?"

"I mean, Jojo can bake all the emotions, not just happiness. Jojo can do that?"

GG nudges my arm to get me walking again. "I know, at your age, it seems important, who can do what. Let me be as plain as the nose. This is not about who can do the baking; this is about the choosing. This is important for you to know, we all *decide* how to bake."

I let that sink in for a moment. Yeah, it sounds like she just said everyone can bake the way I can. This is like trying to swallow a huge bite of peanut butter and jelly sandwich; it gets all clogged in my throat. 'Cause, here's the thing, I sort of thought I was the only one that could bake all the emotions. My mom and Marissa made such a big deal about it, I thought I was unique. Somehow, I now feel a little less awesome sauce.

The whole world looks dull and cloudy gray.

"Oh, my Cat," GG says. "If it helps I will tell you this, some baking is stronger than others."

This perks me up again. "The way I bake, it's way strong right?"

"I understand it is. Your mother told me you have strong, powerful emotions."

I stumble over my own feet. It's really hard to ride an emotional roller coaster and walk at the same time. "I'm curious about something you said before. About Jojo. What did you mean that she can't control her feelings?"

"Jojo," GG pauses for a way long time. "She feels things so strongly. High, highs..."

"And low, lows?"

"Yes. My Jolynn, she worries about the bakery though there is nothing to fear. *L'Amour Bakin'* will always be successful, until it isn't. And then it will be okay, for it has served its purpose."

I try to wrap my head around this. I don't know if it's a comforting, or depressing thought. "Then you aren't worried?"

GG shakes her head. "Worry? My *maman* always said, worry cares nothing for you, so do not waste your time on it." GG smiles at the look on my face. "What I mean is, in this moment, there is nothing to worry about. In this moment, we are strolling down a dim street, at my favorite time of night, with fall in the air and stars twinkling above us. Nothing to worry about here."

"Is that why Jojo can't bake, because she's worried?"

"Worry tends to sour things."

I wrinkle my nose. There is so much information zooming through my head, I'm pretty sure some of my thoughts are seconds away from head-on collisions.

I start talking to sort it all out. "So, you can bake, and Marissa can bake. Jojo, my mom, Granny Penny, and Robyn can't or don't."

GG tips her head to the side. "That is mostly true. Most of those you named can do as you said."

I narrow my eyes in concentration. I really want to understand this, but sometimes it sounds like GG is talking around a huge wad of bubble gum.

"What you're saying is, we all can bake with emotions. Some are stronger than others, and some don't because they don't want to...and I get to choose? So, does that mean we *can* control it?"

"That remains to be seen. I am saying that it is *possible* to control it." GG looks at the sky, "You are shivering, twilight has gone. We best be turning back."

Yeah, I'm not so sure the shivers are because of the cold.

We turn around and start walking at a faster pace. GG's little legs can totally move.

"The dark sneaks up on me when the seasons change. I expect the sun to linger longer than it does in the fall. It is a shame. This time of year reminds me of Levaine."

"How old were you when you left France?"

GG looks up at the sky. "I was thirteen years old when we immigrated to the United States. Papa and Mama chose this small town because it reminded them of our village."

"That's cool." It's like what I was thinking on the drive here when I saw all the crop fields in Snowflake and Taylor. You can be far, far away from home and still catch glimpses of it.

"So, they buy our bakery, make this small town our home, and we live here happily forever after."

From GG's point of view, everything in this town looks lovely.

Cozy.

Homey.

GG pulls me tighter. "Never fear, my Cat. I have thought of a way to give you all the information you need."

I press my teeth together so they don't chatter.

"Until then, what would you say to waking up early with me tomorrow morning?" GG smiles, her teeth gleaming in the dark.

"How early?"

She laughs at my suspicious tone. "Just before the sun, around five. If you meet me in the kitchen when the flour delivery comes, we will do some baking. I would very much love to bake with you."

I guess five isn't the earliest number in the morning, though it definitely isn't my favorite one. The good news is that waking up early means baking, and that is something I love to do no matter what time it is.

"I'm in." I squeeze her hand. "That sounds like the bestest idea ever!"

French Bread

3 C. hot tap Water
1 TBSP Yeast, active dry, not instant
2 TBSP Sugar
2 TBSP Olive Oil
1 TBSP Salt
Flour

Preheat the oven to 425°F.

This recipe is super similar to the white bread from Bake Believe but think of it as 2.0. There are a few more steps and a couple extra things to think about this time around.

I'll even put my serious face on while explaining it, so you don't get the wrong idea.

Ready, go!

First, get your tap water into a glass measuring cup that can hold at least 4 cups. Water should be hot to the touch, but not scalding. If it burns your fingers, it will kill the yeast. And if you kill the yeast, you might as well be making pancakes.

Sprinkle the sugar into the water and then stir in the yeast. Let it sit for about 5 minutes. This is enough time for the yeast to foam up and start to grow, but not long enough for it to overflow onto your counter.

You're welcome.

When it's ready, put it into the bowl of a stand mixer and add salt and olive oil, then about 5 cups of flour. Mix it up, and let it rest for about 5 more minutes.

(I'm really digging the 5s right now.)

Keep adding flour until the dough is sticky, but not wet. Nothing should be shiny here, but when you dab your finger on the dough, it should pull back with you.

Cover and rise for 1 hour.

Flop onto your counter. Meaning flop the *dough* onto your counter, but you can flop onto the counter, too, if you want—I won't judge. Divide into two pieces. You might need some flour on your hands to keep it from sticking to you. That's fine; all the cool kids are wearing flour on their hands, so you're good.

Shape dough into two long, skinny loaves and let rise another hour on a cookie sheet. Space the loaves far enough apart that they won't rise into each other. Take a sharp knife and cut diagonal slits in the top of each one.

Because they're pretty.

Then bake for 15-20 minutes. Golden brown here.

Let cool on cooling racks before you try to cut them or, again, they squish into pancakes.

Brush with melted butter because, why not?

<h1 style="text-align:center">6</h1>

<h1 style="text-align:center">Crepes</h1>

The bakery is quiet and dark when GG and I get back from our walk. Jojo locked the front up tight, so we have to go around the back of the house and come in through the porch. It's a super cozy room with all sorts of interesting things on the walls, I'll have to remember to come back in here and explore later.

"It is past my bedtime." GG yawns. "These old bones love the rest. Good night, love." She kisses both of my cheeks and points me to the stairs.

I watch her disappear around the corner. I'll never be able to wind down with my brain buzzing the way it is. I take the stairs two at a time and start checking for my parents. I find my mom when I peek through the third door on the right, in a room decorated mostly in pink.

Mom lays on the canopy bed with her arm draped over her eyes.

"Hey, Mommy Mom Mom."

"Hey." She doesn't move. Her voice sounds heavy, like it weighs five billion pounds and is carrying a backpack full of rocks.

"Can I..." I take a deep breath. It's too late now; I have to finish what I start. "Can I have my phone to email Tobey?"

Her arm flops off her face as she turns to look at me. "We need to talk about that."

Uh-oh.

I sit on the edge of the bed. It's as fluffy as a hug, so I sink right into the mattress. But I can't relax.

"Cat." Mom sighs and reaches over to rub my arm. "I've been so stressed about seeing—"

"Jojo," I finish for her.

"Yes, Jojo." Mom's hand runs out of juice and drops to the bed. "Really, though, that's no excuse for how grumpy I was during the drive. I feel really bad about that; I was too hard on you and I'm sorry."

"Oh." I can't think of anything else to say for a second. "It's okay."

"Thank you, sweetheart. I want you to know how proud I am of you. You've shown so much maturity these last few months. You followed all the rules we set, without exception, and only baked with Marissa or at school. You've been so good, Kitty Cat, really. I think...I think you are old enough and responsible enough to be in charge of your cell phone on this trip."

I freeze into a Cat ice sculpture attached to the comforter in this super pinky-pink room.

I don't even blink.

Mom boops my nose with her index finger. "For realsies." Her eyes squint into happy lines as she rolls over the bed for her purse on the nightstand. She tosses my phone on the comforter between us. "It's all yours. I just ask that you don't use it after eight. It's a terrible habit to look at your phone right before bed. Your brain needs that time to wind down to sleep."

I reach forward in the slowest of motion. When my fingers touch my phone, a thrill zings up my back. Seriously? I can have my phone all the time? No breaks? No curfews? No more watching Robyn stare at her screen while all I get to look at is the boring cactusy landscape?

"Does it have to sleep in a basket downstairs?"

Mom thinks for a minute. "At home, yes. That is a family rule. Here, I'll let you decide. Just, please put it to bed at eight. I..." She swallows. "I won't even check in on you. I trust you to do what you say."

I roll the phone over and over in my hands, watching the glitter in the case slide down one side and then the other. Not gonna lie, I'm choking up a little here. "Thanks, Mom."

Mom wraps her fingers around my wrist and pulls me forward so she can kiss my forehead. "I love you, Catnip."

"I love you, too, Mom."

"Go email Tobey and have fun." She shoos me away with a smile.

I jump to my feet, pushing buttons to wake up my phone and get into my emails as I walk towards the doorway.

"And Cat?" Mom's voice moves slower now. She's not going to win the stay awake fight for much longer.

"Yeah?"

"Please don't call people 'butt' anymore."

I giggle. "Done and done. Sleep good, Mom."

From Show Low to Boise, longest day ever!
Cat Anderson (kittycat14@email.com) November 22nd, 7:49 p.m.
To: Tobey
Tobey,

Hey! Sorry it took me so long to email you! I know I said I would as soon as we got here, but this was a super busy day!

After the longest car drive of all time, we got to Show Low, and landed right in the middle of a bakery war zone. Like a wild, wild west shoot-out almost. Can you picture it?

The bakeries stand back-to-back, the oven timer beeps, and they take long steps away from each other, the length of a commercial size kitchen. Then they whip around, face to face. The air fills with the scent of baking bread. Sprinkles are fired and boom!

Bakery one falls to the ground.

Which kind of makes sense, because Show Low got its name from gambling cowboys. I researched it before we left home. I wanted to know everything about this place so I wouldn't be an ignoramus when we got here. Turns out Show Low is something people say in poker or something, I don't know, I've never played.

Back to the Bake-Off.

Don't you want to play sinister music right there?

I really think it would add to the suspense.

When the alarm on my phone goes off, it dings and dongs into my dream. Even with my eyes open, I'm not sure where I am or what day it is.

Or *who* I am, for that matter.

I roll over with a groan. With how sluggy I feel, I could have closed my eyes five seconds ago. I pry each eyelid open with my fingers and just hope that they will stay that way on their own because it's going to be really hard to bake with my hands stuck to my eyelids.

With all the strength I have in my body, I roll myself the rest of the way out of the beautiful, soft bed and try to get dressed in the pitch black. I don't want to turn on a light and wake Robyn. She will be a bear all day long, especially since she got a second wind and stayed up super late playing Canasta with Aunt Jojo.

I inch my way out of the room, scooting my fingers along the wall. My eyeballs are useless right now. Good thing there is a little night-light plugged into the outlet up ahead.

Oh, my goshness!

My shirt is on backwards.

For the love of crepes! I look around to make sure no one is watching and flip it the right way. Now, I am officially awake. The horror of someone seeing me dressed like a blindfolded toddler has scared the sleepy right out of me. I check to make sure everything else I am wearing makes sense, then hurry down the stairs into the kitchen.

GG catches me at the door and wraps me up in a hug before I know what's happening. She's lucky I don't actually have ninja reflexes, or I might have done a wicked karate chop in my surprise. Instead, I muffle a good morning into her shoulder.

Today she smells like cinnamon.

Which reminds me of Tobey.

I can't think about him right now or I'll end up staring off into space with hearts where my eyeballs used to be. This is especially disastrous if I'm in charge of the salt measurement, setting the oven timer, or beating anything.

I really hope he answers my email soon. Writing to him last night made me miss his cute face a super lot.

"Good morning! Isn't it a glorious day?" GG holds me by the shoulders, kissing each of my cheeks with a loud smack.

I giggle. "What time did you get up?"

She waves her hand. "Who can tell? My bones creak and my body gets out of bed. It is time to bake!"

The oven beeps and GG feels for a potholder, then moves to open the oven door. Watching her pull pans out of the oven reminds me of the time my mom took me and Penny to see the Nutcracker at Ballet Idaho. It is so graceful and beautiful. Mist comes from the hot dishes, giving the whole kitchen a mystical feel.

"What did you make?" I lean on the counter to peer closer. Whatever is in that pan smells like the best thing ever, but I have no idea what you call that.

"Crepes. I cook them on the stove, then keep them warm in the oven."

"Oh, I've had those before. They have pudding or something in the middle, right? And fruit on top?"

"No, no, no,." GG's eyes twinkle while her mouth turns down. "That is not how to eat a crepe! I show you." She lifts a folded triangle onto my plate, and drizzles something that smells like butter over the top, then dips her fingers in a container and sprinkles white stuff over the top of that. "Powdered sugar." She winks, throwing a bit over her shoulder. "For good luck. Now you may eat."

She hands me a fork.

I remember my profound thought from dinner last night, to just eat whatever they give me without questioning it, and dig right in. "This is sooooooo good!"

GG's smile lights the sky better than the lame morning sun. She opens her mouth to say something, then stops when a shrill bell sounds through the kitchen.

"What's that?" I raise my voice so I can hear my words over the ringing in my ears. The bell was seriously loud.

"That's the flour delivery."

Hold up.

Didn't Jojo say that the flour gets delivered by the Jake guy? So, I am totally about to meet him? My heartbeat speeds to keep up with my imagination. From what I've heard about this Jake guy, he's either a dreamboat or a hairy scary troll that smells like overcooked broccoli.

One of those things, for sure.

GG shuffles to a big steel door next to the refrigerators. My fork scrapes the plate. What the what? I look down and am flabbergasted to see that my crepe is all gone. I was so caught up in the drama of my mind, that I didn't even know I finished eating!

It's like that unexplainable phenomenon when you're watching a good movie and all the popcorn disappears.

So weird.

The doorbell chimes once more, echoing off the walls. As GG opens the door, I lean forward, my elbows slipping on the shiny counters. I don't want to miss anything. It's probably good I finished eating; now I can give my full attention to Jake. Robyn and I need to go over every detail of this guy when we talk later on, so I have to focus.

"Well, hello there, Jake!" GG stands back as she holds the door open with one arm.

A really tall, super good-looking guy walks into the kitchen, his arms loaded with a huge bag of flour.

This is the guy that's trying to ruin our bakery and stressing out Jojo?

I don't get it.

He looks way more hero than villain. Like, he should be wearing leggings and a cape, carrying a princess down a thousand tower steps after defeating a dragon.

Seriously dreamy.

"GG!" He huffs. "It's a pleasure to see you this morning. *Bonne*... How does it go?"

"*Bonne journee.* Good day to you too! Will you be a dear and pour into the bucket?"

Jake moves across the kitchen without noticing me.

I wipe my mouth with the sleeve of my shirt. I hope there isn't anything hairy stuck in my teeth.

As Jake walks by, I catch a whiff of pine-scented air. I reel back, almost falling backwards onto the floor. It's like that moment when you find a worm in your apple after you already took a bite.

Jake props the flour bag on his knee and rips it open before he tips it into the bucket. He turns his head and notices me for the first time. "Hey now, who's this?"

I push my plate away, clamping my lips together so my breakfast can't go anywhere but down. My stomach twists and turns like it's driving up a curvy mountain pass. I turn away from Jake so that if the unthinkable happens, it doesn't happen on him.

Barfing on people is *no bueno*.

Believe me, I know.

As the silence stretches longer and longer between us, Jake's face slowly morphs from friendly to confused.

GG steps in, finally. "This is my great granddaughter, Cat Anderson."

"Ah." Jake nods. "I should have guessed. She looks just like Jojo."

I don't appreciate the way he talks about me as though I'm a puppy in the window of a pet store instead of a person with perfectly good ears right here in front of him. I am also totally unimpressed with the way his eyes dart around the kitchen when he says Jojo's name.

Shifty eyes.

You know what? I don't like this guy.

I don't like him at all.

I scowl.

Jake laughs. "Yep, just like Jojo." He crumbles the bag between his hands, sending a puff of flour into the air. "And where are you from, little Jojo?"

Little Jojo? Seriously? I love Jojo and all, but I'm fourteen years old for pecan's sake! He talks like I'm crawling on the floor in a diaper.

If I hadn't already decided to dislike his stinking guts, I would have started right up. Plus, now that he's said more than a couple words at once, I notice Jake sort of has an accent, like he should be rustling cattle and chewing straw instead of delivering flour.

"My name is Cat," I snap, "not little Jojo, and I'm from Boise." I lift my chin, as if I can take credit for the fact that I'm from a major city in Idaho and not a tiny town in the Arizona Mountains.

Show Low isn't even like *real* Arizona. I mean, not the Arizona everyone thinks of. No desert. No big cactus. No sweltering heat. Only cows and cowboys, which I just decided are nothing to brag about. Stupid place, I am disgusted with it for letting Jake live here.

Jake tips an imaginary hat. "I beg your pardon, Ms. Cat."

He's trying to charm me with his toothpaste commercial smile and fakey good manners, but it's not working. The more charming and adorable he tries to be, the more I want to pour melted butter over his head.

I open my mouth to say exactly what I think about him, but GG literally sticks a spoonful of whipped cream in my mouth and steps in front of me.

"The rest of the flour you may take to the storeroom. Thank you, Jake."

"My pleasure, GG. You have a great day. And you, Ms. Cat, might I say it was a joy to meet you." He whistles as he walks by, carrying the empty flour bag out with him.

I furiously swallow, trying to get all that dumb whipped cream out of the way before GG can close the door behind Jake. I have so much to say, I just can't get the words around all the fluff in my mouth. I finally spit the rest out on my empty plate.

"I hate that Jake guy!" I sputter as I hop off the stool for a drink of water. My mouth is all slimy, like it's coated in wet wax. "Who does he think he is, being all cute in here when he's our bake-off competition?"

Water slides right down the sides of my mouth when I try to drink. GG hands me a towel, I wipe my face and then throw the towel on the counter. It misses, slipping into the trash can. I pick it up and fling it back on the counter, smacking it in place so it doesn't get any ideas about falling again.

"Cat," GG says softly.

"And then he's all 'a pleasure to meet you' like he's a nice person. Well, he's *not* a nice person. Even I can tell that, and I don't even know him. How can you stand to look at that guy?"

"What guy?" Jojo comes into the kitchen, dressed in shiny pink running pants that have black zigzags going up and down her legs. She pulls an oversized hoodie over her tee. The static makes her short hair stick up in all directions, but it looks adorable. Robyn is right behind her, wearing her pajamas and a jacket. She lifts one leg to stretch her quad.

"*Buenos dias, Gata*. You're up early! Are you baking? It smells so good in here."

I study Jojo's face. Do I really look just like her? Our hair is different colors and lengths, but our noses are sort of the same, and our eyes. Yeah, her eyes are just like mine.

"Who are you talking about?" Jojo asks again. This time, she sounds suspicious.

I think she actually knows exactly who I am ranting about but wants to hear it out loud. Why do we humans do that? Like, force people to say the one thing that's going to make us the most annoyed or hurt?

"You know sometimes it is better for us to not know the answers to our questions." GG gives Jojo a sweet smile.

Jojo places a hand on her hip and fixes GG in place with her eyes. How is GG standing there so calm? I'm not anywhere near the beam and I get all gummy worm squirmy.

"We just finished the flour delivery," I blurt out.

"So, you are talking about Jake." Jojo puffs out her cheeks like his name tastes really bad. Which it does, I know, because I totally said his name out loud earlier and it tasted like moldy grapes.

"Yes,." I look down at my feet.

GG reaches out a hand and smooths down Jojo's static hair. "You know you will have so much more peace when you let this go."

"Let what go? I don't know what you mean. I don't have a problem with Jake. I don't even *know* Jake. So, don't you worry about me." She clips her phone to the sleeve of her jacket. "Did you quality check the flour order?"

"It is the finest flour in the White Mountains."

"Did she check it?" Jojo asks me.

I glance at GG, squirming for a different reason now. I don't actually know what Jojo means about checking the flour, but if GG says she did, I believe her. So, I'm not sure what to say.

"Jake does not hurt the flour, Jolynn."

"But did you check? There were weevils a couple months ago, remember? And with the bake-off so close I wouldn't put it past him to do something heinous."

GG sighs, leaning into the counter. "Weevils happen in flour, my Jolynn. It is one of the things. Now, no more worries. Go on your run and enjoy the day."

Jojo works her mouth like there are more words waiting for their turn to come out, all backed up in there, then she swallows them away. "Okay," she squares her shoulders, "You ready, Robyn?"

"Yep."

GG's eyes follow Jojo until she's gone, then they slide over to me. I shift to my other foot, fascinated with the tile. It's so tile-y. All square and grout-filled.

"Cat—"

I decide to interrupt so she doesn't scold me. "Why are you so nice to Jake? He's obviously a creeper."

GG takes my plate and fork. "Oh Cat, he is not the creeper." She rinses the dishes, then stacks them in the dishwasher. "Jake is a sweet boy."

I snort.

GG studies me for a moment longer, then reaches for a chair, which she drags to the sink so she can stand on it. Even then, she moves onto her tiptoes to reach the cabinet over the sink. When she steps down, there is a box in her hands. Two index cards slip out on her way to the counter, fluttering to the floor like butterflies.

I pick them up, not looking at them as I place them in her palm. My brain is thoroughly focused on how icky Jake is, so there isn't room for anything else right now.

"Oh, thank you." GG takes the cards, filing them carefully back into the box. "Someday I will find the time to type these in the computer. These are from my mama. See, Cat?"

She pulls out the first card and smooths it with her thumb.

"Her treasured recipes." GG's eyes grow wistful, then she laughs. "We French, we love our recipes like our children. Especially the pastries." She turns the card, so I get a glimpse of loopy cursive. I recognize the handwriting from Evie's journal, but I am not about to be sidetracked.

"Jake is your competition, and he delivers your flour; how do you know he *doesn't* poison it or something? Like...sabotage?" I whisper the last word to make it as ominous as it sounds in my head.

GG sets the cookbook on the counter and pulls out a long-handled pot all dinged and discolored like it was used in the Revolutionary war.

"Don't laugh, I'm serious!"

"Oh Cat." GG takes both of my hands in hers and looks deep into my eyes. She is a lot shorter than me, but somehow, I feel small. "I am sorry for not being serious to you. I will tell you something. Jolynn, she is a kind, gentle, thoughtful, fun-loving soul. She is this way with all that she meets, except for this Jake."

"I don't get it."

GG looks at the ceiling, "How to say it? Your Aunt Jolynn thinks she cannot stand Jake. She tried to date him but decides she cannot stand him. Why? It is strange, you see, he is a good-looking boy."

I make my best pshaw noise; no way I'm admitting that.

"He is good also." She squeezes my hands. "Jolynn sees only his bad. It is like this: she is not herself with Jake and in return he is not himself with her."

I still don't really get what GG means. "So, they weren't ever friends? Not even before he decided to open his ghetto bakery?"

GG looks at the ceiling. "How do you say it? When they are friends, but not friends?"

I think for a minute, "Frenemies? Is that what you mean?"

"Yes, they love to hate each other. They bring out the very worst in each other. This is important, Cat, very important for you to know." Her eyes get that far off look again, like she's going to the past and the future both at the same time. "My advice to you, dear Cat, is this, do not be judging either of them until you gather more facts."

I want to argue that I saw enough to judge Jake, and I think Jojo has every right to hate his guts. Oh yeah, and everything is obviously Jake's fault. I don't say any of that though. I can't quite agree with myself that it's true. I mean, I want to believe it, because it sounds right, but there is a small part of me that thinks GG has a good point. It probably is better for me to get more information.

And this part, though small, is super-duper convincing.

"Okay," I say, "I'll gather more facts."

"Okay?" GG smiles at me. "But not now. You and I, we have work to do. Let us bake."

Crepes

1 C. Flour
1 C. Milk
2 Eggs, beaten
1 TBSP Sugar
1/4 tsp Salt
2 TBSP Butter, melted

Do you have a crepe pan?

Is that a weird question? Maybe if we were sitting on the beach working on our tans it would be, but if you want to make some crepes, this is a valid concern.

Having a crepe pan is super helpful when making crepes. It's just a flat, round pan that fits on a stove burner. I personally love mine; it's made of cast iron.

So, I give you permission to try this out without a crepe pan, but I don't guarantee they will turn out very round.

Fair enough?

Let's get started!

In a large mixing bowl—no stand mixer here; it's too easy to over mix. Do it by hand. Baker's biceps, y'all!

Whisk together flour and milk. The reason we do this first with just the milk is because the small amount of liquid lets you get out all the lumps early on. When you have a pretty smooth situation, gradually add in the beaten eggs until it's all mixed together.

Add the sugar, salt, and butter; stir to combine.

Now, heat your crepe pan on medium. If you use cast iron like *moi*, make sure it's lightly greased so there's no sticking.

We don't tolerate sticking around these parts.

Using a ¼ - ⅓ measuring cup—depending on the diameter of your pan and how thick you like your crepe—scoop the batter onto the griddle. Tilt the pan around and around and around, like one of those carnival rides people always puke on, so that the batter coats the surface evenly.

Crepes don't take long to cook at all! Super speed masters. Like 1-2 minutes per side. They should be golden brown in spots. Layer the finished crepes on a plate with sheets of paper towels to separate.

Then they don't sweat or stick.

I think I already made it clear how I feel about both of those things.

Okay, here's the fun part!

You can dress them up with cream and fruit in the middle or make them savory with scrambled eggs and spinach or do like GG and sprinkle with powdered sugar. This is why I love crepes—so many options!

7

Cream Puffs

The very first thing GG wants me to do?

Bake happy.

I was thinking that baking with GG means I can really let loose. Like, maybe I can bake something epically awesome. Or even better, bake something with an epically awesome emotion. But no, GG wants to see me bake happy. Just happy. Even though this sounds like the most boringest thing in the whole world.

It doesn't take me long to realize that GG chose happy *because* happy is so basic. I've practiced so much with Aunt Marissa, I can do it easily, almost without thinking now. GG wants to observe me, like I'm a microbe on a biology slide, to see how I do what I do.

That's the theory anyway.

The reality is that I'm so stinking irritated at Jake, all I can think about while I stare at the counter full of flour, sugar and eggs, is throwing each ingredient in his dumb face.

No wonder Jojo's baking is all sour.

I totally get how she feels.

"Cat, Cat, Cat," GG clucks, "you do not do the baking happy!"

"I know." I grit my teeth.

She takes my hands to stop me from cracking eggs like they insulted my mother and leans in to look at my eyes. Her face softens.

"Did I tell you...you look so much like my mama when she was young? It is uncanny."

"Your mama? Evie? I look like her? Really?" I put the eggs down as my brain makes the slow trek out of angry town.

I already want to bake the world a better place like Evie, looking like her would be a super bonus level.

Now that is a happy thought!

I survey the poor eggs, yolks broken and oozing into the whites, and feel the frustration ease out of my pores like toxic fumes.

"I made a mess." I apologize with my eyes.

GG waves her hands over the bowl, erasing the disaster as though she has a magic wand. I half expect to look inside and see the eggs all whole again.

Stranger things have happened.

"This doesn't matter, Cat. Ingredients, we can work with. Feelings are what matters. How do you feel now?"

I stop and think. "Um, calmer-ish, I think."

"That is good. Now, let's think happy. What makes you happy?"

What makes me happy?

Why is that such a hard question to answer? I wonder if it's because happy doesn't really come from things, I mean, there isn't anything that can *make* me happy.

At least, that's what I'm learning, but it's kind of hard to wrap my brain around. Mostly because my brain really likes to point fingers.

Like, point: Bubby makes me so annoyed, because he does sound effects while he plays with his army guys.

And point: when Penny stretches her leg up to her ears during dinner it freaks me out; legs do not bend that way, and they definitely shouldn't do it at tables where people are trying to eat.

Oh yeah, and point: Jake makes me frustrated.

Because he does.

But everyone keeps telling me that no one can *make* you *feel* anything. Like, when GG dropped that bomb last night that not even our baking makes people happy.

Which is super confusing. I know for suresies that the cupcakes I baked made Conner get obsessively in love with me and the cookies from culinary made Tobey sad.

I don't really understand.

Plus, I kind of have a headache now.

"Cat?" GG takes my face in both hands. "Your eyes whirl like windmills. Stop thinking and just say to me, first thoughts, things that make you happy?"

"Glitter nail polish." I bite my lip, pushing away all the other annoying, confusing and frustrating thoughts. "Watching YouTube videos. Hanging out with Robyn. Eating Marissa's Mexican food. Listening to Antonio sing."

GG nods to keep me rolling.

"The sound of lockers slamming at the end of the school day, the smell of raspberries, homemade soft pretzels." I breathe out, and stare at the ceiling. "My dad's stubbly chin, the way Mom pets my head when she's happy, Bubby's freckles. Watching Penny do a *jete*; she looks like she's flying."

My heart fills up my chest like it just took a deep breath and wants to hold it. "This bakery, being here with you. Cinnamon, yeast and butter."

GG claps her hands. "You grab onto each one of those things and hold tight. I will show you how to bake Cream Puffs!"

This time, when GG holds out the old recipe box from Evie, I give it my full attention. I lean over the wrinkled cards, holding my breath in a reverent way. With my eyes, I trace the loops of Evie's handwriting. It is so familiar to me, after all the time I spent reading and rereading her diary over the last couple of months. The way she writes her C's is my favorite, with a curly loop at the top like big, eighties style bangs.

GG's hands linger over the card as she smooths it out for us to read more easily.

"Do you miss her?" I watch GG carefully.

She doesn't answer right away. "It is a funny thing, Cat. It is a funny thing that years and years can pass without someone, and you still feel the empty place where they lived."

I don't know what that feels like. But then, I haven't really known anyone who died and left a big empty space. There was just the goldfish I won at the school carnival three years ago. Glitterbomb was only with me two days before she went belly up, so I don't think I can really relate.

The confusion on my face must be mondo because GG laughs and kisses me right in the center of my forehead.

Good thing she doesn't wear dark red lipstick, or I would look ridiculous because I don't want to wash that kiss off ever. The place where her lips touch feels all glowy, like a magic spell would feel.

Or a blessing.

"Yes, I miss her every day. So, it is good I bake every day, then she is with me." She reaches for a whisk and hands it to me, pointing to the messy eggs in the bowl.

I guess we're still using them. This must not be one of those recipes where the eggs need special treatment. Marissa made a lemon meringue pie for *Tio* Tonio's birthday, and I watched; it was ridiculous! Marissa had to be so careful not to get even the smallest bit of yellow into the white or it was all ruined.

I'm super relieved the eggs I cracked in anger are still usable. I take the whisk and start mixing. "Will you tell me about your mom? I don't know much, and I want to know everything!"

"Everything is much." GG pulls a large pot out of the cupboard and puts it on the stove, lighting the gas burner and turning it down to low.

"Yup."

GG fills a glass measuring cup with flour, then walks to the fridge. "As I told you, my parents came to America when I was about your age." She disappears into the mammoth appliance for a moment.

I'm glad she's not still talking; I think that fat fridge would absorb what she's saying, and I don't want to miss a thing.

GG comes out with her hands full of cubes of butter and starts back towards me. "From France."

"Tell me more about our village, please."

"Well,"—GG begins unwrapping the butter—"it was the tiniest little village near the border of Italy. My grandpapa opened a bakery, the finest in the province. My mama worked at the counter from the time she was seven years old."

I am pretty much done with the eggs, so I reach to help GG. I hold the edge of a wrapper and shake it until the butter plops out. "I could barely tie my own shoes when I was seven."

GG reaches for a wooden spoon. "Well, it is a different time now. Children grew up faster then, but also, they did not live so long, so it is balanced. You are right where you need to be."

I let that thought simmer, and like the way it feels.

Right where you need to be.

"Mama loved to bake, more than all other things, except her family of course. Her papa died right after she and my papa married, so they took over the bakery. People traveled from all over the province to eat there."

"Did she have any brothers or sisters?"

"One brother." GG's face goes smooth, like she wipes it with an eraser. "He came to America as soon as he was old enough to leave Levaine and never returned. Some people are not meant for small towns."

I wonder about that. I mean, I wonder if I am not meant for a small town. It's not like Boise is ginormous, but it is way bigger than Show Low. Could I be content to live in a small place forever? Would I even want to try?

"My uncle, he died before I was born. He was a carpenter of great skill. Many things in this bakery are gifts to my mama from him."

GG plucks the unwrapped cubes of butter from the counter and places them, one at a time, in the saucepan. They sizzle and bounce off the sides of the pot. "Oh! Too hot!" GG lowers the burner and shakes the handle until the butter calms down.

I love the smell of melting butter.

Even when it gets kind of burnt.

It makes me happy.

I'll have to remember that so I can list it with the other things I love the next time I'm trying to calm down 'cause a guy named Jake seriously ticked me off.

GG stirs with the wooden spoon a second longer, then points to the flour. I'm starting to get the hang of working with GG, she doesn't need to say the words out loud for me to know what she means. I pick up the glass measuring cup full of flour; it's way heavier than it looks, so I use both hands and hug it to my belly.

"Pour it in slowly, here, as I stir. Good! Now, where was I?"

"Um." I concentrated super hard on the flour, not wanting to spill any, so I can't remember where she was either.

"No matter." GG shakes her head. "We begin where we begin, and it will be the right place for us."

"Yay!" I shake a little too hard this time, making the flour puff into our faces. "Oops! Sorry!"

"No sorry! This is the experience, the fun of the baking! Do not clean it away!"

So, I don't, and what's weirder, I don't care. I totally could care less that there is flour all over my face and hair. I might look like a depressed ghost, or an albino rhino and I totally don't even give a hoot.

As Granny Penny likes to say.

Oh! I totally remember where GG left off!

"What did your brother make for the bakery? Will you show me?"

"Cat, can you get a cookie sheet from that cupboard? This will be ready in less than a minute." GG scrapes her spoon along the sides of the pot and nods towards one of the cupboards.

I pull it open and grab the closest cookie sheet. I only bang it a little in my effort to get it out. I'm sure the ringing in our ears will fade eventually.

GG goes on like nothing loud and obnoxious happened. "Mama loved to bake, and she was so very, very good at it. These cream puffs we make today were her specialty."

Wait! She didn't answer my question. I watch her for a minute and decide to let that slide. As curious as I am about the things Evie's brother made, I am a zillion times more interested in Evie.

I love that she loved to bake, just like me. I don't think it's a coincidence that we have so much in common. I get a shivery feeling down my back that makes it hard to keep the flour from falling. The shivery feeling climbs to my neck and leaves tingles there.

"Mama was also very beautiful."

My shoulders drop, taking the tingles with them.

Just like that.

I guess I'm not as much like Evie as I thought I was. I dump the last little bit of flour into the pot and set the measuring cup on the counter.

GG pauses her stirring and reaches over to turn off the burner. "This must cool now. We have some time; you tell me what is wrong."

"What?"

"You do this" She exaggerates my slumped shoulders, making herself look even smaller. Her lip puffs out to add to the silliness.

"I didn't!" I push my shoulders way back, like I'm in the military. My blue shirt reflects in her pupils. "Okay, maybe I did."

"Yes, you did. Thank you. Now, why the slump?"

I slide the measuring cup back and forth between my hands, careful to keep it far from the edge of the counter. "I...guess...I'm disappointed?"

"Are you?"

I think for a second. "Yes."

"Why?"

This part is a little harder to get out, like when Bubby stuck a marble in his nose when he was two. I might need tweezers, dish soap, and a clamp.

" I thought I was like Evie."

GG puts her arm around my shoulders. "Oh, my Cat, but you are!"

"No." I shake my head. "I'm not. Not if she was beautiful. I mean..." I take a deep breath. "I'm cute, or whatever. I'm not super gross, but not beautiful. Not like Robyn is..."

GG puts a finger to her lips. "My dear girl, we must have your eyes checked."

"Why?"

"If you don't see how beautiful you are, truly, we need to see about some glasses."

Her expression is so stern, I almost miss the twinkle in her eyes.

She's totally teasing me!

But is she teasing about me being beautiful?

Or about the glasses?

GG reaches for my hand and pulls me around the counter to the stools, where we sit across from each other. "I remember how it feels to be your age. Maybe this seems impossible to you, but I do remember. There will come a time, soon I think, when you will look in the mirror and see what I see."

There is no way I'm asking what she sees.

Even though I'm super curious.

I don't really like it when people are all negative about themselves for attention. I'm not trying to do that; I'm being honest about how I feel, but now GG's going to think she has to build me up and that's just awkward. Nobody likes to sit and wait while someone tries to come up with ways to compliment them.

GG's eyes disappear into smile wrinkles, making her look years and years younger. I think I see that girl she was once upon a time.

"It is good, I think, that you don't see what I see. Not yet. Not until you are older and have some bit of humility also. This, I say, because my dear Mama knew she was very beautiful."

"Oh."

Is it bad to know you're beautiful?

"She knew from the time she was very young. This combination," GG mimes an explosion with her hands, like Jojo did the night before.

When I stop giggling, she goes on, "She made a mistake, as we all do at times—"

"What did she do?"

GG shakes her head. "Mistakes, we know have consequences..."

"Wait, what did she do, though?"

"Last night I stayed awake to think this over. There is much I can tell you about my mama and our family, but I don't think this is the right way. It is like the man who fished."

"The who, what, how?" I scramble to keep up with her thought train.

"They say, you give a man fish and you feed him just today, but you teach him to fish, and you feed him for all his lifetime."

"Okay." I am confused out the wazoo. What does fishing have to do with Evie and baking?

"You must find the answers to your questions, Cat. If I tell you everything, you will have the answers in your head, but not in your heart. When you know in your heart, then you will understand for yourself. I think we are ready to add the eggs."

I follow GG around the counter, back to the stove. She pokes a finger at the lump of dough in the pot while I give the eggs another whisk with the fork, both for good luck and to have something to do with my hands. I wish I could hook an internet cord from my ear to GG's and instantly download everything she knows.

"Do you want to stir or pour?" GG holds a clean wooden spoon in the air.

I look at the glass cup of eggs. "Stir."

GG swats my bottom with the spoon, then holds it out for me to grab.

"Hey!" I snatch it, scrunching my face.

"A swat with a wooden spoon is good luck." GG picks up the eggs and tips some into the pot. "Now, stir this. When it comes together, I add more."

I get to work. As more and more eggs join the mix, I use one hand to hold the pot steady and the other to stir. My biceps burn.

Hey, If I keep this up, I think I will get super buff! I can totally see myself with mega toned baker biceps.

"Do you understand what I tell you?" GG searches my face.

I give myself a little shake. Was she talking and I totally missed it? I gotta learn to focus. "Ummmm,"

GG nudges me with her elbow. "About your question? I don't want you to miss out on discovering the answers for yourself."

"I think so." I blow a strand of hair out of my eyes. Too bad my hands are busy, and I can't tuck it behind my ear; it's tickling my nose.

"When you discover for yourself, then you will never forget, and you will have all the answers you want to know."

Well, that sounds pretty fantastic. All I've had for months is questions; answers would be ding dong dang amazing. But the whole 'figure it out for myself' thing sounds like a lot of work. I mean, where do I even start?

"No, no, no!" GG tips the last of the eggs into the pot and sets the cup down to wiggle her finger at me. "I see you thinking too much again.

No worries, this is a fun game I make just for you. It is a…" She snaps her fingers. "When you search for the prize, oh, what is the word?"

"Like, geocaching?" I give the dough one more stir. It looks pretty combined to me.

GG's face scrunches. "I do not know this word."

"Oh, um…" I press my lips together. "Then, like a scavenger hunt? Or a treasure hunt?"

"Yes! I make the treasure hunt for you."

"Wait, you're going to tell me everything with a treasure hunt?" Excitement whips up in my belly, all white and fluffy like egg whites. I love treasure hunts and easter egg hunts and all the hunts! "Where are the clues? What do I do? Where do I start?"

"We finish this up and I give you the clues." She pulls open a drawer and rummages around until her hand emerges with a cookie scoop. "This is for you."

I squeeze the handle of the cookie scoop a few times without thinking. The lever makes a loud clicking sound each time I release it. What is this scavenger hunt going to be like? I just hope I get to slink around the corner of buildings and army crawl through fields to search for clues!

Okay, maybe not the fields thing. Those are probably covered in cow doodie, and I do not want to crawl through that!

GG sets a cookie sheet lined with paper on the counter next to me.

"What's that?" I point to the paper.

"It is the parchment paper. So, the puffs, they cook the same."

Oh, that's cool. I didn't know about that stuff. I wish I had it when I made chocolate chip cookies. The ones in front were perfect, but the ones in back were crunchy brown.

GG shows me how to scrape the cookie scoop to make the cream puffs all the same size. Unlike chocolate chip cookies, she tells me not to smoosh the dough balls down with my palm. They need to stay rounded so they can puff up. Which makes perfect sense, considering the name.

Once I get the hang of it, GG leaves to get my scavenger hunt.

I pause a sec to take a picture with my phone. Now that I have my phone all the time, I'm going to take a boatload of pictures to document this trip. I try a couple different angles, then stick my phone in my back pocket so I can scoop, scrape, and plop the dough some more. This is harder than it sounds; my arms are all jiggly. Also, my legs are twitchy, and my toes keep popping up in the air. It's hard not to feel impatient, and clocks do not move very well when you stare at them, so I concentrate all my extra energy on making each puff perfectly smooth.

One hundred and fifty million tick-tocks later, GG comes back to the kitchen.

"Here we are!" GG waves index cards in her hand. "I took a very long time, I am sorry. This old brain, I forget where I put the cards, then I forget my glasses!" She laughs. "I did not hide clues; I will give them all to you at once. Once you solve them all, come to me and I tell you everything."

Cream Puffs

1 C. Water
1/2 C. Butter
1 C. Flour
1/4 tsp Salt
4 Eggs

This recipe is proof that it doesn't take much to make something spectacular! Just a note before we start, don't substitute milk for the water. It might be tempting because water is boring, but the added fat from the milk actually keeps the choux from puffing.

Choux?

Bless you.

No, silly! Choux dough is this eggy, light, airy pastry dough that makes cream puffs, eclairs, and churros.

Now that we are all super educated and wise and junk, we can get to baking!

Preheat the oven to 400°F.

In a saucepan, bring water and butter to a boil. Add flour and mix until you get a smooth ball.

Remove from the heat and let it rest for about 5 minutes. All that ball forming can be exhausting!

Now we're going to add the eggs. But slow down, partner, these eggs gotta be patient. Only one at a time. It helps to use a hand mixer, unless you're working on those baker biceps. In that case, get to it!

When one egg is thoroughly mixed in, add the next until all four are done and done.

Use a cookie scoop, medium size, so they are all uniform-ish and drop onto a parchment-lined cookie sheet. They will puff out a little, so give them room to breathe, but mostly they will puff up.

Bake for 25-30 minutes.

Most of the time, I'm a fan of underbaking, but in this case you gotta go full time. It's super important for the puff.

Cool on racks for a few minutes before you cut the tippy tops off with a serrated knife. Pull out any extra dough inside. There shouldn't be much. Then fill with homemade pastry cream.

I think we're ready for pastry cream. How about you? Here's a recipe to try out.

Pastry Cream

2 Eggs
4 TBSP Cornstarch
1/2 C Sugar
1/4 tsp Salt
2 C. Whole Milk
1 TBSP Vanilla extract
4 TBSP Butter

First things first, whisk the eggs, cornstarch, salt, and sugar together, then set them aside. We'll need those later.

Then, pour the milk into a large saucepan and bring to a low boil, stirring the whole time. (A low boil is like a calm bubble: a high boil is spitting mad). You stir the whole time because milk really likes to stick to the bottom of hot pans.

It takes a little while to get to that low boil. Longer than you think, so I suggest having a buddy in the kitchen/on the phone, or a good podcast you are obsessed with. Both make the time speed by.

Now, ladle some of that hot milk into the egg mixture and stir, stir, stir. This tempers the eggs and starts activating the thickening in the cornstarch. Soooooooo technical! Slowly pour the egg/milk mixture back into the pan with the rest of the hot milk and whisk, whisk, whisk some more.

Bump the heat to medium-high and whisk until the mixture thickens. A good test is if you dip a spoon in and it coats the spoon without all dripping off. Another good rule is if it looks as thick as pudding. 'Cause that's what we're going for.

Remove from the heat immediately – so it doesn't curdle – and pour through a sieve, into a bowl, to get rid of all those unsightly lumps. Cool slightly and then fill the cream puff shells.

Refrigerate for at least an hour. These are delicious at room temp, but creamy dreamy refrigerated!

Good luck eating just one!

8

Baked Oatmeal

I bend my knee to rock the old, wooden chair as I wait for Robyn to come back from her jog with Jojo. They are taking forever and a day and a half. If I didn't have an email from Tobey waiting in my inbox, I might do something drastic in my impatience.

Instead, I read it for the third time.

But who's counting?

Cowgirl Cat

Tobey Richards (sweettoothdecay@email.com)   November 22nd, 9:09 p.m.

To: Cat

Hey Cowgirl Cat,

Your vacation is way more exciting than mine. So far, all I've done is play basketball with Liam and dig for earthworms with Conner. Dad's supposed to take us fishing tomorrow morning, but we'll see.

So, a bakery showdown, huh?

I'm glad you asked my opinion; I know exactly what I would do. Get all super-secret spy-ed up and go on a mission to check out the competition. I'd find out everything I could about them so I could crush them.

I am the Tobinator!

But if anyone asks, I didn't tell you to do that. Actually, maybe you should eat your phone after you read this to remove all evidence.

Or at least delete that last sentence.

Then tell me all about it so I can live my dreams through you.

Because I. Am. Bored.

See ya!

Tobey

P.S. You should send me pictures of the stuff you bake.

P.P.S. Speaking of baking, I'm super hungry now. I'm going to walk to Diet Starts Monday tomorrow and buy something amazing.

P.P.P.S. I would make something myself, but I tried to bake biscuits from memory for dinner, and they kind of tasted like baking soda.

P.P.P.P.S. Which tastes like a toilet.

P.P.P.P.P.S. Not that I would know, gross, Cat.

Oh, my goshness! Tobey is so adorable! His email makes me want to dance a flighty jig all over the parking lot. But I don't, because I might scare the customers and because I don't actually know any flighty jigs. I don't even think that's a thing; probably I made it up just now in my rapture of reading Tobey's email.

Since Robyn is nowhere in sight, I'm going to answer him back right away. If today is anything like how crazy busy yesterday was, I don't know when I'll have another chance.

The Tobinator

Cat Anderson (kittycat14@email.com) November 23rd, 7:36 a.m.

To: Tobey

Tobey,

Here's a picture of the cream puffs I made this morning with GG.

Well, just the shells. They are baking right now, while I sit outside waiting for Robyn to get back from jogging. She's nutso; I have on like four layers and I'm still freezing. I don't know why people want to run outside at all, much less when it's this cold.

> *I just realized you totally don't agree, right? I've seen you jogging by my house in shorty shorts when it's freezy cold outside.*
>
> *What is up with you people?*
>
> *Anyways, GG put together a scavenger hunt to help me learn more about my great-great Grandma Evie. She's the one who started this family bakery. Well, her parents did, actually. She brought it to America. Isn't that the funnest? I'll let you know how it goes!*
>
> *And I love your idea for checking out the new bakery, Tobinator! I'm totally going to do it, as soon as Robyn gets back from her run with JoJo. If she ever does. I might be waiting on this porch forever and ever, a thousand-year-old skeleton in a rocking chair that freaks out little kids on Halloween.*
>
> *Oh - and after I start on these clues. They are burning a hole in my pocket. For suresies after that I'll dig out my best spy gear, stage a bakery coup, and then tell you all about it.*
>
> *Also, you have to tell me what you get at DSM. My mouth is watering thinking about their pretzels!*
>
> *Cat*

"Whatcha doing?"

I screech and jump a mile, my phone flying into the air. Robyn catches it with a smooth swipe of her hand and a laugh that they can probably hear all the way back at home in Boise. I stand up and smooth my shirt, then grab my phone back.

"Emailing Tobey."

"Oooooooooooh."

I roll my eyes. "Kindergarten much, Robyn? Where did you guys run? Taiwan? You've been gone forever!"

Robyn leans into a side lunge. "We ran to the cemetery—"

"Ew! Why would you do that? Creepy McCreeperson!"

Now Robyn rolls her eyes. "You are, like, six years old. Actually, *muchacha*, the cemetery is *muy* coolio. We should walk over there later."

"Yeah, and then we should tie ourselves to a railroad track, because that is also a good idea."

"Whatever." Robyn tightens her shoelaces. "Anyways, first we ran over to Jake's bakery; Jojo wanted to see if he's busy."

"Was he open that early?"

"He opens a whole hour earlier than *L'Amour* does."

My heart speeds up so it thumps against my chest. "And?"

Robyn leans to stretch her other side. "It was busy."

With a face that would make a gremlin jealous, I peek into the front window of *L'Amour*. The tables are all full, it's been a steady trickle of people since we opened, but I wouldn't say it's busy.

"Crap-a-doodle-ding-dong."

"Oooooooh, language!" Robyn pushes my shoulder. I shove her back, making her lose her balance and topple into the rocking chair I was sitting in.

"Sorry!" I giggle, pulling her back up. "If you didn't act like you're five, things like this wouldn't happen."

She scoffs. "Whatever, you're the one who said crap-a-doo-dle-ding-dong! Why are you waiting out here anyway? I thought you were baking with GG."

"I was, guess what?" I pull the index cards out of my pocket and hold them behind my back.

Robyn's face drops. "What are you hiding?"

"I..."

"If you spray me in the face with something vile or drop a stink bomb, I swear..."

I reel back in mortal offense. "Do I look like Liam?"

Robyn's head tips to one side, as if she's considering it.

Seriously?

"Maybe around the ears a little." She taps her top lip as I gasp in horror. "Yes, definitely. There's something about your earlobes for sure that have a distinct Liam look."

I shove the cards deep in my back pocket so I can fold my arms and glare.

Robyn leans against the window, laughing. "You should see your face."

"Oh?" I raise an eyebrow. "You mean the face that doesn't look even a tiny bit like Liam?"

Robyn snorts and covers her mouth.

I sniff. "It's just too bad you're being such a bu…I mean booger. GG gave me something super cool, but now I think you're the worst cousin in the world, so I'm going to go share it with the cows instead."

I imagine I hear a low moo, like the herd understands what I said and thinks that's a great idea.

And also, they think Robyn is a stink brain.

Robyn's eyes widen. "What did GG give you? Something about Evie? Something about baking emotions?"

I shake my head. "Too bad for you. You could have known, but instead you had to be a flapperjammie."

"A what?"

"If you don't know…" I toss my hair. "I'm not going to explain it to you."

Robyn falls to her knees. "Cat! You have to tell me! I will go bonkers if you don't!"

I lift my chin as she clings to the hem of my jeans.

"Please, please, pretty please? I'm not good with mysteries! And the last few months, all this stuff we don't know, it is pretty much turning my brain to mush!"

"What brain?" I lift my foot so she will quit pulling on me.

She stops, her hands dropping to the wood porch. "So that's it then?" Her head bows and her ponytail swings side to side. "This is how I die."

"Oh, my goshness!" I swat her shoulder with both hands. She rolls onto her back. Instead of getting up, she crosses her arms over her chest and closes her eyes.

This feels very familiar, not because it's something Robyn does all the time, but because I'm pretty sure I have done this exact thing to Robyn on at least three different occasions. "Since when did you start acting like me, Robyn?"

"Shush, you're ruining my death." She peeks one eye and then closes it tight.

"We have got to stop spending so much time together. I think we are morphing brains. Am I really this annoying?"

"Yes," she says.

Nice.

"Okay." I step over her. "Well, I'm going to go read these cards from GG to the cows and start an epic adventure. Let me know when you're done dying." I skip a few steps down the sidewalk. I'm not sure where the cows are, but I'm sure I'll find them if I walk far enough in any direction.

Robyn rolls to one side, propping her head with one hand. "If I'm not dead anymore, will you show me what GG gave you?"

"Not if you still think I look like Liam." I place one fist on my hip.

"Then you don't, not even a tiny bit."

I wave my arm in a big arc. "Thank you. Come on already! I've been waiting and waiting and waiting for you to get back so I could read one!"

Robyn leaps to her feet with a cheer and is at my side before I have time to blink. "What did she give you? What are these cards?"

I pull them out and hold tight with shaky fingers. "Clues."

"Clues?" Robyn's face wrinkles. "What are they for?"

"Okay, check it! GG put together a scavenger hunt for us to learn more about Evie and baking. Isn't that the *coolest*?"

Robyn squeals her yes.

"These are the clues; we get to choose where to start." I turn the cards over so we can't see the writing. "Pick one."

Robyn waves her hands in the air a few times, like she's working on a magic spell, then yanks a card from the middle. She turns it over so we can both see while she reads it out loud.

"You find me where the weather turns. When it freezes, when it burns. Not without a blush you see, I am red as red can be."

I look up. "Super poetical. Do you think GG wrote this?"

Robyn holds the card up to her face to read it again, her lips form some of the words. "She must have. Hey! She's a poet and we didn't know it!"

I groan, but at least Robyn didn't do one of her horrible, cheese bomb jokes. She went through a hundred thousand of those things during the drive here before my mom, very politely, told us she wanted to shut her eyes for a few hours.

"So, what do you think it is?" I ask. "Something that does weather, like a cell phone app? Maybe the next clue is on GG's cell phone?"

"Maybe." Robyn chews on her lower lip. "But GG's phone isn't red, it's purple. Hey, I'm starving, while we're thinking, let's eat cream puffs. They're ready, right?"

"Probably." I tuck the cards into my front pocket this time and follow Robyn into the bakery. I could put away a couple cream puffs myself; those crepes seem like a long time ago.

We walk by cute old people sitting at the tables. I smile at the cowboy hats and plaid shirts. It's like the bakery is a time machine that took us back two hundred years.

We push through the kitchen doors, just in time to hear Jojo and GG talking.

"Grammy, please, we have to do something. Jake's bakery has a line down the street. If we're going to survive, we will have to change, evolve with the times. Gluten free flour, agave instead of sugar, opening an hour earlier, all of these things might help-"

"No, no, no, no." GG shakes her head with each word as she wipes crumbs from the counter into her hand. "No glutes, no krypto—"

"Keto." Jojo sighs.

"None of that either. Jolynn, I tell you and I tell you we will be just fine. We do not need to change with the whims."

"But we haven't ever changed, Grammy! Other than adding scones and cinnamon rolls, we are the same bakery we were when Evie was in charge! Don't you think that's wrong?"

GG shakes her head.

"I just think it might help, if we were smarter about what we make." Jojo picks up one of the cream puff shells and looks it over. "Cream puffs are not a breakfast food. We should concentrate on things we know people will eat, things that sell well, so that we aren't wasting our time and resources. I just don't know that anyone will come to the bakery for cream puffs at seven in the morning."

"Oh posh!" GG turns away as the oven goes off. A rich, delicious smell fills the kitchen as she pulls out two rectangular pans. "Cat, Robyn, dears, please fill the cream puffs. If no one else eats them for breakfast, we will."

"Absolutely." Robyn rushes around the counter, not looking at Jojo.

"Here." Jojo sighs again, deeper this time, and pulls a covered bowl out of the left fridge. She hands a spoon to both Robyn and I. "Pastry cream."

I watch carefully to see what we're supposed to do. Robyn dollops pastry cream into a shell, then she puts a little piece of cream puff dough on top of the cream, like a cap. GG must have cut off the tops before we came in.

I pick up a spoon and do the same thing as Robyn, except for the part where she pops a whole cream puff into her mouth instead of putting it on the serving tray.

"Hey!" I elbow her.

"What?" Her mouth is so full I can barely understand her until she swallows. "I'm hungry! These are so good; I want to eat them all."

I move the tray so it's closer to me, in case she gets any ideas about following through on that want. I think she totally *would* eat them all.

Jojo still examines the cream puff in her hand.

GG reaches over to scoop some cream onto a spoon and hands it to Jojo. "Fill, eat." She winks. "Do not want to waste our resources."

Jojo shakes her head and does as she's told, then pops the whole cream puff into her mouth. As she chews, she looks at me, her face contorting into many expressions. I try to give the cream puffs my full attention, because it's super awkward being stared at creepily. Jojo swallows heavily, then her eyes suddenly pop open as if someone squeezed her belly really hard.

"Wait a second, did Cat bake these?" She points a finger at the tray of cream puffs.

"Did you, Cat? All by yourself?" Robyn sounds impressed. "You rocked it!"

I turn my face and shrug one shoulder. "GG helped me."

"But you did the emotion, didn't you?" Jojo's voice rises a little with each word. "Why didn't you warn me? Thanks a lot! Now, I'm going to feel all happy while the bakery goes down the toilet." She smiles and grabs another cream puff. "And you know what? That's okay. These really are great, Cat. Good job. Isn't it a beautiful day?" Jojo hums her way out of the kitchen.

My curiosity moves me around the counter to the window in the kitchen door. Jojo sashays through the bakery with her eyes closed. She gives a little twirl and bumps into my mom, who is wiping down a table.

"Oh! Bridget! Have I told you how glad I am that you're here? I am so so so happy!" Jojo wraps both arms around my mom's waist and squeezes her like a lonely anaconda.

"Jojo is hugging my mom," I whisper over my shoulder. There is clatter as GG and Robyn hurry to join me at the door. We jostle around each other for a moment, trying to find the best way for all three of us to see. I barely breathe as I watch.

Jojo finally lets my mom go. "You should go eat a cream puff; they are so good! I'll take over here." She skips behind the counter, where she helps a customer.

My mom stands there, staring at the wall with the most confused look on her face.

"Oh my!" GG covers her mouth with one hand.

"Did you do that on purpose?" I whisper. "I mean, get Jojo to eat so she would be happy?"

GG lets out a little giggle. "Well, no, not exactly. I just thought the blood sugar might be low with her, so some food would help. But it worked out very nicely, yes?"

Mom's eyes snap to the kitchen door; she takes long strides towards us. GG, Robyn and I scatter. GG adds hot water to the sink that steams the air around her face. Robyn slides into the counter stool and starts filling cream puffs like she has been there all her life and has no intention of ever moving. I hurry to the other side to do the same, but barely pick up the spoon when my mom comes through the kitchen door.

I totally think all three of us look like we are anxiously engaged in such important things we have no time to peek at doors.

But I am very, very wrong.

Mom flings one hand behind her, towards the bakery. "All right, what did you do to Jojo? Even for her, that's a little over the top."

"Cream puff?" Robyn holds the tray out to my mom. I'm sure she means well, but she draws Mom's attention to the most incriminating thing in the kitchen.

"Who made those? Cat?" My mom sighs, pushing her bangs off her forehead so they stick up at weird angles. "And Jojo just ate one, didn't she?"

I laugh, nervously. "You're good at this game, Mom. Remind me to never play I Spy, Spot It, or Charades with you ever again."

My mom leans against the wall, rubbing her eyes behind her glasses. "I'm not ready for this. I thought I was, but I was wrong. I'm going back to bed. For a week or so. At least."

GG clicks her tongue. "Bridget. I love you, but you worry too much." She draws her face into an exaggerated frown. "Methinks nothing can be quite as bad as you worry it may be."

To my surprise, my mom smiles. "You are right, Grammy. So very right." She steps further into the kitchen. "Do you have anything to eat that hasn't been baked by Cat?"

"Hey!" I use my most wounded voice.

GG hands Mom a plate of something that looks like cake with syrup on it. I'm not complaining; if owning a bakery means cake is breakfast, sign me up!

My mom sits next to Robyn and takes the plate. "Oh! I love your baked oatmeal, Grammy, thank you."

GG leans on the counter across from my mom. Her elbow lands in a dollop of cream either Robyn or I dropped, but she doesn't notice. "We must talk about this." She waves her hand around and around. "This cream puff and Jojo. My Cat, I have never seen such a thing!"

My mom stops chewing. "What do you mean?" She looks kind of queasy.

GG spreads her hands out on the counter. Her fingers are long and thin for how short and tiny she is. "I have seen many women in our family bake emotions, but I have never, ever seen it happen so quickly. Jojo worried, Jojo happy. Like this." She snaps her fingers in the air.

A shivery tingle goes up my spine as six eyeballs settle themselves on me. GG's, almost black and astonished. Robyn's, sky blue and excited. My mom's, dark blue and troubled.

I try not to inhale any pride, but it's difficult when everyone looks so awed. Well, everyone except my mom. She just looks pukish.

"What should we do?" Mom whispers.

GG pats my mom's cheek. "There you go now, worries, worries, worries. Who's to say there is something that needs to be done? Nothing is wrong here. I look forward to this week of baking with Cat."

Mom pushes her plate away, even though she hasn't finished all her food. "I was afraid you were going to say that. I sort of hoped you would say something along the lines of 'that's it, no more baking; it's too dangerous'." She rests her head on her crossed arms.

Robyn and I gasp in real life horror. Never bake again! What is my mother thinking?

But GG just laughs. "No more worries Bridget, all of it is figure-out-able. You'll see."

Baked Oatmeal

6 C. old-fashioned Oatmeal
1 C. Honey
1 C. Applesauce
2 C. Milk
4 beaten Eggs
1 tsp Vanilla extract
1 TBSP Baking Powder
2 tsp Salt

This is going to be so easy, watch!

Preheat the oven to 350°F.

Mix all ingredients together, mix, mix, mix, and pour into a greased 9x13 baking pan.

*Here's the part where you can add extras like strawberries or blueberries, chocolate chips or nuts, apples or craisins. So many options to fill all the extra time you have because making this recipe is so speedy!

Bake for 30-45 minutes, until a toothpick inserted in the center comes out clean.

Serve with milk or like a slice of cake with syrup drizzled over the top!

Done and done!

9

German Pancakes

Soon, Dad comes into the kitchen with Penny and Bubby, starving their stomachs out. After they sample cream puffs, baked oatmeal, and about a dozen crepes, GG pulls out a big, bubbly pan of something she calls German pancakes. Our actual breakfast. Apparently living in a bakery turns a person into a Hobbit. We just eat all day. Breakfast, second breakfast, elevensises, and etc., etc., and so on!

This German pancake thing is like nothing I've ever seen before. All bumpy and lumpy. It sort of reminds me of the volcano I spent two weeks making for the second grade science fair, after Liam accidentally sat on it.

At least, he says it was an accident.

I have my own thoughts about that.

It only takes GG lathering the whole puffy thing with butter, mixed berry syrup and powdered sugar, for me to decide I will try it. And once I do, I wish she made more.

Germans really have this pancake thing figured out.

When we finish eating, Dad says he wants to take Penny and Bubby to Fools Hollow. I guess that's a lake? I wonder who was the fool who named it. Mom thinks it's too cold to play in the water, but Dad isn't planning on swimming. He just has great memories from growing up and is excited to wax nostalgic with his offspring.

Full disclosure: not super disappointed to miss out on that outing.

III

Robyn and I work on the dishes so GG doesn't have to do them, while Jojo pops in and out of the kitchen with something optimistic to share each time.

"I was thinking, we are going to survive!"

"This bakery is a staple; the locals can't do without us!"

"We make the best scones. You've tried the scones. They are the best scones!"

"Jeff just gave his compliments to the chef; we are going to make it through this!" On her way out this time, she pauses to kiss Mr. Bojangles with a loud smack.

Yes, that would be the mixer.

The mixer.

I exchange a look with Robyn, who grins.

I guess I agree. Super silly/happy Jojo is way better than the super worried version. When she comes back into the kitchen, all of us look up, curious to see what she will do next.

"So, guys, I was thinking...smell my hair by the way, this new shampoo is fantastic!" She leans over, sticking her head in Mom's face. "Smells like mango, huh? Love it! What was I saying? Oh yeah! This whole thing with the bake-off is going to be fine. GG, you are so right! There is plenty of work for all of us in this town!"

The four of us nod like bobblehead dolls. It's all we can do. Jojo doesn't stop talking to take a breath, so there isn't room to talk even if we were bursting to say something. I lose track of what's going on around me because I'm busy watching to see if Jojo hits the floor from lack of air. She talks so fast that her words skip over each other and it's kind of hard to understand what she's saying.

She picks up the tray of cream puffs and wags a finger at me and Robyn. "Susie Freeze just asked if we have cream puffs this morning and then Norman wanted some too, you rascals, I guess you were right." She blows each of us a kiss on her way out again.

Once the cream puffs are sold and Jojo can't eat them anymore to keep her spirits up, it takes about two hours for her happy to wear off. I can tell it's happening because her visits get further apart, and her impersonation of a peppy cheerleader slowly morphs to a battery powered toy running out of juice.

When she returns to the kitchen again, she is the epitome of cha-grined. Which is a super fun word to say out loud ten times fast, plus also means she's pretty much embarrassed.

"You know, that was really not a nice trick you all pulled. I feel like an idiot. Everyone in town is going to think I'm kooky dukes." She slumps onto a bar stool.

GG flicks a towel in her direction; I feel the breeze whoosh past the end of my nose. "No, no, the whole town did not visit the bakery this morning."

"Not helping! Why did you make me eat those cream puffs? The last thing I want to do right now is to feel happy about everything."

"Whyever not?" GG hands the towel back to Robyn, who picks up a spoon to dry. "You notice, Jolynn, that I am quite happy, no eating of the cream puffs needed."

"Well, goody for you." Jojo sticks her tongue out at GG who tweaks her nose. "I think I woke up on the wrong side of the bed. Everything feels like a big, hairy, stinky deal. I might need some chocolate."

"You've come to the right *casa*!" Robyn does a twirl and throws Jojo a baggie filled with dark chocolate chips from the cupboard nearby.

"Hey!" The word bursts out of me, surprising myself as much as everyone else. I accidentally drop a cup full of soapy water on the floor. "Sorry, I'll get it, no worries." I toss the cup back into the sink and dry my hands on the ends of Robyn's towel. "I almost forgot! Robyn and I read one of the clues,"

"Clues?" My mom blinks a few times, transitioning.

"Yeah, GG gave us a treasure hunt to learn more about Evie and our family history."

Jojo raises her hand like we are in—*gasp!*—school and hops on the balls of her feet. "I helped with the rhymes!"

Mom clicks her tongue as her head tips to the side. "Oh! That is a wonderful idea! How fun for the girls!"

"I like for the girls to discover what they can on their own." GG flushes.

"Yeah, so, me and Robyn think the first clue is a weather app. Is that right?"

GG looks at me for a moment, then her eyes stray to my mom. "Weather app? Translation, please."

Mom hides her smile. "There are apps for your cell phone that will tell you the weather, Grammy."

"Why for? I can do that myself." She walks across the kitchen and unlatches a window, turning the crank so the shutter pushes out. "It is sunny today, a chill breeze. No clouds in all the sky."

"Very good point." My mom jabs a finger in the air, her eyes shifting to me.

Like that's going to change anything.

"Retro," Robyn says in an awed voice.

"So, it's not a weather app?" I try to ignore the sinking in my belly. "What else tells the weather? Or did we get the whole clue wrong?"

GG holds up her hands. "I made a vow to stay out, I must seal my lips."

"Is it like the weather on TV? Or...radio?" Robyn chews on her bottom lip.

Speaking of retro.

Those are great guesses for ways people got information before the internet enlightened us on everything we never knew we needed to know. Maybe we're going to have to think with different brains, old school brains, like GG's brain. Just a few decades behind the now.

I mean that in the nicest possible way.

GG's face doesn't change a bit, not a flicker of anything to let us know if any of those were good guesses or not. "I'm sorry, I can't say one word, or I will say too many."

"Mom?"

She shakes her head. "I really think it will be more fun for you to figure it out on your own."

"Does that mean you know what it is?"

She can't hide her smile this time. "I will give you a hint: you won't find the answer on the internet."

Robyn looks up from her phone. "Oh! No?"

"Did you google it?" I lean around her elbow to see the screen. Robyn typed in household *items that tell the weather*. There are a ton of YouTube videos showing you how to make your own weather instruments, but there is also an article about a woman in the Midwest who swears her goldfish can tell when a tornado is coming.

"Do you have a goldfish, GG?"

She shakes her head, confusion all over her face.

"Girls." Mom puts her hand over Robyn's phone, so we are forced to look at her. "Go explore, run around, figure it out. I'm positive if you spend a little bit of time wandering the property, you will find what you're looking for."

Mom, GG, and Jojo exchange amused looks and then, slowly, like they timed the whole thing, turn away from us.

So, I'm not a rocket scientist or a mind reader, but I think that means they aren't going to tell us anything else.

Ratatouille.

I look at Robyn. "Where do we start?"

"I don't know." Her eyes widen. "I really have no idea, Cat!"

"But you've been here a zillion times, by now you should know the place inside out, backwards, front to back!" I slump.

How am I supposed to find something I haven't figured out yet in a place I don't even know all that well?

Yeah, that's not impossible or anything.

"True, I have been here a ton, but we don't usually wander the house looking for weather instruments." Robyn's eyebrows slant down.

My mind jumps on this. "So, what do you usually do when you visit?"

Robyn takes a while to answer, her face all scrunched up in thought. "Oh, we bake and eat and play cards and GG tells stories. She has great stories."

"Like what? What stories? About her life?"

Robyn squints; her eyes unfocused. "I don't know what we're looking for! I can't tell us how to find something when we don't even know what it is!"

"Robyn!"

"What?"

"What stories does GG tell? What do you know that I don't?"

She looks at me like I have cupcakes instead of ears. "I don't know what I know! Quit distracting me, I'm trying to figure this clue out."

I sigh. "Should we just wander around, like my mom suggested? Try and figure it out on our own?"

Robyn wrinkles her nose.

My thoughts exactly, wandering will take forever.

Should we just give up?

Quit?

Call it a day?

Beg for mercy?

That's when movement catches the corner of my eye. A hand beckons from a shadowy corner of the bakery.

"What the..." Robyn whispers.

Jojo peeks out, gesturing more enthusiastically. Robyn and I link elbows, tiptoeing forward. Both of Jojo's palms stop us in our tracks. Apparently, we can't go any further. She cups her hands around her mouth so that's where my eyes focus.

Jojo says something with exaggerated movement and no words.

It looks like 'Mack Poor'.

"What?" Robyn mutters.

Jojo starts to mouth again but then stops, turns her head sharp to the side and disappears.

Well, that stinks. Now what are we supposed to do?

I tug Robyn's elbow to get her attention on me instead of the empty place that used to be Jojo. "What's Mack Poor?" I'm kind of hoping it's a code word for where the weather thing is.

"Mack Poor? I thought she said Ack Morie."

"That sounds like a Star Wars name."

Robyn chews her lip, the hamster wheel in her brain working overtime. "Okay, so, obviously Jojo is trying to help us."

"Are you sure? Maybe she was trying to distract us."

"No way." Robyn shakes her head. "Jojo is the worst at secrets and surprises. I'm positive she was trying to tell us where to go."

"Okay, well, I don't know what a Mack Poor-Morie thing is, do you?"

"Wait!" Robyn grabs my shoulders. "Say that again."

"What? Mack—"

"Back!" Robyn shakes me in her excitement. My eyeballs roll all over like a pinball game. "Say porch, I mean, mouth it."

I steady myself and do what she asks.

"That's it! Look!" She mouths 'back porch' so I can see.

It looks exactly like Mack Poor.

"Yeah!" I fist pump the air. "You're brilliant! Let's go!" I turn in a circle. "How do we get to the back porch from here?"

"Oh my gosh! Bean-up!" Robyn pulls me back through the kitchen doors. We squeeze around tables until we come to a set of French doors. Robyn pulls them open to a narrow rectangular room with fluffy rugs, small glass end tables, a couple worn chairs, and a big couch.

"Back porch!" Robyn spreads her arms.

It looks way different in the daytime than it did last night when I came through here with GG. "Okay, what tells the weather? It's not any of the furniture, right?" This is an obvious question, but I still have to ask it, just in case.

Hey, our family can bake feelings, who's to say our furniture can't tell the weather?

Robyn roots through cushions, pulling out loose change and considering it with a critical eye. "This isn't right. If something was going to measure the weather, it would need to be on the wall or something, right? Somewhere that gets the sun and the cold wind?"

I scan the walls carefully. By the back door, leading outside, there is a large cottage hung on the wall. It reminds me of the cuckoo clock in Robyn's Abuelita's house. *Tio* Antonio told me her great-great-grandfather made it in Mexico, so it's super old and way valuable.

I move to get a closer look. Wait a second! It's not a cuckoo clock! I carefully take it off the wall to look closer. The stone that makes up the tiny house is so realistically carved and chipped; I wonder if someone finally invented a shrink ray and used it on this cottage. Intricate painted ivy snakes up the walls and hangs from the roof. There are tall flowers all around the outside, colorful and so realistic looking I imagine I smell violets and peonies. In the place where the door should be, there is a long red tube with numbers along the sides.

I know what this is!

"Robyn!" I shriek, holding tight to the house, so I don't drop it and ruin everything. "I found it!"

"You did?" She bounces to my side. "Cat! A thermometer! That's it! Why have I never noticed this before?"

We team carry the thermometer to one of the lumpy couches and turn it over and over in our hands. I keep getting distracted by tiny details. On the back, instead of being flat and boring, there is a back porch with bags of flour stacked against the wall. That explains why the thermometer hung lopsided on the wall.

"What do we do now?" Robyn pulls her eyes away from the tiny cat sitting on the corner of the white picket fence. I just noticed it has a mouse in its mouth, the long wormy tail whips around the cat's face.

"GG said she'd tell us a story once we find everything, so I guess we put it back on the wall."

"Oh." Robyn deflates.

I watch her for a second, thinking rapidly. "Do you have some paper?"

Robyn pulls a notebook out of her jacket pocket and holds it up. "Always."

"Write down the word thermometer. Then we have something to show GG to prove we found all the clues."

Robyn perks right back up. She pats her other pockets until she comes up with a bright pink pen. "Great idea! I'll be, like, our scribe. Oh my gosh, this is so fun! Do you have the other clues on you?"

"Always." I grin, pulling them out.

"Let me finish writing... Done! Here." She takes the cards and fans them out for me, face down. I choose one, then we both lean over to read it.

"Beneath the trees I rest, I sleep. No one near will make a peep. Though I slumber evermore. I never sigh, I never snore."

My brain whirls like a merry go round, trying to process what I heard as quickly as possible. I start to say things out loud, because there is way too much to keep contained.

"Sleep, peep, trees, snore."

Robyn chimes in, "Slumber, evermore, sigh, rest."

Between the two of us, we've pretty much said it all.

"I don't know what this means yet, but I have that feeling, Cat." Robyn rubs the goosebumps on her arms.

"Like after we ate that whole bag of marshmallows, and we went all sugar crazy? Me too!"

"No!" Robyn giggles. "You dork-a-lumpalous! That feeling that something is happening, something big. I can't wait to find out more! So, this clue..."

We bend our heads together to read it again, Robyn out loud and me to myself.

"Do you think it's one of the bedrooms?" I say, finally. "Sleep..."

Robyn taps her finger on the side of her pajama pants. "I don't know, that seems way too obvious."

"Where else do you sleep?"

"Oh!" Robyn's eyes widen. "Oh! Cat, the cemetery! I told you Jojo and I jogged by there this morning? It's where people sleep, but don't snore—I'd bet money on it."

"You don't have any money."

She waves her hand to get rid of my words, like they are noxious fumes. "Let's go ask if we can go, it's not far."

"Right now?"

"Why not?" Robyn stands, hopping from foot to foot.

I lean back into the couch. "You're not dressed for the day yet, for one, and you stink from your jog, for two and—"

"Pshhhhhh." Robyn grabs my arm and pulls. "Come on, I can't wait to find the next thing."

I rise slowly, hugging the thermometer close to my side. "Maybe we should wait?"

"For what?" Robyn stops, her arms dropping to her sides. "We want to find all these clues as soon as possible, so we finally know what is up with our family. Right?"

"Yeah, but the thing is...I mean, I'd really love to go right now, but I'm supposed to help with the baking. It's too bad, really, but I can't leave GG to do it all alone, not when they're getting all busy."

"Oh yeah." Robyn's shoulders slump, but only for a second before the optimism kicks back in. "Let's just go ask. Maybe it's not super busy right now, and anyway, it doesn't hurt to ask."

Robyn is gone before I can answer, leaving me all alone.

Which is totally fine, by the way, fantastic even. In fact, I love time all alone in a strange place after people creep me out by talking about cemeteries and junk.

Yeah...

Right.

I carry the thermometer carefully to the wall and place it back on the empty nail. I stare at it for a moment longer, admiring all the details, also putting off the moment I have to go get permission to go to a cemetery.

Cemetery!

That word makes it sound so tame. In my mind it's a dark and loathsome graveyard with dripping black trees and owls that have dangerous 'peck you' yellow eyes that follow your every move. Woe unto those who travel therein! A ghostly chill creeps up my neck. A skeletal hand reaches from beyond the grave.

"Cat!"

I scream my head off and jump onto one of the chairs, my back pressed against the wall like I'm trying to disappear into it.

"What the heck are you doing?" Penny peeks around the door frame.

I place a hand over my heart. I'm pretty sure it's going to leap out and run for the hills.

That's what I would do if I were my heart and had a brain.

It takes a few deep swallows for me to be able to answer. "Nothing."

"Why are you standing on the furniture?"

"I'm not."

Penny raises one eyebrow.

"Okay, I am, but I don't think I need to explain why."

Penny continues to stare at me.

I let out a long breath as I step down to the floor with as much dignity as I can. It's easier to breathe now that my heart isn't trying to escape my chest. Which means it's easier to think of legit reasons why I was tap dancing on the patio chair just now.

I pull my shirt down and smooth out my jeans, mostly to get rid of all the sweat on my hands. "If you must know, I was…"

Penny's face doesn't shift, her skeptical look makes me forget the story I just made up.

"Okay fine!" I throw my hands in the air. "I was thinking about the cemetery and freaked myself out. Then you scared the snot out of me."

"All I did was say your name."

"Exactly!" I poke a finger in the air. "What do you want anyway?"

"Oh." She fiddles with her necklace, a silver ballet slipper on a thin chain. "I heard Robyn asking to go and I want to go too. Can I come with you?"

"You want to go to a creepy graveyard?"

"No." Penny shakes her head. "I want to go to the cemetery. I love cemeteries! Remember that family history class I took last year?"

I shake my head.

Penny sighs. "Anyway, we have a bunch of family buried here. I thought it would be fun to take pictures of the gravestones for my scrapbook."

She has a scrapbook of gravestones. Creepy just got creepier!

My mouth opens to say no, without a good reason, but the look in Penny's eyes stops me. It suddenly occurs to me that Penny is Great-Great-Grandma Evie's descendant too.

"Hey, Pen…" I tip my head to the side. "Do you like to bake?"

She stares at me for a moment. I guess that question was kind of out of the blue. Once she wraps her mind around it, she shakes her head. "I like to eat the stuff you bake, but I don't have time for that with school and ballet and everything."

"Would you want to learn? With me and GG in the mornings?" I offer her the greatest gift ever. After only one day of baking with GG, it's become my most favoritest thing to do. I don't want to share, but my heart bubbles out of my mouth before my brain can stop it. "It's really fun, you might like it."

Penny's face softens. "That's really nice of you, Cat, thanks."

"So, you want to?"

"No, but thanks for asking. I hate getting up early. How about, instead of baking, you and Robyn let me go to the cemetery with you?" She grins until her dimples deepen.

"Deal," I smack her hand. "But only if you promise to protect me if someone's long gone great-great-something-or-another tries to grab my ankle."

"I got you." Penny grins, flipping her hair over her shoulder. "You big baby."

I poke her in the side, giggling as she twists away. She runs ahead and I chase her through the house to the bakery kitchen, like we are both five years old.

And seriously?

It feels good.

German Pancakes

2 TBSP Butter
6 Eggs
1 C. Milk
½ tsp Vanilla extract
1 C. Flour
1/4 tsp Salt

Preheat your oven to 400°F.

In a blender—

Note: I love it when a recipe starts this way because it usually means there will be less dishes. It's sort of the same feeling as starting a story with Once Upon a Time.

—combine all the ingredients except the butter; that's why it's separated with a space in the ingredients line. Eureka! There is purpose to everything we do!

Pulse just until it looks combined.

Put the butter in a 9x13 glass baking dish and melt in the oven. Watch it close—it won't take long. Just 3-5 minutes.

No burnin' the butta!

Pull the dish back out—with an oven mitt, please—and pour the blender contents into the pan, then put into the oven again.

Whew. That was tough, but hang in there, we're going to get through this together. I believe in you!

Bake for 20 minutes.

You know it's done when the whole thing puffs up like eighties bangs and is golden brown.

Plus, also, your kitchen smells amazing.

Serve right away!

Like you want to wait, pshaw.

Super yummy with syrup or jam or berries and whipped cream.

Soooooooooooooo dreamy!

Triple Berry Syrup

Just 'cause I love ya.

4 C. Frozen Berry Blend
½ C. Sugar
2 TBSP Water

Pour everything into a pot and heat on medium. Cover it with a lid until the berries defrost, about 10 minutes. Uncover and reduce heat to low. Simmer for 20-30 minutes, until the berries reduce and thicken. Cool, then refrigerate for at least an hour before using. This will help thicken even more. Yay!

10

Granola Bars

I t's still super chilly in the Arizona mountains while the sun is trying to come up. I swear, each time we pass under a shady tree the temperature drops like twenty degrees. I wonder what GG's thermometer would say about that.

I unzip my hoodie, pulling it around me so it's tighter and I can hug it in place with my arms.

"It will warm up as we walk," Robyn says.

I really hope so, because right now I feel like I'm going to turn into a Cat-sicle, frozen to the bushes on the side of the road for time and all eternity.

"Anyone want a granola bar?" Penny swings a grocery bag in time with our footsteps. Even though I've eaten breakfast twice today, GG still sent us out the door with homemade granola bars and juice boxes. This kind of makes me feel like a little kid out for an adventure, except that we're going to a cemetery instead of sparkle unicorn kitty land.

"I'm good for now." My voice sounds weird through chattering teeth.

Robyn holds out her hand. "I'll take one."

Penny drops a bar in Robyn's palm.

"Do you want me to carry that?" Robyn gestures to the bag with her granola bar before she takes a huge bite.

"Nah, I got it." Penny moves the strap over her shoulder. "But thanks."

Right about the time I think I'm never going to feel warm again, my blood gets moving and the sun starts doing its job. I go from shivering from my bones, to sweating profusely. I have to take my hoodie off and tie it around my waist.

"How much farther until we get there?" I wonder, with no hidden agenda at all. I'm just curious. I don't mind walking forever; this road is really pretty and the air right now smells like farms and pine trees. No need to spoil a perfectly good morning by putting ourselves into the opening scene of a horror movie.

"We turn here. It's just up the road."

Robyn guides us across a street that is still waking up. There are only a few cars moseying along. We turn right, following the road as it curves around like a big snake. Most of the streets where we live in Boise are great big squares. It's interesting to find one that weaves around the land, all twisty and swervy.

Then we veer left, and Mount Everest rises before us.

I stop walking.

"Cat, what are you doing? We're almost there, it's just at the top of this hill."

"Hill?" I squeak. If this is a hill, then I really do look like Liam. "This isn't a hill! This is like the side of a cliff. Where's the elevator?"

Penny swats my arm as she passes me, prancing her way up.

"Come on, drama." Robyn rolls her eyes.

I, however, wait in place for a kindly man with a horse and buggy to appear. Or for someone to get their rear in gear and build an escalator. There is no way I'm climbing this thing. To even consider it, I need months of training, water bottles, and the trail mix with candy in it.

And also, I'd need to lose all of my marbles.

"Cat!" Penny's voice sounds very far away. Like an echo from the great height she's climbed in the last forty-five seconds.

Robyn turns around, narrowing her eyes. "Are you coming?"

"No way! No one told me about Jabba the Hill. I didn't sign up for this!"

"Fine, then, go." She shoos her hands at me. "See you back at the bakery."

Wait, *what*?

Isn't she even going to try to talk me into it?

What the heck?

I tap my foot as I consider my options. It seems grossly unfair that I have to climb a vertical slope to a place I don't even want to go. If there was a rocking awesome shoe store at the top of this thing, then I can see how it would be worth the effort.

Sometimes fate has a wicked sense of humor.

My arms hug my sides. Now that I'm not moving anymore, the wind feels icy. I could go back to the bakery; I think I know how to get there by myself. It will be a lonely walk back, but then I won't be freezing anymore, and I can bake.

I snort, that was the easiest decision-making session of all time.

"See ya!" I call as I turn around.

I only take two steps in the opposite direction before Robyn's voice floats to me on the breeze.

"Hey, Penny? Cat's going back to the bakery. She can't handle this hill."

My foot stops mid-air.

Can't handle...

Can't handle this hill?

I whip around and stare at Robyn's back. Did she just say I can't handle this hill?

I'll show her!

I take a deep breath and sprint forward. The ground rushes up so my shoes are almost vertical on the concrete. My calves start burning after only a couple steps, but I tell them to zip it. Not only am I going to conquer this hill, but I'm going to beat Robyn to the top. Even with her unfairly long legs and super head start.

Instead of thinking about my gasping breath and screaming muscles, I picture all the ways I'm going to gloat when I get up there before Robyn does. I am so wrapped up in magical daydreams, that I barely notice the ground leveling off.

"Ha!" I raise both hands in the air. "Who can't handle the hill?" I dance in place, which is a super dumb idea. My jiggling muscles give out and I collapse onto the cold grass outside the cemetery gate.

I think I'm out of range of the skeleton fingers. At least I hope so because I don't think I can get up now.

Robyn and Penny reach me at about the same time. They stand over me, giggling. I'm too wiped out to even care.

"How'd that go for you?" Robyn asks.

"Not my best idea."

Robyn reaches for my hand, nodding to Penny to do the same. They pull me to a standing position with much groaning.

On my part.

I clamp a hand on Penny's shoulder to steady myself and take a shaky step forward. Okay, so, maybe my legs aren't wrecked. Now that my heart isn't pounding in my ears, I start to think I might live to see fifteen.

Penny breathes in. "Oh, this cemetery is so pretty!"

We stop walking and I look around, trying to see this place the way Robyn and Penny do. Most of the graves are decorated with cheerful flower bouquets and sunlight flickers through leaves, making interesting shapes on the pathway. It is the opposite of dark, dank and dreary.

"Where's Evie's grave?" I study the rows and rows and, oh yeah, rows of headstones.

Robyn makes a face. "Um, I don't exactly remember. I know it's next to a tree."

There are about five bazillion trees surrounding us; they are all different kinds and sizes. Tall, tall trees that cast long shadows over the grass, flowers, and headstones.

I look at Robyn.

She shrugs. "I guess we walk until we find it?"

Yeah, or until we celebrate our one hundredth birthdays, cause it's going to take that long to make it through this whole place.

Rather than express my very valid complaints, I follow the example of my little sister. Press my lips together and start looking at the names on the headstones. That takes way less energy than throwing a tizzy fit and I'm fresh out of energy at the moment.

But seriously, this is going to take forever.

After a little while of silence and searching, I notice how nice it feels with the sun finally raised enough to consistently beat the chill, a bright blue sky and chirping birds. Also, the light breeze swishes my hair against my cheek, leaving a trail of tickles.

Maybe this cemetery is not such a bad place to sleep. I guess I can let it be creepy-cool instead of just creepy.

But I'm still going to watch my ankles.

"I found it!" Penny squeals from a couple rows over. "I found it!!"

I step carefully around the headstones to get to where she is.

Robyn appears at my shoulder, smiling triumphantly. "See, I told you! There's the tree!"

I just roll my eyes.

Penny points at two simple concrete blocks. The grass has really grown wild in this row, creeping up over the stones. My eyes immediately go to the one in the middle.

Evelyn Grace Mareau

Evie! A totally different kind of shiver creeps up my back. I don't know what it means or where it came from, but it's powerful. Goosebumps pop out on my arms all the way to my shoulder.

"This is awesome!" Penny drops the snack bag and pulls out the phone Mom lent her to take pictures. She moves around, trying to get the best shot. The wild grass blots out the bottom right of Evie's headstone. I can't read any of the words engraved under the dates of her birth and death.

"What does that part say?" I ask Robyn.

She peers down. "What part?"

I show her where the grass covers.

"Are you sure it says something? It's probably smooth stone like Grampa Joe."

Grampa Joe's marker just has his name and dates, but Evie's husband—Newell—has a quote at the bottom of his. At least, I think it's a quote. It's hard to say for sure because it's in French.

That there is a whole lot of words I don't know.

"Robby, look, what do these words mean?" I know she's not French, but she's been here with GG. So, for sure she has a better chance of knowing what it says then I do.

Robyn bites her lip. "It's a poem or something. I just remember it's about a bird."

My eyes go back and forth between Evie and Newell's stones. I don't know how I know, but I feel it in my bones that there is something under the grass on Evie's headstone.

Something important.

But I'm not brave enough to start pulling grass off a grave.

Isn't that, like, illegal? Or something?

Robyn loses interest and sits down on the bench under Evie's tree, leaning back with her eyes closed. Penny takes a couple more shots of Evie's grave and then moves down the line, taking more pictures as she goes. Neither one of them seem all that concerned that something monumentally life changing might be right at our feet.

Although...

I have been known to let my imagination run away with me.

It's probably nothing.

With a sigh, I trail behind Penny. Towards the end of the row, she stops and swipes the screen of Mom's phone. "Whoops, I think this isn't our family anymore." She holds the phone out so I can see the picture she just took. "This one. Look, we go from Mareau to Miller. I don't think he's ours."

I bend over the gravestone. "Maurice Nathaniel Miller. That sounds sort of French."

Penny squints her eyes. "Really? You think so? Miller sounds way American to me."

That is an incredibly good point, but something just popped into my head. "Robyn!" I screech, making her jump off the bench.

"I'm awake!"

I wait for her eyes to focus on me before I go on. "Do you remember that Saturday when you made me adopt-a-Grandpa at the nursing home?"

Her face wrinkles in confusion. "Yeah?"

"Remember that old guy sitting by the fireplace?"

She shakes her head. "I remember you acting like a stink brain the whole time and eating most of the whoopie pies."

"What's a whoopie pie?" Penny wrinkles her nose.

I let out a huff that interrupts Robyn's explanation of sandwich cookies with delicious filling, because that's not important right now. "I did not either, your mom made enough to feed Canada. And I wasn't a brat the *whole* time, when I was talking to the guy I was super nice. You can ask him when we get home. His name is Maurice." I widen my eyes to help her along.

"Okay..."

"His name is Maurice; this guy's name was Maurice."

"It's not the same guy, Cat."

I roll my eyes. "Duh, I know that, but Maurice from the nursing home used to live in France, so it might be his family member. What are the chances we find a relative of some random old man I met in Boise?"

"Zilch." Robyn crouches down to look at the headstone more closely. "There's probably a billion French guys named Maurice."

"Or..." I tap my finger on the top of her head many times. "Maurice here and Maurice in Boise are related, and they are also related to us, which means that when we go home, we can visit him again and learn even more about our family! Maybe this guy is our clue!"

Robyn squints up at me. "I don't think so, I don't recognize the name."

I'm not ready to accept defeat. I set my face with the determined look that almost always gets me out of doing stinky chores, and brush the dry leaves away. I want to see his deets, the dates of birth and death especially.

I peer at the numbers and realize instantly I have to give it up. He's just a little older than Granny Penny, and he only died a couple years ago. If he was a family member that lived in Show Low, then Robyn would know who he is. Robyn probably would have had a Thanksgiving or two with him in past years.

Looks like this lead, leads nowhere.

Snickerdoodles.

I should probably leave the detecting to Robyn.

My hand brushes over the cold stone as I consider what our clue might be here. Maybe Evie's headstone? Or the cemetery as a whole?

Wait, does that mean GG's going to tell us a ghost story?

Cause I really hate those things.

I adjust the mounted vase attached to the side of Maurice Nathaniel's stone, I knocked it over when I was searching around, and notice that the yellow, orange, and red chrysanthemums inside look very Fall-ish. And healthy. Someone keeps fresh flowers on his grave.

We need one of those vase things for Evie. I'd love to put fresh flowers on her grave every week. Except that I live a billion miles away so fake flowers would probably be better.

"What are you looking for?" Robyn places a hand on my shoulder.

"The clue." I purse my lips. "What do you think it is?"

"Clue?" Penny looks up from the phone.

Robyn now fills Penny in on GG's scavenger hunt as the three of us walk back over to Evie's grave, nestled between Joe and Newell. Penny leans against the tree, gripping one of the low branches that is probably the main source of shade for everyone in the afternoon. "We have company." She lifts her chin to point behind me.

I take in a sharp breath that sounds like the hiss of a snake.

Jake strolls down the row, carrying a bouquet of wildflowers in one hand. As soon as he notices us, he uses his other hand to remove his cowboy hat and rest it over his heart as he comes to a stop.

"Well, howdy there, Ms. Cat, how are you this fine morning?"

I cross my arms and scowl, which brings a great big smile to Jake's face.

"Just like Jojo. And you are?" He gives a slight bow in Penny's direction, tipping his hat forward so it looks like he's asking for handouts.

I know a thing or two I could give him.

A piece of my mind.

A not so fond farewell.

A swift kick in the—

"Penny." She has the nerve to blush, pink to the tips of her ears.

I snort in disgust.

"Penny, it's so nice to meet you. Are you another niece of Jojo's?"

Penny nods, unable to speak.

"She's my sister." I raise my eyebrow, just so he knows what's what.

"Ah." Jake winks at her before he turns to Robyn. "And you?"

"Robyn. I'm their cousin. But we've met before."

Jake nods. "Yes, ma'am, I thought you looked familiar."

Robyn at least has the dignity not to swoon under Jake's smolder. Though, she doesn't seem to find him as detestable as I do, which I think really shows a lack of loyalty to Jojo. The least she could do is hate his stinking guts. But nooooooo, she offers him her hand and shakes quite heartily.

Like he's a friend or nice person or something.

"Well, what are you ladies doing here this early in the morning? Don't you have a bakery to run?" The smile on his face verges on a smirk.

I want to slap that stinking thing clean off. How dare he talk about our bakery when he's competing to try to put us out of business? He has no right! It's like he's rubbing it in our faces.

"Don't *you* have a bakery to run?" I glare at him.

Jake laughs, a low rumble that sounds like the waves of the ocean. Not that I've been there, but Bubby had an ocean sound stimulator when he was two or three and had a hard time sleeping.

Jake's chuckle sounds just like that thing.

"I do, actually, but I also have employees that can cover for me when I step out for a few minutes."

"Well, la-di-flipping-da."

"Cat!" Robyn digs her elbow into my side. "You are being so rude!"

I don't even feel bad. Actually, I feel like I want to be ruder.

Or more rude.

Or whatever.

"Just so you know, with all of us here to help, *L'Amour Bakin'* is going to beat your bakery in the bake-off Friday." I fling my hair over my shoulder. "*Hoard.*"

"Well, that's good." Jake blinks.

"You won't think so when we win the account, and you don't." I wish I knew more about this bake-off thing, I want to be able to throw scathing words at him, but I only know what little I heard Jojo say.

And, truthfully, I don't really understand most of that.

"Hey, it's just good fun." Jake holds up his hands, the flowers brush his cheek, leaving a line of pollen just under his eye.

Like war paint.

"Ha!" I say so loud Jake takes a step back. "Maybe for you! But for us, it's for real! We're playing to win, Mr. Cowboy Man."

Jake pushes his lips together. "Are you now?"

"Yeah." I look to Robyn and Penny for back up, but they both look at the ground, or the sky.

"Why?"

I falter for a minute. The first thing that comes to mind is 'to win of course', but the words don't come out. Maybe 'to beat your smirk off', but that doesn't want to be said either. I open and close my mouth, as I consider what else.

Jake shields his eyes from the sun to look at me. "You know, this bake-off is just for fun. It isn't really a competition. The restaurant knows all our bakeries; it's a small town. They already decided who they're giving the contract to."

I bristle. "That's what you think! As soon as they taste the amazing things we're baking this week, that contract thingy is coming to us. Maybe you should just close up shop now and save yourself the humiliation."

"Cat." Robyn tugs on my arm, trying to get me to shut up.

Jake's grin widens like he knows exactly what's going on.

Like he's so smart.

Well, he doesn't know anything, and I've had about enough of this whole conversation and his stupid face. "Don't let us get in your way." I wave my arms to move him along.

"Sure." Jake tips his hat again, a deep dimple appearing in his left cheek. "Have a nice day, ladies."

I roll my eyes and stomp off, not looking back to see what Robyn and Penny do. After a few minutes, I hear footsteps behind me. I slow down so they can catch up, but only Robyn does. I look back and see Penny waving to Jake.

When she reaches us, I pull her closer so I can hiss in her ear. "Were you talking to that guy?"

"Jake?" Penny asks.

I roll my eyes. "No, Voldemort."

"I was talking to Jake, Cat."

Now is not the time to explain that I obviously know Jake isn't Voldemort. Especially because I think he might be a dastardly villain after all. "Why were you talking to him, Pen?"

Penny shrugs. "He asked me a question, and then he—"

"Penny!" I groan. "In the future, will you please not talk to super smirky creeplings in cemeteries?"

"But Jake—"

"Cat!" Robyn huffs. "You were so rude to him. What's the matter with you?"

"Nothing!" I try not to screech, but it's hard. There is a lot of emotion brewing in me right now. So much that my logical brain, the part that isn't freaking out about Jake, has to wonder where all the feelings are coming from. Seriously, they are big, even for me. "Nothing's the matter with me. It's Jake. You know? Jake? The guy is trying to ruin our bakery, therefore, our lives."

Robyn leans her head to one side. "I know who he is. I really don't think that gives you a right to be so mean."

I fling my hands into the air and let them drop to slap my thighs, totally at a loss for words.

"Hey, you guys?"

I'm too busy glaring at Robyn to answer.

And she's too busy glaring at me.

"Guys?" Penny says a little louder.

I cross my arms; my eyes narrow even more.

Penny jumps between us, waving a piece of paper in the air. "When I was talking to Jake, he gave me a two for one coupon, I think we should go check out his bakery."

Granola Bars

1 C. Brown Sugar
1 C. Peanut Butter
1 C. Honey
½ C. Butter
½ C. Applesauce
2 tsp Vanilla extract
6 C. Quick Oats
1 C. Chocolate Chips

Preheat that oven to 350°F.

Use a saucy pan—that's a pan that likes to sass—on the stove to melt sugar, peanut butter, honey, butter, applesauce, and vanilla. Just heat to mix, don't boil.

While you're waiting, though it really shouldn't take long, fill a good-sized bowl with oats and chocolate chips.

Just a note, since we're on the subject, old fashioned oats are too dense for this recipe. If you use them, they won't keep the granola bars together and everything will fall apart. That said, if all you have is old fashioned, give them a zip in a food processor or a blender and they will totally work like quick oats.

Magia!

All right, pour the saucepan into the bowl and mix everything up, then pat into a greased cookie sheet, all the way to the corners. Bake for 20-25 minutes.

Make sure you cool all the way before cutting. Like, refrigerating is even better—that way they'll hold up as bars instead of mush.

Tastes great either way, but, you know, granola *bars* are kind of a thing.

11

Blueberry Muffins

"Are you crazy? Why would we go there?" I switch my narrowed eyes to Penny.

She falters, just a smidgen. "It's free-ish, and I thought, maybe now would be a good time to go because he's not there, since you don't like him. I want to see what his bakery is all about."

Something rushes to the front of my mind. Tobey said he would go check out the competition so he could crush them. That's it! I really want to crush Jake, so that's our next step! That's what we're going to do!

"Yes, this is great! Let's go spy on Jake's bakery!" I fling out my hands and make them jazzy to emphasize my words.

Penny and Robyn just stare at me.

They obviously forgot that jazz hands mean you have to be enthusiastic; rounds of applause, fireworks, blimps in the sky, things like that.

Not wide open, fly catching mouths.

"Spy?" Robyn drags the word out like it's attached to a very heavy chain.

I shrug. "Spy, sneak, snoop. Use whatever word you want."

Robyn's face now turns white.

"Uh, I mean, observe, check out, experience..."

Penny shrugs. "I'm game. Let's do it; I am super good at tiptoeing."

I slap a loud high five into Penny's palm and turn to Robyn.

She still looks uncertain, but less than she did before Penny got into it.

Why didn't I think of this before? Having another person around, who agrees with me, means Robyn will go along with all my *loco* ideas without the extra begging and whining I usually have to do.

"Come on, Robby! Penny and I are gonna do it, don't you want to come with?"

#pressurenopressure.

Robyn shifts from side to side. "Someone will recognize us and tell Jojo. This has big trouble stamped all over it."

"Well, what if we change how we look?"

"Fun!" Penny claps. "And we can compare his stuff to our stuff and then we can leave his bakery terrible reviews on google!"

Robyn moves her narrowed eyes from me to Penny.

Penny's arms drop to her sides, and she coughs, her cheeks turning pink. "I mean, we leave him witty, punny reviews on google."

I poke Robyn's side. "That's fantastic! Best idea ever, you are the Queen of Puns."

A little flattery never hurts.

Robyn smiles a teeny bit. "I am pretty good at being punny," she says, "and Jojo has a ton of dress up clothes..."

"Yes!" I start pulling arms. "Hurry up, let's go right now."

She stumbles a few steps and then yanks her arm out of my grasp. "Just don't expect me to say anything or do anything sneaky. You know how bad I am at secrets."

Yes, I am well aware.

We jog across the street and slink around buildings to avoid the front windows of *L'Amour*. I resist the urge to army crawl through the parking lot, mostly because I'm sure it would rip my jeans and I like them a lot.

I barely have time to wonder how we're going to get to Jojo, without anyone else noticing us, when we reach the kitchen door to the bakery.

Like a miracle from the Commercial Kitchen in the Sky, Jojo is in the alleyway, stuffing a trash bag down with the lid. "Hey girls!"

"Hey, Jojo," we answer together, then look at each other.

Who's doing the talking?

Jojo puts her hand on her hip; a dish towel hangs down the side of her leg. "What are you up to?"

Robyn and Penny look at me.

I guess that answers my question.

"We are on our way to Jake's bakery," I say in a rush, trying to catch my breath.

Her brow wrinkles. "Why?"

"Because Jake isn't there right now and we want to spy on him."

"Spy?"

"Check out!" Robyn chimes in. "Take a look at, inspect."

"Google." Penny squeaks.

"Girls," Jojo shakes her head, fists on hips. "I am so disappointed..."

"Sorry..." Robyn shoots me a grumpy look.

"...with myself. I totally wish I'd thought of that!" Jojo goes on. "What do you need? How can I help?"

I beam. "Robyn said you have disguises?"

Jojo claps her hands. "I have tons! Give me just a sec and I'll go grab some, this is fabulous!" She disappears, still murmuring to herself.

"Well, that was easy." Penny lets out a breath.

"Yeah," I rub my hands together, convinced this easy-ness means the Head Bakers have smiled on us and we're doing the right thing. "I just had the best idea! Since we're in spy mode, let's go check out all of the bake-off competition!"

Robyn groans and covers her face with her hands.

"Where's this food truck, again?" I ask Robyn as I adjust the leather pants I chose because they look fantastic, but sad to say, feel terrible. It's like

I'm wearing a deflated balloon. I pull at them every few steps to decrease the serious chafing going down.

Robyn looks at the note in her hand. "Jojo said it's usually parked next to Pizza Hut on Mondays."

"And Pizza Hut is where?"

We turn the corner, and my question is answered. Just a block ahead, thank goodness, cause these thigh high black boots also look much better than they feel.

Penny giggles. "Cat! You totally look like Catwoman! I keep expecting to see a tail coming out of the back of those pants!"

"Awesome!" I sashay down the sidewalk, then trip on my heels.

How do people walk in these things?

Robyn sets me back on my feet. "We all look ridiculous. Like Halloween ate our Middle School drama club and threw it all back up."

"Yep!" I smooth my black silk shirt and continue walking. I can't wait to check out this food truck we're going to. Jojo said it specializes in cinnamon rolls and bacon. That's it. One type of cinnamon roll and twenty-five types of bacon. Unless that cinnamon roll is magical, I'm ninety-nine percent sure they are not going to be any competition for us.

"How much money do we have?" Robyn asks for the third time.

Penny is our treasurer. "Fifty bucks." She still sounds awed. It probably is the most amount of money she's ever held on her person. "And the coupon from Jake."

"And remind me again what we're doing?" Robyn's voice quivers.

"Easy peasy." I spread out my hands to wipe away all doubt. "We just buy stuff and eat it."

"But, like, what do we say?"

I look at her. "Hi, I'd like to buy a fill-in-the-blank."

"That's it?"

"Yep."

"Okay." Robyn takes a deep breath. "I can do that. Wait, but, what if Jake beats us back to his bakery? I don't want to run into him, he will totally recognize us. Let's go there first."

"But we're already here, goofus. Plus, we're in disguises," I say, like *duh*. "This is going to be awesome. Now, get into character."

"I wish I was at the dentist," Robyn mumbles.

"That is the dumbest back story ever." I shake my head, then place my hand over my heart. "You have to think of something better, like this, I am a famous stunt girl for teen actors, passing through on my way to California for the holidays. Penny?"

She fluffs her clown wig. "I am a makeup artist in town for a much-deserved break." She smiles with satisfaction, her fake gold tooth glinting in the sun. "Your turn, Robyn."

"I am not going to survive."

"Sure, you are," I lightly punch her shoulder. "And, you are?"

She looks at her sparkle ruby slippers and sighs. "I am a Smurf."

"That's the spirit!" I flip a stand of her long blue wig hair over her shoulder and stride forward, positive Robyn and Penny will follow. When I reach the window of the food truck I lean with one elbow, I'm pretty sure it makes me look cooler.

If that's even possible.

Robyn and Penny join me just as a grandmotherly woman with rosy cheeks comes into view. She looks up from a clipboard and startles so badly, it clatters to the floor. Instead of picking it up, she stares at us and blinks very slowly.

"Hi! My friends and I would like to buy a cinnamon roll and, uh, bacon." My eyes glaze over as I look at the choices, so many choices. "What's your favorite flavor?"

Her mouth closes and opens again without any sound.

I toss my head, so my short, pink bob sways next to my ears. "It's okay if you're in awe. We have that effect on people."

She just stares. "Pepper."

I'm gonna assume that's her favorite bacon flavor and not the beginnings of a mental breakdown. "Great then, a cinnamon roll and pepper bacon please."

The woman moves like she's stuck in jelly. Picks up her clipboard, grabs a pencil, scribble scribble scribble. She can't take her eyes off us even when she's taking our order. I wonder if she will be able to read her writing when she looks at it later. I never can when I write without watching.

"Coming...right...up?"

"Yes!" I smack my hand on the window ledge, making her drop her clipboard all over again. When she stoops to retrieve it, I hustle Robyn and Penny out of sight of the window. I think this poor woman is starstruck; she just can't do anything with our awesomeness in sight.

"That was humiliating!" Robyn hides her face in her hands. "I seriously might never recover."

"Oh, come on, Robyn!" I grab her arm and wiggle it. "I thought you don't care what people think of you. I thought trying to impress people is a total crap shoot."

Penny gasps.

"Pardon my French." I straighten my shoulders. "But seriously, Robby, what's the big deal?"

Robyn swallows. "It's not the same thing and you know it, Cat. When you are yourself it doesn't matter what others think of you, but when you're dressed like a really bad Disney original movie reject..."

"Really? You think so?"

Disney originals, now that's the big time.

Robyn grimaces. "Don't look all flattered, wait a second, why doesn't this bother *you*? You're the one that's always worrying about embarrassing yourself in front of other people. Why not now?"

"Well, first of all, thanks for blabbing my darkest secret—"

"Nah, I knew that." Penny picks at a rhinestone sticker on her index fingernail.

"Wait, really? How..." I give myself a shake to focus. "Never mind. Second, nobody knows us here. It's like when we go to the mall and pretend to be different people to flirt with guys."

"Don't tell Penny we do that!"

"Already knew." She squints harder at one of her nails.

Robyn eyeballs me. "You promised you would never tell a soul!"

"I didn't!" I raise my hands in self-defense. "I swear I didn't!"

"She didn't." Penny looks up. "But I have eyes and ears, and you guys are not subtle."

Well, that's a disappointment.

Robyn sighs the great sigh of resignation. "Just, tell me again why we had to dress up?"

"I think it's fun." Penny moves the beauty mark from her left cheek to right above her lip. "We should totally do this when we get home!"

"Oh, Penny." Robyn peeks through her fingers. "What has she done to you?"

"We didn't *have* to dress up, but Penny's right, it's fun! Plus, it was Jojo's idea."

"And that"—Robyn points at me—"Is the only thing I can think of that makes Jojo less than perfect. I blame you for corrupting her. How did you work your dark magic so quickly?"

I bat my super long, thick eyelashes that are held in place with magnetic eyeliner.

"Order up!" a voice calls.

Since there is no one else around, I assume that means us. I put out my hand for money, cause Penny is our treasurer, and go alone to the window. The three of us together are too much for one person to handle.

"Cinnamon roll and ba—" As soon as the poor woman sees me standing here, she loses her words again.

Poor dear.

I leave her a nice tip in the jar next to her frozen hand and wave a cheery goodbye.

I hope she'll recover soon.

"Let's see, let's see!" Penny leans over the Styrofoam container, holding her breath.

"Hang on, Robyn, do you have your handy dandy notebook? Let's document all of this."

Robyn whips it out and holds up her pen.

"First of all, the presentation is boring; Styrofoam never inspired anybody."

"Frugal, though." Robyn writes. "What was the name of this place? I forgot to look."

"Great Buns." I ignore my little sister and her eruption into high-pitched giggles.

Robyn stares. "For reals, Cat."

"I'm serious!" I pull out the receipt. "I wouldn't make that up."

More staring.

"Okay, maybe I would, but that is for honest truth the name of the food truck!"

Penny giggles with her words. "Well, let's see how great these buns are then."

I open the container, the first thing that happens is peppery bacon smacks me in the nostril, the second thing that happens is disappointment.

The cinnamon roll looks fantastic.

This might be a problem for *L'Amour.*

Penny rips off a piece and chews slowly, making quizzical faces that are hard to take seriously. Especially with her heavy on the nasal British accent. "The dough is soft, the cinnamon overpowering, the frosting delightful, but they don't use butter."

"What!" My hand freezes over the bun.

No butter?

Robyn takes a piece. "How can you tell?"

"Oh." Penny holds up a hand. "I know butter. Mom used to always buy that imitation stuff that tastes like wax until Cat made her buy real butter. Now my taste buds wig out whenever I eat something with the fakey stuff."

My eyes well up. That was seriously the most beautiful thing Penny has ever said! And I am the proudest person in the world that my little sister is a butter detector.

Superpower, indeed.

"The bacon is good," Robyn says, but starts coughing mid-sentence. "Maybe a little heavy on the pepper."

I'm not even going to try it.

I do pinch off a little of the roll though and wish the whole time I chew that Tobey was there to connoisseur with us. He would be able to tell if the cinnamon roll was any good just by holding the styrofoam carton in his hand.

I miss that guy.

"Okay." Robyn looks at us. "I've got our observations written down. Are we really going to Jake's next?"

"Yep!" I brush crumbs off my hands. "We're ready. We can do this. But if anything goes wrong, start talking in Spanish and run."

"I don't know very much Spanish," Penny says, her eyes wide.

I put a hand on her shoulder. "Me neither. I'm going to use Pig Latin."

"I can do that!" Penny grins.

"Yay! Then off we go."

A surprising short time later, Robyn, Penny and I step through the chimes of Jake's bakery. Which is not actually called Jake's bakery at all. A flashing pink sign spells out Diet Starts Monday.

I grab Robyn's elbow and hiss in her ear. "This has the same name as that place in Boise!"

"What place?"

"The one I went to with Tobey, when we first met him, by the pool?" She still looks confused, and a little nauseated. I don't think she can hear a word I say over the gremlins in her head. "Never mind, let's just do this."

Penny steps forward, but Robyn ducks behind me.

I squirm away. "What are you doing?"

"People are looking at me!"

"They are not." I check and confirm that no one is paying any attention to us. "You're just paranoid."

"Yeah, because I feel like an idiot!"

"I think you look amazing." Penny smiles, showing her blacked-out front tooth. "I love that blue wig. I wish I saw it first."

"I wish you did too." Robyn stares regretfully at a spot on the ceiling. "Wanna trade? I look like a mutated Smurf robot."

"No." I shake my head. "You look like a rock star. Now come on, let's get some stuff and get out of here, hopefully without seeing Jake." Even with disguises, I so don't want to run into him again. Twice in twenty-four hours is more than enough for me.

I adjust my leather pants and sashay to the counter.

Only to be pulled back by the crook of my elbow.

"Cat!" Robyn's hot breath blasts my neck. "I don't have money! Do you have the money? We can't pretend to buy stuff if we don't have money! That's actually called stealing! I'm too young to go to jail!"

Now people are staring. Robyn's shrill voice might permanently injure everyone's hearing.

Penny runs a hand through her rainbow afro and has to yank to get her fingers out. "I have the money, Robyn, remember? It's okay."

"That's right." Robyn nods, taking deep breaths. "Okay. Okay."

Penny and I exchange a satisfied look.

This sibling of mine is proving to be a valuable member of our team. I should have promoted her from annoying little sister a long time ago.

I square my shoulders. "Anything else? No? Good! Then, let's go."

Robyn and Penny follow me to the counter. As we get closer, the smell of butter gradually overpowers everything else. I refuse to be moved. I refuse to like any of this stuff, even if my traitorous nose thinks the smell is so good it is now making my rebellious mouth water.

Knaves!

They should know better. No matter what, this place isn't going to be as good as *L'Amour Bakin'*!

"Cat, look." Robyn points to the display case where a teenage girl slides the fresh baked pretzels into place. Steam makes the glass foggy.

Curse this Diet Starts Monday! They have found my only weakness, the chink in my armor, my Waterloo, my Achilles heel! Homemade pretzels are my very most favorite thing in the whole entire world!

Come to think of it, pretzels are kind of what started this whole shenanigan. If I hadn't eaten that pretzel, that day at the pool, I would still be perfectly content to eat the frozen junk food my mom always brought home. I would never have known what I was missing, and I would probably never have felt the need to bake.

I wonder if these soft pretzels are some kind of sign from the Bakers in the Sky, telling me I'm in over my head.

Maybe this is a bad idea.

Maybe we should go.

Penny slips between Robyn and I to stand in front of the cashier. Too late.

"Hi," she says, like she's a totally normal girl wanting to buy things to eat and not like she's the enemy, scoping out the competition, with fake freckles all over her cheeks and one gold tooth.

While Penny chats it up with the cashier—Marshall, according to his name tag—and Robyn twirls one of the thousand jangle bracelets around her wrist, I take in every detail of this bakery. It's smaller than ours, but much nicer. New and clean and shiny. Jake must have built this recently, or completely renovated an old building. There's no marks on the walls or scuffs on the floor.

Too bad for him because scuffs and marks build character, which means we have lots and lots and lots of character at our bakery.

Take that, Jake!

I can totally tell a dude decorated the place, there's animal heads on the walls and old tin canisters on a shelf along the ceiling. There are zero bright colors, which makes me itchy, just gray and white and dark gray. There aren't any chairs or tables either. If you wanna sit, there's a long bench in front of the front window. I think that was a dumb idea. Paris style tables and chairs are much better.

Palate-less drones line up for their turn to come in. I need to do something, before they enact the worst mistake of their lives and support this bakery.

When I turn back around, I come face to face with a boy about my age. He waits in line with a woman that's gotta be his mom. They have the same reddish hair.

I catch his eye and smile. "Hey!"

He looks at me twice. The second time, he leans back like he wants to get away from me.

But that's just silly.

"What's your name? I'm Cat."

"Oh." He looks at my clothes again. "I guess that makes sense." There's a long pause until his mom nudges him. "I'm Blane."

"And I'm Dorothy." His mom extends her hand.

I shake it twice and then make a grab for one of my fake fingernails that wiggles off with super bad timing. "Nice to meet you. Have you been to this bakery before?"

He shakes his head and looks away. There's no way he can convince me that staring at glassy-eyed animal heads is better than talking to me.

Robyn elbows me. "What are you doing? Do you know them?"

"Yeah," I hiss under my breath. "We just met, so now we are bestest friends, duh."

More important than that though, I am on a mission to save these people from themselves, so I have to ignore Robyn and her poking now.

I do such a good job I think I deserve a medal.

Or at least a refrigerator magnet.

Okay, a sticker that says, 'you are special'.

I flip my hair out of my eyes and turn on my most dazzling smile. "Is this your first time here?"

Blane blinks multiple times, his head following the movement of my swaying like he's mesmerized by the glam. I ask my question again, with the utmost patience because I know it's hard to concentrate on boring words when someone looks this amazing right in front of you.

"We come in every Monday morning," he says, finally, "for the donuts."

Donuts! I don't think we have donuts at *L'Amour*. How can we not have donuts on our menu? People love donuts. This is a super bad oversight.

I give a tinkling laugh, like nothing is amiss, even though I feel super unsettled now. "Wow, you must really like it here. Are the donuts good?"

He shrugs, looking at the toes of his brand-new cross trainers.

I try again. "It's kind of a small town to open a new bakery in, you know, with all the other bakeries around here." No matter what I do this guy won't look up. I must be out of practice. Since I fell for Tobey, I haven't flirted all that much.

Dorothy nudges Blane again. His face is pained when he finally looks up at me, and then scuffs his shoes on the tile.

Ha! Scuff number one!

Take that, Jake!

Oh wait, I forgot I don't want Jake's bakery to have character. I wait for Blane to shift away and then try to smooth out the scuff with the toe of my boot. I totally fail, the scuff is now bigger and scuffier.

"I guess." Blane says.

I try to think, what were we talking about? All that's in my brain is scuffs. Oh, wait! The bakery. Specifically, how this is a small town for more than one.

Dorothy smiles with kind eyes. "Show Low alone isn't large, but there are a lot of other, little towns, that aren't far away. People travel back and forth frequently."

"Yeah?"

"Clay Springs, Pinetop-Lakeside, Heber…" She ticks each name off on her fingers.

"Wow!" I bat my luscious eyelashes and feel one start to slip. My left eye waters.

"Are you okay, dear?" Dorothy's smooth forehead disappears into concerned wrinkles.

I wave my hand and try to maneuver the lash out of my eyeball without taking it off all the way. That would just be freaky. "Fine, I'm fine. So, you think there are enough bakeries for all of them to stay in business?"

Blane gives me a strange look. "There aren't really any other bakeries, just in the grocery store."

Robyn opens her mouth, but I poke my finger in her side. She becomes super interested in the pattern of the floor tiles.

"No, that's not right." His mom pats his shoulder. "There's the old bakery off main street."

"Yeah, I guess, but it's French." He uses the same tone I use to describe Brussel sprouts. "What are you going to get here?"

His mom looks pleased that he's no longer inspecting the tops of his shoes, but I am less than pleased that he blew off our bakery. Robyn huffs next to me. I reach for her arm and squeeze to calm us both down. It's about a minute before I can get any words out.

"Um, I haven't decided yet."

"I'm getting a blueberry muffin." Blane bounces on the balls of his feet. "My dad brought a mystery bag home last night. There were blueberry muffins in it, and they tasted so good."

Whatever.

Like Jake can make anything better than GG; she is from France, which is, like, the birthplace of bakeries. I know, I watched a whole food network episode about it.

Robyn's shoulders are scrunched to her ears and her face is slowly morphing into the color of a super ripe tomato. I think we might need to go. But first, I have to convince this misguided boy that he wants to leave this horrible place and go to *L'Amour*. How do I do that super-fast?

"Oh, yeah, muffins are yummy." I hold up my hand to block my mouth from Marshall the cashier, all sneaky like. "But you know that French bakery we were talking about? It's actually amazing, they have cream puffs and macarons in all different colors and scones..."

"What's a scone?" He scratches his cheek.

I purse my lips, digging deep for patience. But really, how am I supposed to have a serious conversation with a dude that doesn't even know what a scone is?

I stretch a smile that feels fake, even to me. "It's like a biscuit, only sweeter and usually has something like blueberries inside."

"I like blueberries."

My heart bubbles. "With an almond glaze, it is just..." I kiss my fingers.

Robyn leans over, her face so bright red she looks like part of the American flag with that blue wig on. "If you haven't tried *L'Amour Bakin'*, you need to. It's the best bakery in the White Mountains, in fact, do yourself a favor, ditch this line and go there instead."

Blane twists his face until he looks super confused. "If it's better, what are you doing here?"

"An excellent question."

My limbs stick in place like someone just zapped me with a freeze ray. Robyn squeezes my hand so tight I start to lose feeling.

Together we turn around.

Blueberry Muffins

2 & 1/2 C. Flour
1/2 tsp Salt
I TBSP Baking Powder
1/2 C. Sugar
1/2 C. Butter, melted
4 Eggs, whisked together.
1 & 1/2 C. Milk
2 C. fresh or frozen Blueberries

Preheat the oven to 400°F.

Combine all the dry ingredients in one bowl, then combine all the wet in another bowl, except not the blueberries. So, you have a dry bowl, wet bowl and blueberries.

Ultimate Showdown!

Okay, not really, but it sounded cool, right?

Put cupcake wrappers into muffin tins and spray lightly with cooking spray.

If you're using fresh berries, toss the blueberries in with the flour, make a well in the middle and pour in the wet stuff. Fold together until there aren't any dry pockets. It should still be super lumpy.

If you're using frozen blueberries, do the dry and wet mixing thing above with the blueberries separate, then fold them in at the very end. The reason is frozen blueberries defrost really fast and we don't want them discoloring the batter.

Scoop batter into cupcake wrappers and let rest for 30 minutes, then bake for 15-20, until golden brown.

12

Coconut Cream Pie

B usted.

Busted.

Busted.

Jake stands behind me with an amused expression on his face. "Hello, Ms. Cat."

I can't believe it. Our disguises totally let us down.

"We, uh..." My eyes skip around the room, looking for something to say. This is the worst timing ever. If Jake was three seconds later, we would have slipped out of this place like we never existed.

Penny takes her change and reaches for a brown bakery bag. She hugs it to her chest, jostling around for a better hold. Robyn gives Jake a harrowed look and hurries to Penny. They whisper for a second, then Penny hands the bag over. It must be heavier than it looks.

Good, I hope everything in it is as dense as rocks and breaks all our teeth.

Wait.

Just kidding about that last part. I just hope the food is nasty, that's all.

Jake follows my gaze, a smile playing around the edges of his mouth. "Yes? You were saying?"

I narrow my eyes. "We were just checking out your bakery, to see if it's as good as *L'Amour Bakin'.*" I raise my voice so everyone in the tiny room doesn't miss a word, "You know? The perfect bakery that's been here forever, just over there, the one that is the best bakery in the gray mountains."

"White mountains." Jake breaks into a full grin.

I avoid looking at his stupid face. "That's what I said."

Robyn and Penny huddle next to me. Jake crosses his arms across his chest, probably to make his muscles look bulgier.

He's so self-absorbed.

"Listen," Jake raises his voice, "*L'Amour Bakin'* is a fantastic bakery. If you want to head over there, make sure you ask about their lemon cookies." He points at an older couple sitting at one of the benches. "Frank, I know how you and Teddie like lemon, you won't regret it. But hurry, they are only open until twelve." With an amused glance in my direction, Jake disappears through shiny doors that probably lead to the kitchen.

"Let's go." Robyn brushes my arm just as I'm getting really worked up. I forget all about Blane and his mom as I follow Robyn and Penny out the door. My shoulder brushes against a girl, one of many, who are entering as we exit. I wish I didn't have such good hearing; their comments make it really hard to see straight.

"Jake is soooooo gorgeous! I think I'm in love."

"Right? I come in everyday and order a muffin just so I can look at him!"

"Me too, Irene!"

"I know! His hair! His eyes!"

"Have you seen the way he counts out change? He is adorable!"

I resist the urge to punch the wall. I have fantastic self-control, plus the wall is brick and that would hurt really, really bad.

We walk in silence around the side of the building, out of sight of the entrance. Like we all share the same brain, we gather around the bag and open it.

It smells delicious.

Dang it.

Robyn, Penny and I just stare at the stuff inside.

"That was rotten luck Jake came back while we were there." Robyn sighs.

"The worst." I poke at one of the pastries inside the bag. I hate that it's soft and tender to the touch.

Penny breathes deeply. "It was good he didn't throw us out or something, he was actually really nice. He wasn't even angry we were spying."

Whatever. The guy's a saint.

I rub my belly, which is the definition of unsettled. I don't want to eat anything right now. "How about we go to the other bakery before we sample anything else? I want to make sure we get there before our disguises droop and look totally weird."

Robyn studies me for a minute, her face all scrunched. "You don't think we look weird already?"

"Nope." I pull off the eyelash that was giving me trouble in Jake's bakery and smooth it back onto the magnetic eyeliner.

"I agree with Cat." Penny rolls the top of the paper bag and takes the pen from Robyn to mark a big DSM in one corner. "This way, we can try the stuff from Jake and the stuff from this other place at the same time."

I point at Penny. "Yes!"

"Fine." Robyn sighs. "The next place isn't too far, if we wind around this way, it's almost on the way back to *L'Amour.*"

"Fabulous." I take long steps, ready to put as much distance between myself and Jake the snake as possible.

"Cat?"

"Hm?"

"It's this way."

I spin on my heel and, without missing a step, take off in the direction Robyn is pointing. "What's the name of this place?"

"Uh." Robyn squints at her handwriting. "Pie in the Sky."

"Cute."

We walk in silence. I don't know about the other two, but I'm just singing random Taylor Swift songs in my head, trying to drown out my thoughts. I don't want to think about anything right now.

As our pace starts to slow, I narrow my eyes. "Is this the right place?"

Robyn consults her handy dandy notebook one more time, then looks around with squinty eyes. "Oh, look, there's the sign. We're in the right place."

I see the sign too, but I'm not convinced. Penny hides behind me, so it's up to Robyn to take the lead on this one. She squares her shoulders and walks up the swaying front porch of a tiny, peeling RV. Before she has a chance to knock, the door swings open to reveal a guy with muscles the size of Thor and a tattoo I feel like I need a permission slip to look at.

Penny closes her eyes, trying to disappear.

"What?" The word comes out so much like a grunt I almost miss it.

"Oh...uh, we're looking for Pie in the Sky?" Robyn tries a smile, can't make it stick, so bites her lip instead. "Is this Pie in the Sky? We're looking for Pie in the Sky."

"You said that." His voice sounds like gravel under our van tires.

"Are you Pie in the Sky?" Robyn squeaks.

"I'm Blaze."

"Pretty name."

I look around, trying to figure out what numb-skull said that, when I realize it was me! Apparently, under extreme stress I spout stupidity.

"You think so?" The scowl disappears from Blaze's face. "No one has ever said that to me before." He rests his hand on his heart and leans against the door jamb.

"No?" I hiccup. "That's weird."

"Yeah, it is. I picked Blaze as my name to represent the blazing of a new me. From the ashes of my old life, it's symbolic, you know? Anyways, ain't nothin' prettier than a blaze of fire." He stares off into space; a single tear glistens in the corner of his eye.

After a moment of silence, Robyn tries again. "We're looking for Pie in the Sky. Are...are we in the right place?"

Blaze snaps his attention to Robyn. "Yes, ma'am. This is Pie in the Sky bakery, at your service." He waves his arm to the side but doesn't move his hulking body, so I'm not sure if we're supposed to cram inside his RV, or what.

I think not.

Actually what I think is that my mom will destroy us if we go inside that thing. Her Spidey Mom Sense is probably tingling right now. I wouldn't be surprised to see her marching down the path, snorting like a rhinoceros with allergies.

"Do you...have a...menu?" Robyn whispers, her eyes huge.

Blaze crosses his arms and makes the mistake of looking at one of his gargantuan biceps. He eyes it, flexes, examines it some more. Then goes from arm to arm, making his biceps jump back and forth and back and forth. He might keep going forever except that Penny sneezes and snaps him out of his bicep trance.

"Oh, what?" Blaze looks at us.

"We're looking for Pie in the Sky," Robyn squeaks.

I think the stress is getting to her.

"Right, whatcha want?"

"Pie?"

I mean, are there other options at a place called Pie in the Sky?

"Coming right up." Blaze closes the door, leaving us on his rickety porch wondering if we should make a run for it. At least, that's what I'm thinking. I can't speak for the other two. But judging by the shaky way Robyn sinks onto the top step and Penny's whimpering, I think they're with me.

We didn't tell him what kind of pie we want. What is he making in there? I wonder if there is there only one type.

"Is this real life?" Penny whispers in my ear.

I squirm, rubbing away her tickly breath. "I think so." I'm not really into pinching myself to check if I'm dreaming, or I might be tempted to. This is the most random experience I have ever had.

And that's saying something.

"He isn't competition for *L'Amour*, is he?" Robyn leans toward Penny and I, her eyes on Blaze's door. "I mean, his kitchen is tiny, how can he handle a restaurant account?"

"Maybe he's a wizard," Penny peeks out of my armpit. "He looks like Hagrid, doesn't he?"

He's not nearly as hairy, and more muscle than fat, but if I squint my eyes and sort of tilt my head upside down, he totally does.

"I ain't a wizard." His voice floats out one of the windows. "And, so you know, I'm shooting to use the high school kitchen. They let me rent it, real cheap."

I whisper, "Did he hear us?"

"Yes, ma'am," he growls. "And I think I know just what's going on here."

I lean back; my legs feel wobbly. Penny presses into my side to keep us both from falling over.

The door opens again, this time with Blaze in a pink, frilly apron that I kind of want to borrow, even though I would never in a bazillion years have the guts to ask him. He carries a square bakery box the same color, tied with white tulle. "Nothing gets past me; I know who you all are." His eyes glare into my soul. "Y'all are from one of them reality shows! I'd recognize ya anywheres," He jabs an oven mitt at Penny. "Ain't you that famous make-up artist?"

Penny yips and dives out of sight behind me, except that her poofy wig sticks out about half a foot on either side.

"Yeah, I thought so. Don't you worry, your secret is safe with Blaze." He holds out the box.

Penny passes her purse up to Robyn, who pays the guy, then the purse and change get passed back to Penny.

"You girls have a good day now. Be sure to mention old Blaze on your fancy show. Bye now."

Our lasting image is a pink oven mitt, waving in the doorway.

We sort of wander around in a daze after that. I honestly have no idea where we are and am more than happy to sit when Robyn eventually directs us to a bench along the main road. My eyes are unfocused as I stare out into the abyss.

What the what just happened?

Robyn tugs off her blue wig and shakes out her hair. It tickles my neck, but I make no move to brush it away. She lays the wig carefully in her lap and folds both hands over it.

Penny pulls her knees up to her chin and disappears into her arms.

I lose track of how long we sit there, stuck and frozen and practically traumatized.

Except that my belly lets out a roar that pops Penny's head right up.

"Was that Blaze?" Her voice is so high-pitched it hurts my ears.

Robyn blinks. "Blaze?" She erupts into giggles that quickly escalate into belly laughs and tears. "Blaze? And his pie baking trailer!" She tries to say more but can't get any words through all the laughing.

Then Penny starts in, rolling onto her back to hold her stomach. Her legs hang off the bench, shaking with each giggle. I am about to give them both up for looney when I hear a snort escape from my nose.

"B-B-Blaze!" I guffaw so loud an older couple walking towards us crosses the street, checking over their shoulders to see if we've succumbed to madness yet. I don't even care, I just clutch my own belly and laugh.

And laugh.

And laugh.

"Holy cow, I am starving!" Robyn wipes her eyes and reaches under the bench for the bakery box. "Should we see what old Blaze can do?"

I swallow another round of snickers; I have to stop now because my tummy muscles are super sore. To distract myself, I lean over the box. Inside are three miniature pies. One has a crisscross pattern on top with dough, like Marissa does to her apple pies. The other has meringue, so probably lemon, and the last one has a topping that looks like whipped cream. Who knows what's under that?

"Do you think they're safe to eat?" Penny's breath is hot on my arm.

"Only one way to find out." Robyn pops the cream pie out of the little disposable tin and takes a bite. "Oh wow! That's good!" A blob gets stuck on the corner of her mouth. She hands the pie over to me, wipes her mouth, and reaches for the meringue.

I nibble at first, just until the cream makes my taste buds sing, then I take a huge bite.

It is good!

Really good.

The coconut filling is thick and dreamy. The biggest surprise is that the guy uses real whipped cream, with coconut extract instead of vanilla. A few months ago, I would not have known or cared about any of that, but now I can tell with one sniff.

I pass the coconut cream to Penny and take the meringue. The lemon is so subtle the marshmallowy meringue is what comes through, and it is delectable.

Robyn hands me the last pie. I smell the cinnamon apples before I taste them. At first glance this pie seems like it will be the least memorable, but I am totally wrong. Little bits of caramelized pecan make each bite super exciting.

We pass each teeny pie around once more, and then they are gone. I look at the empty box sadly. There isn't any more to eat, which is a pity cause there's no way I'm ever going back to Blaze's RV to get more.

"Wow." Penny leans back. "Just, wow."

"That was fantastic." Robyn's face clouds over. "Do you think people feel this way after leaving *L'Amour*?"

"Absolutely!" I nod, trying to make it true. "They all leave and they're like, let's go back, that was so good, I need more right now."

"Yeah?"

"Yes!" I reach for Jake's brown bag. It's time to make ourselves feel better with his inferior food. I pull out one of the big blueberry muffins and divide it into thirds and give Robyn and Penny a piece.

Penny stuffs the whole thing in her mouth. "This has been a weird day. I mean, Blaze, weird, but then, at the bakery, did you feel weird there?" She has a hard time pushing out coherent words around that hunk of food.

"What do you mean?" I turn my piece of muffin over and over in my hands.

"I don't know." Penny swallows with a gulping noise. "It was fine at first, but then, when Jake came in, I felt all weird. Kind of tingly and nauseous."

"Yeah." Robyn puts her piece up to her nose. "I sort of felt it too, like I was just electrocuted or something."

"How do you even know what it feels like to be electrocuted?"

Robyn shoots me a glare; I think her fun-o-meter ran out. "You know what I mean. Something was definitely weird in there."

I can't deny that what they say is true, but I don't want to talk about it anymore. I take a small bite of muffin, then swallow and glare at what is left in my hand. "This is really good, too."

Robyn takes courage from me and finally puts the thing in her mouth. Her shoulders slump forward as she groans. "Aw poop, *gata*. It is really good."

Penny nods, licking crumbs from her fingers.

"Seriously." I crumble the top of the bag, so I'm not tempted to reach in and eat anything else. I'm no longer sure it will be gross, and I just want to keep believing it is without reality interfering. "It's super unfair. It would be so much easier if this stuff was disgusting."

Robyn nods, her wig slipping off her lap. She catches it before it hits the dirt. "Right? Our bakery is better, of course, but this is really, really yummy too."

"I'm so glad you approve."

Robyn and I jump a mile and a half into the air. Penny squeals and grabs the bakery bag out of my hands, clutching it like a shield.

Why does he keep doing that?

Jake looks down at the crumbs in our laps. His voice rises to a super high falsetto. "I'm super glad you like, like, my baking and stuff. I'm so glad you think it's sooooooo not disgusting." He crosses his arms and leans against the streetlight pole.

The bakery bag rustles in Penny's shaky hands. I grip her arm to get her to hold still. Robyn glances at me, her face confused. Here's the thing about Robyn, she's so sincerely nice she hardly ever gets it when people use sarcasm. I usually have to confirm that it is what she thinks it is.

I nod and mouth the word *mocking*.

Robyn purses her lips. "We didn't mean to upset you; we were just curious about your bakery."

A smile twirls around the corner of Jake's mouth. "I have to tell you girls; it's pretty satisfying to hear people from *L'Amour* compliment my baking."

This is one of those moments when it's hard to tell if the person expects an answer, or they just paused for dramatic flair.

"It's good..." Robyn begins but doesn't know where to go next.

"I don't need your approval to know I'm good. I plan on being the best bakery in the White Mountains. You can take that"—he gestures toward Penny and the bakery bag and she squeaks and ducks her head—"back to your Auntie Jojo and tell her she's got herself some serious competition."

"Jojo didn't tell us to go to your bakery." Robyn twirls one of her rings around her finger. "We decided to come on our own and—"

"Compare?" Jake raises an eyebrow.

I suddenly have visions of Penny, Robyn, and I flying through the air.

Because he picks us up with his angry hulk strength and throws us of course.

I don't know, it makes sense to me.

Robyn's cheeks begin to flush. "No... Jojo didn't tell us to go to your bakery. It was our idea." Robyn shifts to face Jake more fully and holds out a hand. "If you want to be mad at us, fine, it was our idea, but leave Jojo out of it."

Jake smirks. "Yeah, sure. And those aren't her costumes either. Nice try girls, I know Jojo's style, she's too chicken to come check me out herself, so she sent her minions."

Robyn clamps her mouth closed.

It's time for me to talk. Up until this moment, I wasn't sure if my tongue was going to let me. It feels all dry and way too big for my mouth. "Robyn's telling the truth. We did come on our own, okay? We wanted to see what your bakery is like."

Jake's lips set in a thin line, he raises an eyebrow into his cowboy hat. "So, Jolynn didn't put you up to it?"

"It was my idea." I meet his eyes and toss my head, super sassafrass.

"I see." He fixes me with his gaze. It's like the ultimate staring contest. Too bad he doesn't know how amazing I am at staring contests. I throw my shoulders back and concentrate every effort on not blinking.

Also, on breathing, cause that's important too.

As the tension builds, Robyn starts to get antsy, her hands twitch against my side, her feet bounce off the ground. I'm not totally sure what has her so keyed up and there's no way I'm breaking eye contact to question her.

"I think we need to go now." Penny's small voice peeps out from behind me, she moves to her feet but stays crouched down, like she's trying to stay unnoticed. The bag crinkles with her movements, undoing all her effort.

Jake looks away, but before I can even enjoy my victory, he takes two long steps to Penny. She closes her eyes as he reaches for the bag, but all he does is ease it out of her arms. "Muffins, a couple different kinds," He shuffles through the insides. "Donuts with glaze and with sprinkles. You'll notice *L'Amour* doesn't sell any of those things."

"We noticed." I grumble.

Penny nods and then shakes her head, then nods again. "But we only had time to try the muffin before you caught us."

Jake's long, low chuckle fills the air.

I look at Robyn and am totally stunned speechless.

This does not happen to me often.

Robyn's face is bright red again, her hands clutched and shaking. The line of her jaw that I can see from this angle is tightly clenched.

I have never seen Robyn this upset before. She never gets mad. Irritated? Frequently. Annoyed? Often. But never, ever mad.

The world might actually be coming to an end.

I'm with Penny; we need to go now. When the world implodes, I do not want to be standing on a corner in Show Low Arizona. I tug Robyn's arm, wrenching her angry eyes away from Jake's face, where she might be trying to mentally pepper his face with pock marks.

Jake quirks a smile. "Well, off you go then." He hands the bag back to Penny. "You girls have a nice day. Thanks for the business."

I have to fight the urge creeping along my legs to run screaming down the street. Penny shifts the bag to cover the goosebumps on her arms. I didn't even notice I have them too until just now.

"This is *loco*!" Robyn mumbles, rubbing her arms so fast I imagine I see sparks. I'm so happy to see her doing normal things again like talking and goose-bumping. Maybe we are going to get through this after all.

We walk so fast, *L'Amour Bakin'* comes into view right away. There is a fat line out the front door that winds around the building to the back.

Robyn stops walking, touching my elbow so I stop too, and Penny looks back at us curiously.

"Before we go in there and it gets super busy and we don't have time to talk, I have something to say."

"What?" Penny's eyes widen to beanie boo size.

Robyn braces herself, "Cat, you were right."

"I know!" I nod emphatically. "But what are you talking about specifically?"

"Jake." Robyn jabs a thumb back the way we came. "You were right about Jake. He's a big, fat, stinky..."

My shoulders tense, waiting for the climatic word.

"Butt."

Penny covers her giggles with the bakery bag.

"Robyn!" I clap my hands onto my cheeks. "Such language! Do you kiss your mama with that mouth?"

She smacks my arm. "Stop it, I'm serious. We have to do something. Did you hear him? Talking about Jojo like that? He's trying to hurt Jojo, he's trying to break her heart. On purpose!"

"Yeah." I totally agree.

"What can we do, though?" Penny wonders.

I wonder too. We can't burn his building down, for obvious reasons, or buy him out, or offer him a lifetime supply of baked beans to leave town, or-

"We bake." Robyn folds her arms, her blue eyes stormy.

"Wait." I squint at her, making sure I heard what I think I heard. "Are you saying w—"

"Yes! We bake him something, some emotion, that will make him go away."

Penny's eyes get wider, if possible. "Can we do that?"

"How much does she know?" Robyn asks me.

Before I can answer, Penny chimes in. "Cat told me we have a family gift, and we can bake our feelings into food and make other people feel that way too. I didn't believe her at first, but then she gave me cookies,"

"That's right." Robyn presses her lips together. "The calm cookies."

"Yeah, and they totally changed how I felt. So, I know she wasn't teasing like that time she told me that raisins are dried up rat dookie."

"That's what they taste like!" I defend myself.

Robyn shakes her head. "Yeah, anyway, focus here. What emotion can we bake that will make Jake go away? We can make him forget, I guess that's not an emotion though, that's just, like a *problemo* in his *cabezo*. Um, maybe we can make him bake terrible, like if we make him feel stupid, so he reads the recipes all wrong or gets mixed up and bakes really bad? Then people will stop going to his bakery and start coming to ours instead. That might work, but is stupid an emotion? Sometimes I feel stupid, but it's because I don't know something. Is that a real feeling? Could we bake him to not know? No, that would be the forgetting thing again, I think. What else, what else? Oh!" Robyn snaps her fingers right in my ear, I wince and give it a good rub. "I got it! Let's bake him apathetic! That's totally an emotion."

"Apathetic?" Penny wrinkles her nose.

"It means you don't care. If he doesn't care anymore, he will stop baking! He won't be our competition! We will totally stay in business, and everything will be fine. And since Cat's baking is so super powerful, we might even get him to leave town because he stops caring. This is totally going to work!" Robyn turns to me, her eyes shining. "Do you think apathetic is the right emotion? Cat, you're being super quiet. What do you think?"

"What do I think?" I stop walking and wait for Robyn to look at my face. It's really important that I have her full attention so she can't misunderstand the words about to come out of my mouth. "I think you are crazy pants! Have you completely lost your mind? There is no way in this wide green universe we are going to bake Jake anything. That is the worst idea ever!"

Coconut Cream Pie

Filling:
2 C. Coconut Milk
1/2 C. Sugar
3 TBSP Cornstarch
3 Egg yolks
1/4 tsp Salt
1/2 C. shredded unsweetened Coconut
1/2 tsp Vanilla extract
2 tsp Coconut extract
1 baked Pie Crust

Topping:
2 & 1/2 C. Heavy Whipping Cream
1/2 tsp Coconut extract
2 TBSP Powdered Sugar

Are you ready for some fun?

In a large pot, whisk together coconut milk, sugar, and cornstarch. Heat to medium and bring to a boil. Keep whisking until your arm burns or—if you're super innovative—until the hand mixer gets too whiny.

Take the pot off the heat just for a second while you whisk the egg yolks with salt. You want them to get frothy, because that's a fun word to say.

Now we're going to temper the eggs. This means we ease them into the heat, so they don't curdle. That is also a fun word to say but not at all a fun thing if it happens. To temper, splash some of the warmed milk into the eggs and stir together. Then, add the whole mixture back into the pot, put back on the heat, and stir together some more.

Now we stir until the whole mixture gets thick. Think pudding thick, cause that's what we're doing here, people, making pudding—or, really, custard.

When you think you've got it, remove from heat again and add shredded coconut, vanilla and coconut extract. Stir to combine.

Pour the whole shenanigans into a bowl and cover with plastic wrap. Press the plastic wrap into the custard, like touchy-touchy to prevent skin from forming. There are many things that should have skin, custard is not one of them.

Chill 1-2 hours.

While you're waiting, whip the cream with sugar and coconut extract until thick enough to form peaks. That just means that when you lift the whisk out of the bowl there are parts that stay standing without any help from you.

Now is also a good time to make your pie crust, or defrost it, whichever you're in the mood for today.

No judgement here.

When the custard is all the way chilled, pour into the cooled pie crust and top with whipped cream. If you could put heaven on a plate, this would be it.

13

Berry Breakfast Tarts

Cat, the Cream Puff Queen

Tobey Richards (sweettoothdecay@email.com) November 23rd, 11:23 a.m.

To: Cat

Hey, Cat!

Why are you so mean to me? Those cream puffs look really good, I just drooled on my phone. What do you think? Should I pack it in rice?

Maybe, when you get home, you can show me how to make cream puffs. Now that I saw them, I need to eat them. You know, I think I might be addicted to sweets.

But not as bad as my brother. I made the mistake of taking him with me to Diet Starts Monday. We got there as soon as they opened this morning. I wish I could tell you the cinnamon roll was good, but I wouldn't know, Conner yanked it out of my hand and shoved the whole thing in his mouth. The whole thing! It sounds like I'm exaggerating, but it's the honest truth.

I wanted to shake his hand and punch his lights out at the same time.

But the trip this morning wasn't a total loss. I came up with a poem on the walk home.

"Cinnamon rolls can't be beat. I would eat them in the street. I would eat them stale or dry, I would eat them 'til I cry. But no rolls for me today, my dumb brother is going to pay."

Then I thought of at least ten ways I can get back at him. Unfortunately, I can only do two of them without getting grounded.

I guess I'll just have to go back to the bakery tomorrow. Without Conner this time.

Speaking of bakeries. Did you decide to do about the other bakeries? I hope you're going to ninja spy. If I was there with you, I would make you do it. Actually, I'm going to make you do it remotely.

This is me making you. Don't you have an uncontrollable urge to dress in black and buy some nunchucks now?

Go, go ninja spy, and tell me everything so I can pretend like my vacation is as cool as yours.

Tobey

P.S. Nate says Hi.

P.P.S He works at Diet Starts Monday; did you know that?

P.P.P.S I wonder if he can get me free food, like the stuff that doesn't sell?

P.P.P.P.S I should call him.

P.P.P.P.P.S Do you know his number?

"Pshaw," I say under my breath. Like I would have Nate's number. Like I would ever call Nate. Nate is the worst. Maybe the only person worse than Nate is Jake.

But that's a close second, for sure.

"Cat!"

I look up from my phone and almost ram into Penny for the fourth time. "Sorry!" I say, even though it's not completely my fault; Penny keeps swerving in front of my feet because she's staring off into deep thought land. To passing observers, the two of us probably look like we're complete loony birds.

This might be what Mom's talking about when she lectures on using cell phones responsibly.

But I have a really good reason for phoning and walking. It's called distraction. As in, distraction from the fact that Robyn wants to throw me in the garbage since I refuse to emotion bake Jake.

Also, distraction from the plethora of emotions that are swarming my own belly.

My belly, which knows everything, keeps rumbling at me. Normally I would think it's because I'm hungry, but that's impossible after our bakery stakeouts and hobbit-like breakfasts. Besides all that, I know the rumbling is because baking Jake is the worst idea ever.

I have to wonder what is wrong with the universe where I'm the one trying to talk Robyn out of baking emotions. Is it just me, or is that all backwards and stuff? Seriously, was she not there the whole time I kept baking cupcakes and bread and cinnamon rolls to undo the love and the hate?

Plus, I don't even like Jake. So, I really resent the fact that I'm sort of protecting him here.

Yeah, lots of feelings.

Good thing there was an email waiting for me from Tobey. Tobey is the perfect distraction. But it isn't working as well as I hoped. Not with Robyn's death glares, and with me tripping over everything.

I put my phone in my pocket and concentrate on walking back to the bakery without maiming myself or anyone else around me. We make it with only one more stumble stepping off the curb and a flat tire for Penny.

Oh, yeah, plus I almost fall face first into the gutter.

But we don't need to keep bringing that up.

Robyn stops outside the kitchen door and takes off the rest of her costume stuff. She organizes when she's upset, so she takes a really long time folding everything up and stacking it perfectly.

Penny and I wait, semi-patiently, with mounds of accessories in our arms. Robyn gives a martyr sigh and folds all our stuff too, then we open the door to the kitchen.

Once inside, I get sucked into a tornado of flour and pastry cream. People are running all over the place, like organized chaos. My mom washes dishes so quickly, her hands are peach blurs. She doesn't even stop washing when she peers over her shoulder at us.

"What in the world took you so long? Never mind, don't answer, doesn't matter. Robyn and Cat, go help Jojo at the register, she's swamped. Penny, come dry for me, would you? How do they do this on their own every day?" It's obvious my mom doesn't expect an answer; she's already showing Penny where the towels are, so it must have been one of those talking to herself questions.

My dad squeezes by with a huge bag of flour on his shoulder, just like Jake did this morning. But unlike Jake, my dad is red-faced and huffing.

And also, he doesn't make me want to practice projectile vomiting.

Bubby skips along behind him, singing a song he made up about donut dinosaurs.

It's not bad actually.

I follow Robyn's straight, angry back with a sinking feeling that is so not pleasant. I don't remember the last time Robyn was this mad at me, and I've done a lot of stupid things over the years.

A lot!

Plus, I'm a little mad at her, so there's that too.

I mean, seriously, what is she thinking?

We push through the kitchen doors into the bakery, GG's face lights up when she sees us. "Oh, I am so happy you are here to save the day. Robyn, please put these berry tarts into bakery boxes. And my Cat, I show you how to work the register. Don't look worried, it is easy as tarts."

"Pie," I correct her.

"That is what I said."

This is not the time to wallow in my frustration. GG needs my help.

But pulling my brain to the present is tougher than it looks. I still want to grab Robyn by the arm and yank her outside to hash this whole thing out. After our walk in the crisp mountain air, I think I'm calm enough to talk to her without ranting about how many marbles she's lost.

In retrospect, that might be part of the reason why she's so upset at me.

"Working the register is easy. You will see." GG grabs my wrist and tugs me along behind her to the backside of the counter.

The forbidden side.

I shake out my shoulders and watch carefully while GG demonstrates how to use the register to check out four customers. By the time the man with his box of tarts rings the bell on his way out the door, I feel ready to do it on my own. GG stays right by me, greeting customers and telling me what they want to order, even though they just told her, and I can hear them. I push buttons, take money, and hand over receipts for the longest half an hour of my life.

Just kidding. Actually, that was world history in seventh grade. I think I lived a thousand and one lives in that class. Like the Egyptian Pharaohs thought they were going to do. I'm actually way older than fourteen.

Jojo runs back and forth from the kitchen to the display case, refilling things, while Robyn helps box and bag whatever people order. When those thirty minutes finally mosey on by, the display case is completely empty and there is still a line out the front of the store.

GG raises her arms like she's about to conduct a symphony orchestra. "Just one moment. We will be back with some more for you to choose." Then she pulls Robyn, Jojo, and me into the kitchen.

"Please tell me we have more to sell?" Jojo falls against the kitchen counter pretty dramatically for a grown up.

"More breakfast tarts." My mom pulls her hands out of the dishwater to point. "Drew just got them from the oven."

Dad pops up from behind a cabinet. "Also, scones, uh, plain and triple berry. On the cooling racks over there."

Jojo darts to the cooling racks and stacks trays in her arms. Right about the moment I'm positive she's going to drop everything on the floor, she stops loading and brings them to the counter where we wait. The smell of browned butter makes my mouth water.

There's no time for thoughts like that, we are way too busy. GG fills a basket with breakfast tarts that look like the pop-tarts my mom used to buy for us before I learned about homemade food. Robyn and I carry them out while Jojo and Dad move trays to the display case. Within thirty minutes everything we have is all gone for reals this time.

"Holy guacamole." Robyn plops into a chair, covering her face with a dish towel like she's trying to hide. It's not going to work. The dish towel is bright yellow.

Super bad camouflage.

"Yikes-a-bee." I sink into a chair next to Robyn and have all my hopes dashed when she scoots away, turning so I have a fantastic view of the back of her head.

"Is it always like this?" Mom fans herself with one of the glossy menus she swiped from the rack near the register. "It can't always be like this; how do you survive?"

Jojo reaches for the empty display trays and starts wiping them out too. "We barely make it through every day." She wipes invisible crumbs off the counter.

I know they are invisible because I barely got done wiping everything down and I actually did an amazing job. Not like at home when I just slap the rag on the table, or whatever, and call it good.

GG gives a tinkling laugh and eases onto a bar stool. "Oh Jojo, you are so silly! The people here know us, they are so patient. But it is with luck that we have you to help us serve them all today." She opens her arms. "It is wonderful you are here to keep us baking."

Penny sits up straight and peers out the front window. "There's someone walking by; did we turn off the OPEN sign?"

"Um..." Jojo crosses the room in a few long strides. "Nope, it was still on. Thanks, Pen." She flips the switch, letting the whole world—or the whole town, at least—know that we are closed.

Penny still stares out the window, her head moving slowly, as though she's watching something move. She concentrates so hard, I get curious and tug on her sleeve. "Who's out there? I can't see."

Penny doesn't answer.

Robyn pulls the towel off of her head; I thought she was rotting under there, and watches Penny curiously. She sits up taller to stretch her neck towards the other window.

Then she hunkers down.

"What is it?" I whisper.

She shakes her head, glaring at me.

I poke her. "Robby!" I can't believe she's being this ornery. Is she really going to hold a grudge forever?

Penny mouths a word. It looks like she's saying the letter 'A', but I know it's not that because of the look of terror on her face. There's only one person, besides Blaze, that would make Penny look like that.

Jake.

Wait, is he out there? Is he everywhere we go today? Because this is becoming a problem for me.

I start to stand up, to see for myself, but Penny shakes her head. She turns around, pulling the curtains together, tight behind her back. "The bakery's closed for the day, now what do you do?"

Jojo yawns. "Take a nap."

GG *tsks*. "No, no, no, we prepare for tomorrow!"

"What are you girls up to?" My mom asks, sounding amused. She doesn't wait for any of us to answer. She crosses the room to Penny. "Why do you have a fake beauty mark on your cheek?"

Penny rubs at it with her knuckle, trying to keep the curtains closed at the same time. It is very entertaining to watch her; she looks like she's doing the chicken dance. Good thing she's so flexible.

"Penny!" Mom laughs and pulls on the curtains. At least, she tries to. There's a bit of a tug of war between the two of them before Mom gives an exasperated grunt and yanks.

She peers out the window.

I scoot in my chair, sliding so my nose is level with the table. If something is about to explode, only my hair and my eyebrows will singe. On second thought, I grab the towel Robyn discarded and put that over my head. My eyebrows can be penciled in, but my hair is super important.

I try not to move, even when I breathe. Robyn goes completely still as well.

Great minds.

Except for the part where hers is still mad at me.

That's not a great part.

Jojo stands up and stretches her hands over her head. "What is going on over there?"

Robyn shrugs.

I fold over to hide my head in my knees.

Penny tries to disappear into the curtains.

"I don't see anything." Mom moves to look around the other part of the windowpane. "Just someone walking away from the bakery, that's all. I guess they saw the sign switch to CLOSED."

"That's right," I say quickly.

Too quickly.

"What's right?" My mom gives me a strange look. "What are you talking about?"

Dad leans against the counter near the register. "Is it just me or are our girls acting a little wacko?"

I swallow so hard I'm pretty sure they can hear it in Boise and Timbuktu. "Are there any more cream puffs?"

"Okay, now why are you asking about cream puffs?" Jojo sounds amused.

"Cat?" Mom prompts, in a commanding tone.

"I asked..." I sigh. "Because I want Jojo to eat cream puffs before I tell you guys why we were staring out the window."

"That's interesting," Dad says.

"Why do you want Jolyn to be happy before you tell her something?" GG smiles in a way that makes it seem like we are all sharing a hilarious joke.

I sigh again. "Because then she won't get all ticked off at Jake out there."

"Jake?" Jojo sucks in a sharp breath of air. "What about Jake?"

Robyn slumps in her chair, giving me a nasty look. "He was just walking by. We saw him walking by. Just passing, he's totally gone."

"Well, good thing he kept walking," Jojo says with a sardonic smile.

GG clucks her tongue.

"It is!" Jojo insists. "I can't be held responsible for what I say, or do, when I'm around that—"

"Jolyn!"

"—guy." Jojo finishes.

Mom takes a deep breath like she just ran a marathon. She glances at Dad, then opens a can of worms that are actually explosives. "Why do you hate Jake so much, Jojo?"

Jojo blinks. "I...I don't *hate* him...exactly..."

GG coughs, lightly.

"Okay, fine. I hate him. He's a dirty, low-down, no-good, sarcastic, cocky, booger maker."

"Is that a technical term?" My dad raises an eyebrow.

"Jojo!" Mom giggles. "Are you twelve?"

Jojo turns with flashing eyes, but a smile on her face. "No! It's just the plain truth."

I totally agree, but I'm not about to say so. Especially since I'm the only reason Robyn and I aren't currently scheming a way to transform Jake into something other than the booger maker that he is.

"Then"—Robyn doesn't look up, tries to keep her voice neutral—"you don't want to be friends with him or work with him?" She shoots me the smallest look.

I see what she's doing here. If Jojo says she hates Jake, then Robyn has evidence that we should bake him.

Because Jojo needs our help.

Robyn should save her brain power for inventing a way to keep eating yummy food without getting stuffed. I love Jojo more than sparkle nail polish, but there is no way Robyn can convince me it's a good idea to bake Jake. I did not go through the most traumatizing twenty-four hours of my life back in August, to turn around and do the same thing all over again now. Baking to manipulate people's emotions is so not cool.

Robyn should know this.

"Friends with Jake?" Jojo laughs incredulously as she shakes her head. "No, no stinking way. He knocked a big hole in that ship. It didn't sail; it sank."

"Oh." Robyn rests her cheek on her hand. "I see." Her voice is as airy as over-whipped cream.

"It's sweet of you to care, Robs, but the truth is, I can't work with someone I don't trust, and I don't trust Jake. There might have been a time when that could have been different, but there's really no point in visiting a fairy tale past. So, I'm just going to keep doing what I'm doing, get over this so I can bake again, and everything will be fine. I know it."

There! Maybe now Robyn will let this whole baking thing go and be my friend again. It's obvious Jojo's at peace with the way things are.

"You know what would be really great?" Jojo leans forward with a twinkle in her eyes, "It would be *really* great if Jake would close his bakery and leave town. Then I wouldn't have to see him ever again. Problem solved!" She throws a towel in the air and catches it with one hand.

Or maybe not.

Robyn sits up straight, sending a triumphant look my way.

I still don't think she's right.

I don't like where this is headed at all, so I'm going to employ distraction technique four. Or is it eight? I need to start writing these things down. Anyway—changing the subject—that one.

"Hey, Penny, where's the bakery bag?"

"What bakery bag?" Mom raises an eyebrow.

Rats, I forgot we sort of didn't tell Mom about the part where we went and spied on the competition bakeries. Also, I didn't really change the subject since we're still knee-deep in talking about Jake and his dumb bakery.

I should have gone with my gut and brought up cheetahs.

Penny hurries from the room and I twirl a lock of hair around my finger so tight it leaves marks when I unroll it. "We just bought some stuff from other bakeries."

My mom isn't fooled for a second. Neither is my dad, even though I thought he wasn't actually listening to any of this because he's been doodling on a napkin this whole time.

Tricksey.

"Did you girls go spy on Jake's bakery?" Dad squints at me.

"Well..." I pause to try out the loophole that 'us girls' didn't actual-ly go, because we were in disguise, so we weren't really us. See? I think it can work until I catch a glimpse of Mom's face.

So, that's a big no.

She's not going to buy anything but the total truth.

The silence that follows builds up like a Lego tower. With each second that goes by—and believe me, I notice every tick of the clock—tension feels as thick as pudding with too much cornstarch. I don't know why, but something about the intensity of GG's, Dad's, *and* Mom's eyes combined makes me keep thinking about all the things I've done that weren't the best choices ever.

Baking without permission...

Taking my mom's clothes and shoes without asking...

Using my baking powers on people without telling them...

Trying to get Tobey to fall in love with me...

Spying on Jake's bakery...

I can't take it anymore!

"Yes! We spied on Jake's Bakery, and the other bakeries, too!" I clap my hand over my mouth.

My words bring stares.

Grounded for life stares.

Scrub toilets with your toothbrush stares.

Never again see the light of day stares.

"You. Did. What?" Mom's voice is low and very, very dangerous.

I check out my shoes. They are not super interesting, but it's way better than taking the full brunt of appalled looks. Especially from GG. She doesn't look mad, just disappointed.

And that is a thousand times worse.

"Wait!" Jojo stands up. "Grammy, Bridget, Drew. Before you really let the girls have it, I totally had part in this. I encouraged the girls to go, I gave them dress-up clothes."

"Beauty mark." Mom presses her lips together, putting the pieces together.

"It seemed like a good idea at the time." Jojo gives a rueful smile.

I lift a hand to grip the top of the table and pull myself into a standing position too, even though my legs are super tired. It just doesn't seem right to plead our case while lounging halfway under the table. And I can't let Jojo take the blame. It really was my idea in the first place.

Well, actually, it was Tobey's, but I'm not about to blame it on him either.

"Let me tell you the whole story. It will make sense, I promise."

I hope.

Mom's left eyebrow lets me know she is waiting patiently for an explanation.

Very patiently.

I take the deepest breath in the world. "Well, first we went to the cemetery for GG's clue."

"GG's what?" Dad lifts an eyebrow now too.

With his and mom's eyebrows all synchronized, my chances of surviving this experience plummet.

"I give the girls a scavenger hunt to teach them of our family history." GG explains, for which I am very grateful.

I clear my throat, fiddling with the hem of my shirt. "Anyway, Jake was at the cemetery too, so we decided it would be the perfect time to scope out his bakery."

"Scope out?" Dad taps his pen against the countertop.

"Yeah, so, it's not spying, because we just wanted to see what we're dealing with, you know? Scope out the competition. Plus, he gave us a coupon, so it's like he invited us. Right?"

"Did you have coupons for the other bakeries as well?" Dad asks.

"No, but since we were in the mode, we also went to the Great Buns food truck and Blaze's pie trailer thingy."

Holy cow, why did I bring that up? My mouth is totally leaking!

"Excuse me?" Mom tips her chin downward.

"Oh!" Jojo giggles. "Blaze, he's such a dear. What did you think of his pies?"

"So good," Robyn says.

I send her a grateful look, which she ignores. Well, mad at me or not, I'm still super happy she said something. I was feeling kind of alone and abandoned until she did.

"It was just for fun." I swing my arms at my sides. "We bought things to sample from each place to see what we're dealing with. And we brought some home to share. Wasn't that nice?"

On cue, Penny bursts back into the room, swinging the big brown bag. "The pies are gone, but we got a lot of stuff from Jake's bakery."

Jojo is pretty random about her reactions to anything to do with Jake. So, I'm thinking she's either going to try something he baked and calmly compliment it or grab the whole bag and throw it to the ground so she can stomp it to crumbs of death.

It could go either way.

She moves to Penny like someone going through water. Slowly, she opens the bag and looks through it. After a few minutes, she says, "Interesting."

"What?" Robyn can't help it; her detective mode won't sit idle during a time like this.

Jojo looks through the bag once more and then purses her lips, gazing at the ceiling. "We don't sell any of these things."

"No?"

Jojo bites her bottom lip. "What does that mean?"

"What *does* it mean?" Robyn blurts, unable to let the silence drag out like this.

With a sigh, Jojo closes the bag and walks away. "I'm going to go make sure we turned the stoves off."

"Wait!" Robyn reaches out a hand. "You didn't say what you think it means!"

Jojo stops walking without turning around. Her voice hangs in the air above us like dark, heavy clouds, like a backpack full of history books, like gallons of chocolate ganache.

"I don't know what I mean. I don't even *want* to know what I mean. I wish Jake would just disappear."

Berry Breakfast Tarts

Pastry:
1/2 C. Butter
1/4 C. Sugar
2 Eggs, room temperature
2 & 1/2 C. Flour
1 & 1/2 tsp Baking Powder

Filling:
Your Favorite Jam - about 1/2 C.

In a stand mixer, cream butter and sugar until light and fluffy.

(Side note; don't you love creaming things? It makes me think of marshmallows, fluffy clouds, and hockey games.)

Add eggs, one at a time. Room temperature is important in this recipe because they will incorporate better, making a better crust.

Trust me, I know all about incorporations.

In a separate bowl, mix flour and baking powder. Whisk them just because you can.

Sprinkle—another thing I love—the flour mixture into the butter mixture and combine the two just until it forms a dough. Divide the dough in half and refrigerate for one hour.

Why?

Thanks for asking, because this allows the butter to harden and the dough to rest. We pretty much just made pie crust here, and pie crust needs to be cold to be flaky. It also needs to be flaky to be fabulous.

At least, I think it does.

Preheat the oven to 375°F.

Lightly flour the counter and roll out one of the dough halves. Cut into ten rectangles. Place on cookie sheets, with space to grow, and use parchment paper.

'Cause it rocks.

Do the same thing with the other dough half, except not the thing where you put it on the cookie sheets. Just leave it on the counter for now.

Spoon 2 TBSP of your favorite jam down the center of the dough on the cookie sheets. Then top with the dough that is not on the cookie sheets and crimp the edges together with a fork so they stay closed.

When you've formed all 10 of your deliciously delectable breakfast tarts, whisk an egg white and brush it over each one. This will make them brown up all beautiful and you can sprinkle big sugar granules on top and they will stay put.

Yay for more sugar!

Bake for 15-20 minutes, always check it at the lower time, and cool completely before eating. It's worth it, even with the browned butter smell making your mouth water. That hot jam will really burn the taste buds off.

14

Lemon Cookies

I hate it when myself wakes me up at three in the morning for no apparent reason.

I don't have to use the bathroom; I didn't have a weird dream; and I for suresies didn't eat any weird combinations, like pickles and peanut butter.

There's nothing keeping me from falling back asleep. Except for maybe my super overactive brain. Yep, there it goes, thinking thoughts I can't even identify because they fly out my ears so quickly.

I stare at the dark ceiling and wonder what to do with myself for the next hour. Maybe I should just get up; GG is probably already in the bakery. Yesterday she told me she goes to work as soon as she wakes up.

Anything sounds better than laying here trying not to think my thoughts.

I move slow-mo to make as little noise as possible. Robyn is a bear when she wakes up too early and since she's already mad at me, I don't even want to see what that looks like. I slip on my shoes, because the old floor has splinters, and start to stand up.

"Where are you going?"

I shriek, covering my mouth to keep from waking the whole dang town.

"What the heck?" I squint towards Robyn's bed. "Are you awake?"

She's all snuggled to one side, hugging a blanket. It's too dark to see if her eyes are open or closed. This better be Robyn talking to me and not the creepy old stuffed animals lounging on the bookshelf cause if it's them, I'm going to freak out.

"Duh," she says. "Where are you going?"

I puff up like popcorn in the microwave. "What do you mean *duh*? I have lots of reasons why it might not be you talking to me. Uh, one, because you haven't talked to me since we saw that dumb Jake." I hold up my fingers even though there's no way she can see them. "Two, because you never wake up this early, and three..."

My mind goes blank.

Whatever, two is good enough for now.

Robyn props up on an elbow. Now that her eyes are open, the whites' kind of glow in the dark. Not gonna lie, she's giving me the willies.

"So, where are you going?"

I fold my arms. "Why do you care?"

"Don't be like that." She sits up all the way, pulling a pillow in her lap.

"Like what?"

"Cat!"

"What?" I fling my hands in the air. "Seriously, Robyn? You ignore me half the day yesterday and want things to be hunky dory in the morning. What's that about? You never get mad at me, *never*. Not the time I traded bikes with you without asking first. Not the time I took your new box of crayons and broke them all. Not the time I borrowed your rhinestone jean jacket and forgot to give it back!"

"I didn't actually know about the jacket. Do you still have it?"

"I think, under my bed. Do you want it back?"

"No. You can keep it."

I purse my lips. "I'll give it back. As soon as we get home."

"That would be nice. Thank you."

We sit in awkward silence for a very long time. Finally, Robyn sighs. "Listen, I'm sorry. I don't know why I got so mad, it just bubbled and exploded before I had time to think about it."

"Yeah." I can relate to that, actually.

She reaches out for my hand, misjudges because of the dark, and her arms flop back down to the pillow. "I'm really, really sorry, Cat. I hate fighting with you. And I know I was being a—"

"Yes." I nod, because I totally agree she was.

"*But*," she says in a loud whisper, "I had a good reason."

"Listening."

She shifts, pulling the pillow closer. "I'm super worried about Jojo. She's having a hard time and there's nothing we can do to help. You know how bad I hate that! But then, *then*, I realized there is something we can do. I played it all out in my mind, everything like, fell into place and I was so excited. I guess I got mad cause I was disappointed you didn't agree right away."

"At all."

"What?"

"I don't agree at all. Robyn! After all that junk with Conner and Tobey, I can't believe you would even think about baking emotions like that again! I mean, do you remember what happened?"

I have my doubts, because, if she did remember, there is no way she would want to do it either. Robyn makes a grunting noise, a shrugging noise, an 'it doesn't matter' noise.

"Robyn! You know what happens when I bake emotion like that. Chaos! Anarchy! Indigestion!" I pause to breathe. "Baking Jake is the worst idea I have ever heard, and you know I've had some pretty rocking awful ideas. I can't. You have to get that; I can't do it again."

My heart beats all over the place. Three times in the last month alone I woke up from a dream, no, a nightmare, totally drenched. I was running down the hall at Tobey's house with Conner chasing me like a maniac.

Yeah, still not funny.

"I remember what happened, Cat, and I do get it. But, I mean, what if we were intentional this time; like, extra careful? What if we planned it out? You have to admit, last time we were kind of random."

Whatever! I spent a boatload of time thinking through that scenario with Tobey, so, I don't want to disagree, but I totally disagree.

Though...

I guess Robyn couldn't know all the planning that was going on inside my head. I guess I can see how it might have seemed random. And yeah, the making sour bread thing was completely sporadic.

I was provoked.

The point is, there is no amount of planning that can guarantee baking emotions is going to work out the way we want.

I try to tell Robyn all these things, except that my tongue is suddenly too big. I don't know why it's being so uncooperative. I'm sure I could make Robyn understand where I'm coming from if this dang thing would get out of my way.

"Cat." Robyn stands up, her shadowy form and glowing eyes stop right in front of me. "I know I was a brat yesterday. I'm sorry. Let's start over, okay?

"Okay?"

Robyn pulls me to the bed, so we sit side by side. "Hey Cat, how are you?"

"Fine." I wonder if I should start checking under the sheets for her marbles.

"Good." She nudges my arm. "Now you."

I clasp my hands in my lap. "And how are you this fine morning?"

"Great! Thanks for asking. Hey, I was thinking, you know how Jojo is super upset about Jake? You know how she said she wishes he would just go away? Well, I'm worried about her, and I want to help her. Can you think of anything we can do?"

Wait a second.

I know this trick.

She's trying to get me to say what she knows I know she wants me to say so it looks like it's my idea.

Sneaky Pete! She's good.

I open my mouth and then close it again. This needs some serious thinking, not casual responding.

What are my options here?

The obvious, and most easy, is to agree with Robyn and then plan to bake Jake some emotion that will make him go away. I mean, I want him to go away as much as the next girl, but the thought of sneaking into the kitchen and lighting candles to cover the scent of baking, and lies, makes my belly seize up like I ate a whole batch of cookies all by myself.

What if it doesn't work?

And what if it does?

This is such a bad idea, on so many levels.

On the other hand, if I disagree with Robyn again, will the rest of my life be like last night?

Because that was miserable.

I don't know what I would do if Robyn really never talked to me again. I know I drive her nuts, and it goes both ways sometimes, but we are a team.

Catman and Robyn.

Speaking of selfishness, even though we weren't just now, is it selfish to do this when my motivation is to keep Robyn from hating my guts forever and ever until the end of time?

My guess, just a hunch here, is yes. Yes, that would be selfish.

I know what the right thing to do is. I know it. The right thing to do is look at Robyn in the gray light of dawn peeking through the windows and tell her no way, José.

I open my mouth, then forget what I was about to say when I see her big, pleading blue eyes.

She just wants to help. This could help. I mean, we did help Penny, so there's a good chance we could help Jojo, too.

Right?

Oh, cream puffs, what's the point? We all know I'm going to do it. All this thinking is giving me a headache.

"Fine." I snatch a pillow to smack Robyn in the face. "I'll do it, but if we get caught, I am totally blaming the whole thing on you.

Robyn's face erupts in a grin. "Deal."

This is the fastest day of my life.

No really, it's ridiculous. Everything from my morning bake with GG, to walking to the florist with Jojo for fresh flowers, to talking about menu ideas for the bake-off, all of it goes by in such a blur I don't even have a chance to look for GG's next clue. Penny picked this one, she's had it all day, pondering over it so we know where to go next.

If we ever get a free second, that is.

The sun is already going down.

Any minute now Robyn's going to deploy her distraction technique—unnumbered because it's too epic—to keep everyone out of the bakery for the next hour and a half so we can bake something to change Jake.

I'm so nervous I can't sit still. Every movement out of the corner of my eye makes me jump like a startled cat. I keep imagining everyone is looking at me suspiciously, and if they happen to say my name, I'm sure the words to follow are 'I know what you're planning'.

When Robyn takes the grown-ups away from the kitchen with some random excuse I don't listen to, I turn the framed picture of Evie face down because she keeps staring at me with those eyes.

"Hey, Cat?"

I screech and whirl around so fast I almost fall on my bum.

"Whoa!" Penny holds out her hands. "Are you alright?"

"Fabulous." I rub my knee where I banged it on the cupboard. "What's up?"

Penny smooths a piece of paper, "Do you have a sec? I was looking over this clue and-" She leans closer. "Are you sure you're okay?"

I laugh, a little maniacally, and wipe the counter with my sleeve. "Fine, fine, fine. What did you want to know about the clue?"

"Have you read it yet?"

I shake my head. That might not be true; I may have read it, but if I did, I totally can't remember. I barely know my own name right now.

"No worries. I'll read it to you, because I really need another perspective." She clears her throat and reads a cute rhymey clue about stars or something. I totally don't know because my hands are shaking so bad I have to confine them to my armpits.

Penny finishes reading and scratches her chin with the pen lid. "I thought it might be on the telescope, there's one in the attic, but I don't know... It doesn't feel right. I also looked all through the house for star and moon shaped stuff. This clue is tricky. I don't know if it means actual moon and stars. It could be, like, a metaphor or something. What do you think?"

I honestly can't remember what we are talking about. I blankly stare at Penny until she realizes I got nothing.

"Okay, well, I think I'll go ask GG if I'm on the right track with the telescope."

"Sounds great." I say, too quickly.

"Yeah," Penny gives me a strange look. "So, if you think of anything, I'll be in the attic."

Hold on.

I open my mouth to stop her, because I think the attic is the scene of Robyn's nefarious plot. Then, I realize this might be perfect. Penny can keep them all up there longer, helping her find the clue.

"Okay." I wave my hands to shoo her on her way. "Good luck."

"Do you want to come with me?"

I shake my head so fast I get dizzy. "I'm super busy."

"Doing what?" Penny looks around the empty kitchen.

"Um, waiting for Robyn."

"Well, she can come, too."

"No!" I take a deep breath; I am too young for this kind of stress. "I mean, Robyn and I have stuff to do, you know, girl talk and stuff."

Penny's face drops. "I'm a girl."

Butter buns!

I'm not trying to be a jerky lerky; I'm trying to keep Penny out of the trouble that is for sure coming our way. As I try to think of a way to explain myself, I realize I can't keep this up. It's time to come clean.

I shake out my shoulders and hold a hand toward Penny. "Okay, here's the thing. Robyn and I are going to bake."

Penny brightens.

"I mean, bake-bake. Like, *emotion* bake."

"You caved?" Penny says, in an excited whisper.

I put my hands on my hips. "I like to think of it as weighed my options and made an informed decision that baking Jake is the right way to help Jojo."

Penny coughs into her hand. "Caved."

"Whatever." I roll my eyes. "The point is we didn't tell you because the less of us involved, the better. We're talking Azkaban levels of busted if this doesn't work out. But maybe you can keep the adults distracted in the attic for like an hour while we do this thing? Whatcha-think?"

Penny nods, slow at first until it gains good momentum. "You got it! I'm on it."

I watch her skip through the kitchen doors and collapse on a barstool with my head in my hands.

This is how Robyn finds me.

"All set. The adults are occupied sorting all those tons of boxes in the attic to find stuff to help us learn more about the bakery, and then Penny came up and begged them to have mercy on her and help with the clue so we... Are you okay?"

Why does everyone keep asking me that?

I'm super.

"Let's just do this." I hop off the stool. "How are we going to cover up the baking smell this time?"

"We're not." Robyn claps her hands. "Get this, I asked permission to bake! I said we want to bake a treat for everyone. A surprise."

It will be a surprise all right.

"And before you ask, we'll both bake. I'll make one batch for everyone else, and you make the one for Jake."

"The one with emotions?" I grip the sides of my head like doing so will make this all go away. "Ugh!"

Robyn pauses to smile at me. "It's going to be fine, Cat."

So she says, but my belly is still not on board for this thing. I try to concentrate on happy thoughts, but all I can see is images of large craters where small Arizona mountain towns used to be. I'm not sure if that's because of what happens when I bake emotions or if that's predicting what will happen when the parental units find out that we did this again.

I'm going to combust into a million pieces! I have to think about something else. And just like that, my brain turns into my friend instead of my enemy.

"Wait a second, remember when you told Jojo you're a terrible baker? Why did you do that? You're really good at baking."

Robyn looks uncomfortable for a minute, then pushes it away with a shrug of determination. "I don't want her or GG to ask me to bake. I mean, I can't do the emotion thing."

"Neither can Jojo."

"Well, not right now, usually she's really good at it."

I place a hand on Robyn's arm. "Does it bother you that you can't bake emotions?"

"Maybe." She doesn't look at me. "But, whatever, let's do this before anyone comes in. I'll use the old mixer, you use Mr. Bojangles. Then we can bake at the same time."

I get that swirly feeling in my midsection again and wish we could keep talking about Robyn's issues instead of doing this. I guess she's right, though we don't have a lot of time. Plus, she and I are so close to normal again, I don't want to risk getting her super ticked at me. It stinks when your best friend hates your guts.

"So, uh..." I fiddle with the speed lever on Mr. Bojangles' side. "Did you figure out what emotion you want Jake to feel so he will go away?"

"Yes!" Robyn's eyes light up.

"Yeah?"

"Apathy."

I blink. "And that is what again?"

"Seriously, Cat, don't you pay attention at all?"

"No."

She swats my arm. "Apathy is when you don't care, and since the emotions you bake are so strong, maybe we can get him to stop caring so much he leaves town."

Yeah, that, or we might get him to stop caring so much he stops eating or using deodorant or binge-watching Netflix...

Have I mentioned this is a really bad idea?

I used to think Robyn knows me so well she has half of my brain; now I'm starting to think she's lost her mind completely. It's just really stinking bad that I'm already in this too far to back out now.

Farewell, cruel world.

"Are you even listening?" Robyn snaps her fingers in front of my face.

"No," I say, again.

This time Robyn ignores my attitude and repeats, very patiently, like I'm two years old, everything she said when I wasn't listening.

"You need to feel like you don't care about anything. So, I got to thinking, what does Cat care nothing about? Nothing-nothing, things so boring, they turn your brain to mush so you lose all desire to do anything. It was actually harder than I thought, but I came up with politics and school, volunteering and charities—"

"Hey!" I sit up straight. "I care about charities and volunteering and school." I'm not even going to try and argue the politics thing, it's too much of a stretch.

Robyn gives me a shrewd look. "Do you?"

"Yes?"

"Is that a question or are you telling me?"

I let out a huff. "I care about those things, okay? Just because I don't do them without you making me, and just because I sometimes throw baby fits until you have to bribe me to go with you doesn't mean I don't want to do it."

"Okay." Robyn nods, but not in the agreeing kind of way. It's totally the don't-believe-you-and-think-you-are-full-of-it way.

"Fine, what's the plan?" I ask in a dull voice.

Robyn brightens and lifts her bulging backpack onto the table. "I brought my textbooks; math is a good place to begin. You read, and I'll start gathering supplies."

"You brought textbooks on vacation?" I pull out the math book and blink at the glistening cover. I'm bored already. "What are we baking?"

"Lemon cookies," she says over her shoulder. "Remember? Jake said he loves our lemon cookies."

Lemon Cookies

Cookies:
1 C. Butter
1 C. Sugar
1 Egg
1 tsp Lemon Juice
1 tsp Vanilla extract
1/2 tsp Salt
1/2 tsp Baking Powder
2 & 1/2 C. Flour

Glaze:
1 C. Powdered Sugar
1-2 TBSP Milk
1 tsp Vanilla extract

Preheat the oven to 350°F.

In a stand mixer, cream together the butter and sugar—yay! Until light and fluffy—yay again!

Add the egg and mix well; scrape the sides if you need to. Stir in lemon juice and vanilla.

Turn the mixer off. This is important because we're about to add the flour and we don't want gluten to form. Gluten is great for keeping bread together, but not so good for cookies. And the gluten won't form until flour mixes with wet stuff.

Add the flour, salt, and baking powder to the bowl, then turn on the mixer and just mix until there aren't any more dry spots. A couple turns of the paddle will do.

Scoop medium-sized cookie balls and roll them in powdered sugar—'cause why wouldn't you do that?—then place on a cookie sheet. Don't overload, like 15 per sheet so there is room to grow.

Bake for 10-14 minutes. The edges should look dry and the middle puffy, but not wet.

After they cool for 10 minutes or so, mix the glaze ingredients with a fork and drizzle over the cookies. The glaze will dry into them and become one with the cookie. In the yummiest way imaginable.

Now you know everything there is to know about lemon cookies! Go share them with your friends. It's hard to feel gloomy when you eat a lemon cookie!

15

Madeleines

I follow Robyn through the front door of Diet Starts Monday, just minutes before the time the little sign on the door says they are supposed to close. Jake keeps his place open way later than we do, all the way until seven. That's like, twelve hours he's open.

Overachiever.

A sense of satisfaction rolls over me as I survey the empty bakery. Maybe staying open isn't helping him after all.

Hold on.

The display is empty of all goodies. So, he sold out. Dang it!

But wait, there's a bunch of brown paper bags on the counter. Those have got to be full of all the leftovers. That means he didn't sell out. Phew!

I am riding an emotional roller coaster here.

My hands shake under the wrapped plate of lemon cookies. They look beautiful and delicious, with yellow cracks around the powdered sugar. I push the plate into Robyn's hand, so I don't drop the whole thing on the floor.

Cause I'm totally going to.

A woman comes through the kitchen to the main bakery and stops when she sees us. "Oh!" She grasps her heart. "You startled me. We hardly ever have people come in this late, even with our five-dollar mystery bags." She laughs, gesturing to the paper bag soldiers. "Do you want to buy one?

"What's in it?" Robyn's voice wavers, she clears her throat and tries to look confident.

"Well now, it's a mystery!" She laughs again. "We just fill them with whatever is leftover and try to sell it. You look like a couple of risk takers; how about a couple bags to go?"

Her smile is friendly, but I can't smile back. All I can think is Jake is nowhere to be seen.

Our big idea will fizzle like a birthday candle that's too close to the icing if Jake isn't around. Why didn't Robyn, with all her planning and scheming, think of that? Why didn't I? What are we supposed to do if Jake isn't here?

Robyn gives me a frantic look.

No way *Jos*. I can't save the day now, I'm way too frazzled. My hands won't stop shaking and I think I have heartburn. I don't actually know, because I never have before, but there's this weird fire when I swallow and I have an unexpected urge to burp.

I wonder if people can spontaneously combust?

"Girls?" The woman's face drops to a look of concern. "Is there something I can help you with?"

"Uh..." Robyn drags the word out for a very long time.

In the wake of her monotone, I blurt, "Is Jake here? We have something for him."

The woman laughs so loud it bounces off the walls. Now it sounds like a bunch of her clones are mocking us too.

"You and half the town, sweets!" She now gestures to a table full of wrapped treats. "If there is one thing this town agrees on, it's that Jake shouldn't stay single much longer!"

Is she...

Does she think...

We *like* him?

Oh, gross!

I think I just threw up a little in my mouth.

"Is he here though?" Robyn asks, her face light green.

The woman puts her hand on her hips, about to give us the old heave-ho, I imagine, when Jake strolls in from the back.

"Hey, Shannon, do you know where... Well, lookie here."

Oh please, did he really just say lookie? He sounds like a grandpa.

"These girls brought you something, Jake, wanted to give it to you themselves." She gives him a knowing look and then leaves the room, shaking her head and muttering under her breath. I really don't want to know what she is saying to herself.

Robyn steps forward, holding the plate of cookies out like an offering. I'm a little satisfied to see her arms shake, too. Good to know it's not just me wigging out around here.

"What's this? A peace offering from the great Jojo?"

"No!" Robyn snaps, then takes a deep breath and replaces her glower with a smile. "Cat and I made them for you. To apologize for spying on your bakery yesterday."

"Really?"

I nod, because I can't do anything else at the moment. It would be a super bad idea to open my mouth even a tiny bit.

Jake unwraps the plate and brings it to his nose, inhaling deeply. "Lemon cookies. These are my very favorite."

"Are they?" Robyn says, shooting me a look to speak up. She's just going to have to be content with my presence at the moment.

Jake doesn't answer; he's too busy scarfing. I reach out my hand to stop him, one cookie is probably enough to get him apathetic. With how powerful my baking is, the whole plate might sink him to the floor right now. But Robyn pushes my arm down and holds it there, so all I can do is watch. It's kind of beautiful and disgusting at the same time. In about three minutes, he inhales everything on the plate.

I bet he would have licked it if we weren't staring at him.

"Wow." He sighs, pulling the plastic wrap back over the plate, his eyes longing. "Those were really good. Tell Jojo she outdid herself."

"I told you, she didn't—"

"Yeah, right, she didn't make them." Jake winks as he tosses the plate in a huge trash can behind the counter. When he turns back around, he presses his lips together. "Well, thank you..."

His words trail off with obvious meaning. Like, it's time for you to go already. But the thing is, we can't. I mean, I want to see what he's going to do next. It only took Conner a couple seconds after he swallowed to turn into a raging love maniac. But minutes keep ticking and Jake has a very confused look on his face.

"That was real nice of you ladies..." he tries again.

Robyn grips my hand, digging her fingernails in.

"It's closing time, you see..." He points to a spot next to my head. I turn automatically and stare at the big clock near the door.

A clock that looks like a moon.

I squeeze Robyn's hand, but she doesn't look, she's still watching Jake. I bet my unicorn slippers that the clock is the clue for GG! I don't know how I know. This has to be it though, I'm all hot and tingly and there's this weird buzzing in my brain. Plus, it's sort of old timey and rustic like the thermometer at the bakery.

What I don't know is why GG would choose a clue for our scavenger hunt in Jake's bakery. That seems a little weird.

Doesn't it?

"How do you feel?" Robyn blurts, like she's been holding the words in for a while. They come out with a whoosh of air.

Jake looks at her strangely. "I feel great, thank you. It's been fun and all, but I think it's time we say goodnight." Completely ignoring our protests, Jake ushers us out the door and locks it behind us. With a cheeky wave, he turns off the sign light, plunging us into semi-darkness.

"I don't get it." Robyn chews her bottom lip. "What happened? Why didn't it work? Why didn't he slump? He's, like, *more* energetic now then he was before he ate a cookie. He's cleaning the baseboards!" She flings her arm back towards the bakery. "Did we do something wrong?"

"I don't know." I stop talking and pull out my vibrating phone. There are, like, five messages from my mom, wondering where we are. I text that we're coming and pull Robyn away from the bakery. "We'll figure it out later. Right now, you need to use your big brain to come up with a good reason why it took us twenty minutes to take out the trash."

The smell of vanilla whacks me in the face as I step through the back door of the kitchen. GG has on oven mitts and pulls two trays of golden-brown goodness out of the oven. They look like seashell shaped cookies, but they are puffy like cake.

Jojo leans so close to whatever it is that her nose almost touches. If she had a magnifying glass, she could be a baking inspector.

If that was a thing.

My mom paces the length of the kitchen. When she sees us, she stops. "Where have you two been?"

I look at Robyn; this is the big moment, her time to shine. Her eyes fly around the room, looking for something brilliant to say, which is just...brilliant.

I sigh. "Did you find anything interesting in the attic?"

"Nuh-uh!" Mom puts one hand on her hip. "That's not going to work today, missy. I know all about those distraction techniques of yours. You answer my question first."

What?

How in the world did my mom figure out my system? I purse my lips, considering her. She might be a mind reader after all. This is not good.

I push my hands into my pockets, trying to disappear into a super amazing slouch, when my eyes land on Penny. I stand straight again, 'cause this distraction technique is totally going to work!

"Hey, I think we figured out the next clue!"

It is the perfect thing to say. Mom gets all emotional again about GG doing this for us. She gushes so much she completely forgets about what Robyn and I were or were not doing.

"What's the clue?" Penny leans her cheek into her fist. "GG wouldn't give me any hints."

"I think it's a clock." I look at GG. "Is that right?"

GG lifts her chin. "I will not say yes or no." Then she winks.

I take that as a yes. Robyn does too since she pulls out her notebook and writes the word clock under Evie's gravestone.

"What are those things?" I walk over to Jojo, who stares at the pans of cookies with a disgruntled look.

"GG, I don't know." Jojo taps her chin. "I don't think this is…enough… What do you guys think?"

"There are a lot of them, whatever they are. What are they?" I ask again.

Jojo presses her finger into her top lip, her face totally troubled. "Madeleines."

Okay, that did not answer my question.

"I *love* Madeleines!" Robyn jostles my elbow trying to get a closer look. "They look like cookies but are totally like fluffy cake. Best. Combination. Ever."

I knew it! Cookie cakes.

"I love them too." Jojo runs her fingers through Robyn's hair. "But, there's going to be stiff competition at this bake-off. You know, you ate Blaze's pies. I think we need pizazz, something spectacular, that makes us stand out."

"How do they taste?" Mom asks, "That's what matters, right? That the food is good?"

"Maybe." Jojo shrugs one shoulder.

GG takes off the oven mitts and layers them on the counter. "We do whatever you want."

"I love your Madeleines, GG," Jojo struggles for words. "I just don't think they are exciting enough. Does that make sense?"

GG squeezes Jojo's elbow. She begins flicking cookies out of the pans onto cooling racks. Robyn snatches one and breaks it in half for me.

It's pretty delectable, no question, but I agree with Jojo. The madeleines look totally plain. If we eat with our eyes before our mouths, then these cookies wouldn't even make it to the lips. Maybe we could jazz them up with icing and sprinkles.

I open my mouth to suggest this, when Penny clears her throat, drawing my attention to her. With wide eyes, she jerks her head to the door.

Yeah, we have bigger things to deal with right now.

"Thanks for the yummy treats." I grab Robyn's wrist and tug. "We gotta go."

"Where are you going?" Mom asks.

"Just upstairs."

"Really?."

"For reals. We're going to our room to chillax. It's been a busy day. Wanna come, Pen?"

Mom's lips turn into a smile. It wasn't my plan to smooth Mom over by inviting Penny to go with us, but, well, that worked out nicely now, didn't it?

The three of us hurry up the stairs without talking. It isn't until we close the door of mine and Robyn's room, that we all start jabbering at once. I raise my hands in the air to get the other two to simmer down, because I'm pretty sure that the thing I have to say is the most important thing.

"I'm ninety-nine percent sure the moon clock is the clue. If it isn't, I don't think it matters cause GG's going to tell us what she tells us no matter what, right? So, let's pick the next clue!"

"My turn, my turn." Robyn hops off the end of her bed.

I open the nightstand drawer where I keep the clues. Wait, what? There is only one left now! I hand it to Robyn. "Decisions, decisions."

She closes her eyes and makes a big deal about choosing the card. She's so weird.

Robyn reads aloud, *"Well done you, for getting this far! Now, do you want to wish on a star? Or find a clover, or catch a dream, or kiss a horseshoe, strange though it may seem? Will luck be with you? Time will tell. I want you to know that we wish you well."*

In the pause that follows, I wrinkle my nose. "That makes absolutely no sense."

"We'll figure it out." Robyn taps the card against her leg. "What I want to know right now is why didn't our baking work on Jake?"

"You gave him the cookies?" Penny's eyes light up. "What happened?"

Robyn tosses the clue on her bed and starts pacing the floor in front of the vanity table. By the looks of that rug, this is not the first time someone has done this. "It didn't work." She turns on her heel and stomps the next round. "Nothing happened. Nothing at all."

"What did you bake for him?"

"Lemon cookies," I say.

Penny shakes her head.

"Oh, you mean what emotion?" I pull at a thread on my bedspread. "Apathetic. Robyn made me read her math textbook and I pretty much lost the will to live."

Penny makes a very impressive gremlin face.

"Yeah, nothing sucks the fun out of life like that does. Trust me. While we were making the cookies, I could barely muster the give-a-darn to crack eggs."

"And nothing happened when Jake ate the cookies?"

Robyn grips the top rung of the rocking chair in the corner so hard her knuckles turn white. "Nope, *nada* darn thing."

"That's weird." Penny picks up the clue and smooths it over her knee. "When I ate the cookies you made for me, I felt calm and peaceful almost as soon as I swallowed. Maybe he didn't eat enough?"

"He destroyed the whole plate!" Robyn shakes the chair, making it rock on its own after she lets go in a very horror movie kind of way. "Like a whole dozen cookies. They were smallish, but still. All gone, and...nothing!" She plops down onto the edge of the bed.

Total dejection.

I leap to my feet. "Hold on!" And then I run out of the room, down the stairs, through the silent bakery to the kitchen.

"Don't mind me, I'm not here." I run to the second fridge and root through the vegetable container until I find a bag of cookies buried underneath. I shove them up my shirt, which is the worst idea ever because the bag is freezing, but very necessary, and grab some string cheeses. "Just need a little snack, going now!" I clutch my belly with one hand to keep the cookies in place and wave a handful of sting cheese in the air to prove my words.

I am out of there before anyone has a chance to say anything. Once clear of adults, I sprint the rest of the way to our room.

"Ta-da!"

"Why did you go get string cheese?" Robyn looks up from picking at her nails. "You can't seriously be hungry right now."

"What are those?" Penny points to the bag of cookies.

I give Robyn a look and toss the cheese stick to Penny, who opens it right up and starts pulling off strings of cheese.

Robyn just shakes her head and starts picking at her nails again.

"Listen!" I make her jump before she looks at me with big eyes. "I didn't give Jake all of the cookies, just in case something went wrong, like remember how Conner made me dump all those cupcakes on the front porch? I stashed the other dozen I made under the vegetables where no one would ever find them."

"Good thinking!" Penny says with her mouth full.

Robyn rises, stepping slowly toward me. "Those are apathetic lemon cookies?"

I swallow hard. "So now, all we have to do is eat them and see if they work."

"Oh!" Robyn brightens. "I totally get it, if the cookies make us apathetic, then we didn't do something wrong when we baked! Let's try them!"

Now, this is the part I didn't think through very well. The eating them ourselves part.

"Only one of us should eat them." I open the plastic bag, then push the top back together to seal it. I have the strangest urge to toss them in the trash can.

"It shouldn't be you, Cat, because you've never actually tried your own baking before, so we don't know how it will affect you the same way it affects other people. You might be immune or something."

"Maybe..." I drag the word out for a long time. "I'm not immune to your mom's baking, though."

"That's true, but she is immune to her own baking."

"I didn't know that!" I feel like someone withheld the secret formula for hair lightener. "Why didn't you tell me that before?"

After all these years, after all we've been through.

"Well, I don't know for sure." Robyn takes the bag from me. She opens it and picks a cookie, holding it up to the light. "But she eats her own stuff all the time and nothing changes."

"Maybe she's just always happy?"

"I don't know, it doesn't matter." Robyn now moves the cookie next to her eye like a monocle. "I'll do it. I think it has to be me, unless you really want to, Penny?" She extends the cookie toward my sister.

Penny swallows hard and clears her throat of all cheese strings. "I guess I can, but, what if it works? How will you help me feel better again? I mean, when I ate Cat's calm cookie, I felt super chill for almost a week. I don't want to be all slump-a-lumpus for the entire vacation."

"What?" I stare at my sister like I've never seen her before. All this withheld information, don't people know some of this might come in handy while we're trying to figure things out? "Why didn't you tell me it lasted that long?"

Penny shrugs.

"Guys, you're forgetting something super important," Robyn says, setting her mouth in a firm line. "This cookie isn't going to do anything. It didn't work for Jake. We're just testing it to be sure."

Penny does not look convinced.

"I'll just do it." Robyn puts the cookie to her lips and takes a deep breath. "Okay, here I go." After another pause, she closes her eyes and shoves the entire cookie in her mouth. I want to look away, but I can't. I watch every chew of her jaw until the cookie disappears with a swallow.

Robyn doesn't open her eyes.

"Robyn?" I reach out a hand, but don't touch her. "Robby, are you okay? How do you feel?"

"Tired, I can't open my eyelids, too hard." Her words come out heavy and slow. "Carry me."

And then she drops to the floor.

Madeleines

1/2 C. unsalted Butter, melted
2 Eggs - room temperature
1/2 C. Sugar
1 tsp Vanilla extract
1 C. Flour
1/2 tsp Baking Powder
1/4 tsp Salt

Preheat the oven to 350°F.

In a stand mixer, beat the eggs and sugar until thick, high speed for about 7 minutes. Stir in butter and vanilla.

Whisk the flour, baking powder, and salt in a bowl and then fold into the egg mixture. Just barely mix it.

The batter should be thick and shiny.

Like Rapunzel's hair, except, not really like that.

Cover the batter and chill for 30 minutes.

It's always good to chill.

Now, there are such things as Madeleines Pans. While they are super cool, if you don't have one, no worries. You can totally use a mini muffin pan. If you don't have one of those, you can scoop dollops onto a cookie sheet and if you don't have one of those, well, may Mr. Bojangles have mercy on your soul.

Bake for 10-15 minutes until golden brown. Dust with powdered sugar before serving.

16

Chocolate Muffins

"Is she dead?" Penny covers her mouth, dancing around Robyn's still body. "Is she dead? Did she die? Did we totally kill her?"

My heart leaps into my throat.

She isn't dead, is she?

I kneel next to Robyn's side and roll her over so I can lean my ear on her chest. A strong movement pounds against my cheek. I let out a thousand breaths' worth of air.

"She's not dead. She's breathing."

"What do we do? Should we get Mom and Dad?"

"No." I bite my lip, trying to think through the chatter in my brain and Penny's hysteria. This isn't really a problem. Robyn is fine. She's reacting to the apathy. No big deal. She just needs to sleep this off and she'll be good as always.

Probably.

"Help me, Penny, let's get her into her bed."

Penny stops dancing and starts wringing her hands. "You don't think we should tell someone?"

I shake my head. Since we aren't technically supposed to bake with emotions on our own... No, I think that is a terrible idea. "Let's get her into bed. We can say she went to sleep early. I'm sure she will be all better in the morning."

"Really? You think so?"

I swallow the icky feelings rising in my throat. I can't stop re-membering Tobey's angry eyebrows after he ate the bread I made for Conner. His feelings most definitely didn't wear off. In fact, I had to make cinnamon rolls to fix everything.

But maybe I don't need to worry about that. The cookies didn't work for Jake; maybe this is like that.

Only different.

I look at Penny. "I think our best bet is to let her sleep this off, and then we'll figure it out in the morning. Help me carry her."

"Okay." Penny lifts one of Robyn's legs, loses her grip and it drops to the floor.

Robyn groans and mumbles, "Too hard."

"Careful," I whisper.

Penny nods; both of her lips disappear because she's pressing them together so tight. We do an awkward shuffle to lift Robyn, then slowly shimmy our way to the side of her bed.

"Cat!"

My mom's yell startles me so bad I almost drop Robyn. I stop moving, using a knee to prop up Robyn's back and take a deep breath.

"Yeah?"

"What's all that noise? What are you girls doing up there?"

"Um..." I look at Robyn, and then at Penny. "Getting ready for bed?" I want to kick myself for that question mark at the end; I wanted it to come out super assured and totally the opposite of suspicious.

"Already?"

Footsteps start up the stairs and my heart tries to leap out of my throat. Using my head to gesture to the bed, I also widen my eyes, so Penny knows this is serious business. We have to get Robyn settled before my mom gets in here.

Penny and I heave Robyn onto her bed with strength that comes from nowhere. I read once about a lady who lifted an entire car because her baby got stuck under it or something. Same thing happens now; it's like a miracle.

Penny dives under the bed just as I pull the covers up to Robyn's shoulders and Mom appears in the doorway.

"Oh no! Is Robyn asleep already?"

I smooth out the blanket, so I don't have to look at my mom or answer her questions.

"Rats Marissa, I'm sorry, she's asleep."

I peek over my shoulder and see my mom talking on her cell phone, not even looking at me. I finally feel like I'm getting enough oxygen to my brain so it can think rational thoughts instead of frantic ones. Like, I should have taken off Robyn's shoes.

And why in the donut holes did Penny dive under the bed?

"I will, yep, uh-huh, you too. Love you, bye." Mom pushes a button on her phone and tucks it into her back pocket. She walks over to me and brushes my hair out of my eyes. "Big day, huh?"

I let out a long breath. Yeah, this morning feels like a thousand years ago. I get hit with a wave of exhaustion and wish everyone would go away so I can follow Robyn's example and crash.

"You look so tired. Maybe I should tell Grammy you're sleeping in tomorrow?"

"No!" Shaking my head makes my hair go right back in my eyes. "No, that's okay. I want to help bake. I'll be fine. I'll just...go to bed...now?"

Mom kisses my head, her eyes as far away as her thoughts. "If you're sure. Sleep well Kitty Cat." She walks to the light switch and pauses there while I collapse in the empty bed. I don't bother putting on my pajamas, but Mom doesn't seem to notice. She blows me a kiss and turns off the light.

"Oh! Have you seen Penny?"

I fake a snore, so I don't have to answer.

That isn't lying, is it?

After a minute, Mom's footsteps take her down the stairs where I can't hear her anymore. I'm so tired I barely find the energy to roll over. "Pen? You still there?"

"Yeah." She peeks her head from the dust ruffle.

"I'm going to sleep now, you good?"

"Can I just stay here forever?"

I yawn, "Mom will notice."

Penny sighs and drags herself out from under the bed. "Good night, Cat."

"Night, Pen."

On her way out I hear her mumble, "This is just a bad dream, everything will be normal in the morning."

What in the world is normal?

Ever heard of autopilot?

I think that's what got me out of bed at four, and into the kitchen to bake with GG. For sure, it wasn't my brain who did it, with all the muck and worry going on in there. We make a boatload of chocolate muffins for breakfast. The bakery doesn't sell them, but GG tells me she craves them a couple times a week. Since I'm still sleepy, and – oh yeah– it's chocolate, I go along with whatever she says. I don't feel like I wake up all the way until my mom and Jojo walk into the kitchen around seven.

Jojo wears her running shoes and looks perplexed. "Yeah, I shook her and everything, she's out."

"That doesn't sound like Robyn." Mom slides onto a bar stool. "She likes her rest and all, but she isn't a heavy sleeper. I wonder if she's coming down with something?"

I drop a muffin pan that clatters to the floor. Of course, everyone looks at me. I bend low to pick it up, just glad it was empty, and I was washing it, so I didn't have to be all guilty about ruining perfectly good muffins on top of everything else. My cheeks feel sunburned as I straighten and put the pan back in the soapy water.

"Hey, Cat?" Mom's voice sounds worried.

I wonder if I can get away with pretending like I don't hear anything.

Yeah, this kitchen isn't that big, and Mom is like two feet away from me. I don't think that's going to work.

"Mmmm hmmm?"

"Robyn went to bed early last night; do you think she's feeling all right?"

I consider my options. If I say yes, when there's obvious evidence that she's not okay, then I'll look suspicious. But if I say no, then that's going to make them ask me a lot more questions. I'm saved by the ringing of a phone. I look around for it because I have a sudden urge to kiss it.

Jojo reaches for the land line on the wall and answers, "*L'Amour Bakin,* this is Jojo."

And then there is a lot of silence.

A whole lot of silence.

I just decided silence is a zillion times worse than angry voices.

Jojo says only one more word—bye—before she hangs up the phone. She doesn't say anything else for a long time, just watches her fingers tap on the counter.

Finally, she looks up.

Right at me.

"That was an interesting phone call."

I concentrate every effort on the spot of grease I'm scrubbing. I'm pretty sure it's been there for a thousand years and wouldn't come off if I straight up bleached it, but there is no way I'm meeting Jojo's eyes right now. I feel the trouble hanging over me like a pinata, and I don't want to be the one to bust it open.

"Who was it?" my mom asks.

"Jake."

My shoulders tense for the downpour.

"He called to thank us for the lemon cookies."

I suck in a sharp breath. He called to say thanks? Why would he do that? What a jerk!

"Funny thing, but I don't remember taking him any lemon cookies. How about you, Cat?"

The corners of my mouth drop to my chin. Where is Robyn right now? She is supposed to be here so I can blame everything on her this time!

"Cat?" Mom's voice is not to be trifled with.

I sigh and turn around, wiping my hands thoroughly on a kitchen towel. "Yes?"

"Yes, you're listening, or yes you remember taking Jake lemon cookies?"

"Um, both?" I say in a small voice.

My mom lets out a breath that has my name in it, all hot and angry.

GG stands between my mom and Jojo, a hand on each of their arms. "My mama always said, it is no use getting upset until we have all the facts. Get the facts, she said."

They stare at me with questions in their eyes.

I open my mouth, with no idea how I'm going to explain this, and words just start flowing into the air. I talk so fast; I forget about that one little thing called breath and have to pause twice to catch it.

"Let me get this straight," Mom says when I finally stop spewing. "You girls decided to bake Jake apathetic so he would close his bakery?"

It sounds so bad when she says it like that, but I nod, because I know if I try to explain the whys or defend myself at all, it's just going to get hotter in here.

Quiet as a mouse.

Man, I wish Robyn wasn't all apathetic right now. I never have to face the consequences of my rotten decisions alone. This is super uncomfortable.

"Cat Anderson!" Mom begins, on what is sure to be the beginning of my path to a cold, dark cell guarded by Dementors.

"It didn't work!" I blurt. "Nothing happened, he's fine."

"Well, I could have told you that." Jojo crosses her arms and leans against the counter. "I tried baking him months ago and it didn't work then either. I wish I'd thought to use apathy; that's brilliant!"

Mom gapes at Jojo. "You baked an emotion on purpose? To manipulate someone? Jojo! How could you?"

Oh no, Mom's doing the thing. The thing where her pent-up frustration zeroes in on one place. It doesn't feel right to let Jojo take all the flack for what I did.

So, despite my super strong survival instinct, I burst out, "It's fine, Mom, he didn't feel anything, his bakery is still open, and we figured out the next clue, so it's all good, right?"

Mom pinches the bridge of her nose. "Cat..."

Penny bursts through the kitchen and skids to a stop, her face morphing from upset to devastated. It's not good, whatever she's about to say, that's for sure.

She clamps her mouth shut. "What's for breakfast?"

"Good morning, Penny," Mom says in a dangerously nonchalant voice. "How are you?"

We are in so much trouble, I can't even.

Penny's eyes flicker to me, she knows Mom almost as well as I do, just a few years behind. I wish I could help her out, but I don't have any surprises up my sleeve today. I think we're just going to have to own the fact that our lives might possibly be over.

Right now.

In this kitchen.

Such a tragic end.

"Fine, how are you?" Penny says finally.

Mom gives her a tight smile. "Why in such a hurry?"

"I'm...not?"

Mom continues to stare. I watch the breakdown in Penny's resolve happen in front of my eyes, like someone sped up the filming of a landslide. She covers her face with her hands, "Robyn won't get up, she says it's too hard. It didn't wear off. We are so dead!"

In slow motion, at least that's how it feels, Mom's neck swivels to me.

"Um." It's amazing how my brain shuts off just when I need it most.

Amazing, but not awesome.

Or epic.

"Yes, Cat, you were saying?"

I wipe at the counter with the towel in my hand. "Also, I was about to mention that Robyn ate a cookie to see if they worked, 'cause it didn't work on Jake, and now she's a zombie slug."

I feel, more than see, my mom swell with anger.

"Good morning!" Dad's cheery voice smacks the tension like a mallet cracking ice. Bubby echoes the words cheerily from his lofty perch on Dad's shoulders. When no one responds, Dad takes in the scene, and then asks Mom, "Everything okay?"

She's too red and puffed up to answer. Dad lifts Bubby off his shoulders. "Hey, sport, why don't you go look for four leaf clovers in the backyard?"

Bubby skips away, not knowing he's being sent to his doom. I've spent fourteen years looking for clovers and never found a four leaf anywhere. Which is too bad, because I could really use the luck right now.

"What's going on?" His eyes come right to me, like I'm the obvious one to answer the question. I think that's totally unfair, there are plenty of people in this room who would make Mom turn into a cranberry.

Ok, there's not.

Sigh.

I think that's called wishful thinking.

The trouble is that I don't know what I can say, since I don't know how much my dad knows about this baking emotions thing, so I open and close my mouth in a very goldfishy way.

GG wraps her arms around my mom's waist, bringing her back to life.

Mom takes a deep breath. "Cat broke some rules, Drew. I'm processing. Maybe... Do you want to go find clovers with Andy?"

My dad steps back, his eyes wide. "Are you trying to get rid of me?" His voice is light, but his face falls.

"We just need to sort some things out," she says, gently.

"Without me?"

Mom doesn't seem to know where to look. Her and Jojo exchange glances that bounce off each other.

"Do you really want me to leave?" Dad's voice is very, very small. It's also very, very unlike him.

I think I broke my whole family.

Who knew little choices have such big, fat consequences.

"No!" Mom reaches for his hand. "No, I don't want you to go. It's just complicated."

"Tell him," GG whispers, so quietly I can't hear the words; I just see her lips move.

Mom's eyes fill with tears, overflowing. It's like someone twisted the handle on the faucet behind her eyes. "I can't!"

"What?" Dad softens, he wraps Mom up in a tight hug that is usually uber embarrassing but doesn't really bother me all that much right now. "What can't you tell me?"

"Wait, you haven't told him?" Jojo looks from Mom to GG to Dad, her voice full of surprise. "He doesn't know?"

"What don't I know?"

Mom pulls away, her eyes searching for me, where they stop. "Cat, I am so disappointed in you. After all the things we've talked about, you went and did the same thing all over again. I thought I could trust you."

Okay, that hurts.

I open my mouth to defend myself, tell my mom how I didn't want to do it, how Robyn got so angry about it, how our intentions were so good, how it isn't my fault.

But the truth is...

It is my fault.

I baked the cookies with emotion.

I broke the rule.

"I'm sorry." I look down at my bare feet, which are actually freezing cold on this tile. I should have put on some socks.

"Wait!" Jojo holds up both her hands. "Wait a second, I am totally confused. Why are you so disappointed in Cat for baking? Her heart was in the right place, right?"

I nod as hard as I can.

"There. I knew it. She was just trying to help me, weren't you?"

I nod again.

"Yes," Mom agrees. "But she knew it wasn't allowed and she did it anyway. There are other ways she could have helped you."

"But..." Jojo's mouth works like she's not sure if she should say what she wants to say.

Most of the time, I think that struggle means to be quiet, but I don't know how to communicate that to Jojo without talking. Talking out loud would bring everyone's attention back to me and that's the last thing I want right now.

"But, Bridget, you did the same thing." Jojo reaches out for my mom, like trying to give someone candy after you accidentally break their favorite toy.

Not that I know what that looks like.

I'm super careful with other people's things.

Mostly.

My mom's eyes go wild, she hops from one foot to another. "I'm not having this conversation right now, I'm going to go check on Bubby."

Dad pulls her back, keeping her suspended in the kitchen. "He's fine, Bridget. I think you're needed more in here."

"I can't..." She tugs away from my dad. "I can't do this."

He moves closer, looking deep in her eyes. "You can."

Mom takes a deep breath and then melts. Completely dissolves into tears, right here in front of everyone. She tries to tug away from my dad and cover her face at the same time. "I can't... You won't... You don't know what I did."

My heart swells so big it hurts in my chest. It physically hurts me to see my mom struggling so bad. I fly to her and squeeze her guts out. "Mom, we're good for anything, remember? It's okay."

"It's not." She shakes her head. "It's really, really not. I...did something...horrible."

"Bridget." GG's soft voice is like that ointment stuff you put on cuts. "Nothing is as bad out here as it is in your mind. I promise you will be glad to say these words. It will help."

They lock eyes for a very long time.

"Okay." My mom swallows. "Okay. But if I'm going to do this, I need some chocolate."

GG winks. "I have just the thing."

Chocolate Muffins

3 ripe Bananas
2 Eggs
1 tsp Vanilla extract
1/2 C. Honey
2 & 1/2 C. old -fashioned Oats
1/4 C. Cocoa Powder
1 & 1/2 tsp Baking Powder
1/2 tsp Salt
1/2 C. Chocolate Chips

Blend it up, blend it up, yeah-yeah!

Excuse me, I don't know what just happened there.

Moving on. Preheat the oven to 375°F. Put cupcake wrappers in a muffin tin. In a blender, place your bananas, eggs, vanilla, honey, cocoa powder, oats, baking powder, and salt.

In case you weren't counting, that's all the ingredients except the chocolate chips. Aren't you glad I'm here to tell you these things? I sure am!

Pulse until blended.

Stir in the chocolate chips with a spatula, you'll need it later so it's good you're breaking it in now.

Pour the batter from the blender into the muffin cups, almost to the top. Use a handy dandy rubber spatula to get out all the extras from the bottom and sides.

Bake for 13-18 minutes until the muffins are dry when you poke the top or check them with a toothpick. It should come out clean. If not, add a couple minutes cooking time.

It's hard, I know, but wait until they cool before you eat them.

17

Dreamy Chocolate Cake

I nibble a chocolate muffin and wait patiently for Mom to start talking. GG and Jojo sit on either side of Penny. My mom and dad are so close together she's practically in his lap. The only thing bothering me right now, is the silence. I have this feeling, this epically awesome feeling that something is about to rock my world. I just hope it's a good rock, like eating chocolate for breakfast, and not a bad rock, like finding out you have incurable feet warts.

Mom swallows the last of her food and washes it down with a swig of milk.

"Okay." She steels herself with a big, deep breath. "Drew, do you remember how I told you I had a crush on you the minute I saw you?"

He nods, his muffin totally untouched on the napkin in front of him. I don't know what's weirder, hearing my parents talk about crushing on each other or my dad not eating. "You told me it was when we had physics together senior year."

My mom shakes her head. "I told you that, but it isn't true. You won't remember. The first time I saw you was way before that. It was only the second day after we moved here. You came into the bakery with your mom, and I fell in love with you that instant."

"That's—"

221

"I know that's nuts, to feel like you're going to marry someone at that age. I know."

GG smiles. "Not all that unusual."

"Is that what you can't tell me?" Dad asks.

Mom shakes her head again. "No Drew, I don't even know where to begin."

"I got this." Jojo lifts her hands, drawing our attention to her. "Listen up Drew, our family can bake our feelings into food. As in, whatever we feel when we bake, other people feel when they eat. We change how they feel."

Mom groans, dropping her forehead to the table.

"But..." Dad looks around the kitchen.

GG laughs. "We do not do that! Jojo! So naughty! We can, yes, but we don't. We just bake happy. We want to help people, see?"

"But sometimes we bake other emotions," Jojo insists. "To change how someone feels on purpose, when it's really important to us."

"Yes." GG bows her head. "Sometimes we do that, too."

My mom slowly lifts her eyes. "You were so popular, Drew; everyone wanted to date you. I knew I didn't stand a chance. You know that chocolate cake, at the Physics party our Senior year?"

"How could I forget?"

"Remember how I only gave you a piece and then accidentally dropped the rest in the dirt?"

"I—"

"It wasn't an accident!" Mom groans, her head drooping again, so she's talking to the table. "I didn't want anyone else to eat it because I..." She takes a deep, shaky breath. "I baked love into it. I wanted only you to eat it so you would fall in love with me."

"Bridget—"

"That's why you love me, that's why we got married! Drew, I'm so sorry! I told myself what I was doing was okay because it was just so you'd notice me and give me a chance. But...my baking was so strong you fell hard, and... I'm so, so sorry. I haven't been able to look myself in the eyes for fifteen years. This secret has cankered my soul."

Jojo silently applauds, then reaches over to rub my mom's back. Penny's eyes widen when they meet mine, but I shake my head. I had no idea. I wouldn't have been able to even guess.

Now it all makes sense.

No wonder mom quit baking. No wonder she didn't want me to do it.

I remember how relieved I felt when Tobey didn't eat those cupcakes that made Conner cuckoo. I will never forget the moment I realized I didn't really want Tobey to act that way toward me.

My poor mom.

All these years.

But, our family, I mean, what now?

What happens next?

My dad's face is unreadable. "I..."

Mom looks up, her eyes bright with tears. "I know, you must be so hurt and confused. I love you, Drew, so much. I can't stand the thought of losing you. I also can't stand one more minute knowing you only love me because I made you. I will completely understand if you want to leave me." Her words get smaller and smaller as she ends this sentence, until the word 'me' is barely audible.

There is silence for only half a second, then my dad...

Starts laughing.

I stare at him in awe.

He's cracked!

My mom's face crumbles, she moves to stand up.

"I'm sorry!" My dad gulps, he gently pulls her back down in her chair. "I'm sorry. I know this isn't funny. I had no idea."

"No one does," Jojo says. "It's sort of a family secret."

My dad snorts and laughs harder. Mom is so appalled she can't even look at him. She twists her wedding ring around and around her finger, inching it to the top.

I tell her to push it back in place with my super mind powers.

"Hold on." Dad raises a hand while he downs a full cup of water. He sets it on the table and takes both of mom's hands in his.

"Bridget, I did not fall in love with you because of a cake!"

"You don't believe me," Mom says sadly, like she expected this all along.

With good reason. Who would believe something like this? It's completely impossible.

"No." Dad shakes his head.

"It's true, Drew," Jojo says.

GG nods. "You are welcome to read my mama's journal."

"Cat can do it, too, Daddy. We can show you."

Dad smiles at Penny, and then looks at the rest of us. "You misunderstand me. It's not that I don't believe you. That's not what I'm saying. I'm trying to tell you that I already knew you guys do that."

"You. Know?" Mom blinks. "What do you know?"

"I know about Evie, the bakery, and emotional baking." He ticks things off on his fingers as he says them. "All of it."

"Drew, what are you saying?" Mom looks upset, I mean, more than before.

"Wait a second." I point at Dad. "We never told you about Evie; we never said she was part of this baking thing."

He shakes his head. "You didn't need to. Like I said, I already know."

"Wait, really, how much do you know?" Jojo tips her head to one side, tugging on the ends of her blue hair.

"As much as you do." He spreads his arms wide.

"How?" Jojo asks, "How do you know?"

"I have ears." Dad points to the sides of his head. "Also, I used to hang around the bakery all the time when I was a kid, trying to get the guts to talk to Bridget. I picked up on some things."

"Huh." Jojo stares off into space. "I wonder who else in this town knows what we can do and never said anything?"

"Bridget," Dad coaxes until she looks at him. "I remember that day we first met, right after you moved here. I thought you were beautiful."

Mom's cheeks turn pink.

"I wanted to ask you out all through high school, but my timing stunk. There was always another guy one step ahead of me. No matter how hard I tried to get my locker near yours or finagle a class with you, it never worked.

Until senior year. Finally, we ended up in physics together. I still didn't have any hope; I'm so average and you are so extraordinary."

Mom sob-laughs.

Happy-sad.

"When I ate that cake, I had no idea it was like a love potion. I already was so crazy in love with you, it couldn't have made a difference in how I felt. All it proved to me was that you were interested in me, too, because you gave it to me. That's when I upped my game. That's when I decided I finally had a chance with you."

Mom closes the tiny space between them, snuggling into Dad, wrapping her arms around his neck so she can kiss him.

Now, normally, Penny and I might have screamed and covered our faces while making gagging noises, but today, we both watch with hands clasped and starry eyes.

But then, the kiss goes on and on and on.

It lasts so long, I start examining the tile at my feet.

Jojo clears her throat and threatens to throw ice water on them.

Finally, they break apart, both looking so happy they don't even seem to care they were totally making out in the kitchen, in front of their daughters, sister, and Grammy.

Yeah, that's not awkward at all.

"Seriously, you two, people eat in here." Jojo throws a napkin at them.

They are too busy staring at each other to notice.

It's, like, super weird.

"Okay, glad that's resolved." Jojo turns her back on them with an indulgent sigh. "On to the next. Why don't you girls tell me again what happened with Robyn?"

Happy for the distraction from my gushy parents, I jump right in. "She tested the cookie we gave to Jake, because she was annoyed it didn't work and wanted to prove it, or something. Wait a second, what did you bake for Jake? What's that about? Why didn't you tell us?"

"Oh." Jojo fiddles with a bracelet on her wrist. "Well, that would be because I was embarrassed. I totally baked him to love me."

"What?" Penny and I stare at each other with huge eyes.

"Yeah, well, I knew it works because I helped your mom do it for your dad. Of course I didn't know all that other stuff." She waves her hand. "But it doesn't matter, I still would have done it. It's not that I love Jake, that's not why I baked love. I think I wanted him to be crazy in love with me so I could string him along and then tell him to beat it."

GG tuts.

"I'm not proud." Jojo shakes her head, but laughs. "Really, I'm mortified. But I did what I did and, like you, it didn't work. I've been so confused and stressed about everything that's going on, my baking soured. Which just goes to prove that this is all Jake's fault."

"Wait, why didn't it work?"

Jojo shrugs. "No idea. GG?"

GG gives Jojo a look that would have thrown her in timeout if she was like twenty years younger. "That, I do not know. But I wish you had talked to me of this sooner."

"Aunt Jojo?" Penny asks in a small voice.

"Yes, cutie pie?"

"Do you"—Penny clears her throat—"do you think you hate Jake so much because you really love him?"

"No!" Jojo's eyes look like Bubby's when we run out of fruit loops. "No, no, no, no! That's not it at all. I don't love him; I can't stand that guy. It's so ironic, really, that the more I try to avoid him, the more I get thrown in his path. I just can't seem to get away from him."

I totally know how that feels.

Jojo waves her hand over the table. "All this serious talk. Way too heavy for a Wednesday morning. I'm just making a wild guess here, but I don't think Robyn's apathy is going to wear off." She stands up, heading to the kitchen. "What say we take Robyn some muffins, so she can stop impersonating a... What did you call her? A zombie, something?"

"Slug."

"That's right, a zombie slug. As pleasant as that sounds, let's go snap Robyn out of it."

I glance at my mom and dad.

"They'll be fine." GG winks.

I wrinkle my nose. I didn't even know people could look at each other that long without blinking and I'm the one who rocks at staring contests. "Will the muffins work for Robyn? Don't I have to bake her the opposite to snap her out of it?"

"Maybe, but before we do that, let's try. You helped GG with the baking, no?"

"Yes." I nod.

"And she had you clear your mind, bake happy?"

"Yes."

"Then it's worth a shot. If the muffins don't work, we'll come bake something different. What do you say?"

"What do you think?" I ask Penny.

"Let's do it!"

We fill a plate and follow Jojo up the stairs. I hope Robyn can muster the energy to eat.

"Wow." Penny leans over to whisper, "This has been a super weird morning."

"Seriously!" I agree.

Robyn is going to be so ticked she missed it.

Creamy Dreamy Chocolate Cake

This recipe is super advanced, but totally worth the time and effort. No worries, we got this!

1 C. Water
1/3 C. Cocoa Powder (The higher quality, the better it will taste!)
2 C. Flour (unbleached all-purpose works just fine.)
1 & 1/4 C. Sugar
1 tsp Salt
2 tsp Baking Soda
1 C. Buttermilk (This is not the recipe for substitutions, use the real stuff!)
1/2 C. Butter
2 large Eggs
1 tsp Vanilla extract

Preheat the oven to 325°F.

Prepare three 8-inch cake pans. Cut parchment paper or wax paper to fit the bottom. Place inside. Grease bottom and sides. Don't skip this step or you'll be chiseling the cake out of the pan in chunks; I don't care how nonstick the pan claims to be!

Boil water and remove from heat; stir in cocoa powder until smooth.

Combine flour, sugar, salt, and baking soda. Whisk together to remove lumps.

With a hand mixer or stand mixer, beat eggs and butter until light and fluffy. Stir in vanilla. Add flour mix, alternating with buttermilk, just until combined. Stir in cocoa mixture.

Divide the batter between the cake pans and let it rest on the counter for 30 minutes at room temperature.

(This is super important! It allows the leavening to settle so we don't get a sink hole in the middle of the cake while it's baking.)

Bake for 30 to 35 minutes, or until a toothpick inserted into the center comes out clean. Place cake pans on a cooling rack for 30 minutes. Invert onto a wire rack to cool an additional 30 minutes before icing.

The cake is now done and uniformly baked and amazingly delicious. You can eat it as is, with milk or ice cream, or frost it however you want, or you can cause a sensation!

Let's talk epically awesome! Let's talk about three layers... Ganache filling and White Chocolate Swiss Meringue Buttercream! Oh my goodness! Are you with me?

Let's do this!

But first, let's stick those pan-less, partially cooled cakes into the refrigerator for about an hour so they are ready when we are!

Ganache:

3 C. Semi-sweet Chocolate Chips (Again, good quality tastes best-est)

1 & 1/2 C. Heavy Whipping Cream

4 TBSP unsalted Butter, softened

Use a double boiler to melt chocolate chips with cream. If you don't have one of those, a stainless-steel bowl over a pot of boiling water works just as well, just be careful you don't knock it off.

It's been known to happen.

When the mixture is smoother and more gorgeous than Chris Pine, add the butter. Stir until melted and combined.

Pour the mixture into a bowl and let cool until steam no longer rises, then cover it and leave at room temperature for about an hour.

Let's get those cakes now!

Put one cake layer face down on a cake stand or plate. Cover with 1/3 of the ganache. Continue to layer cake and ganache, make sure the tippy top layer of cake is placed upside down.

Bottoms up, bottoms down!

Refrigerate again to set ganache, and let's make some Swiss Meringue Buttercream! This is my favorite part!

White Chocolate Swiss Meringue:

3/4 C. White Chocolate Chips. (Guittard is a great brand. I don't like the taste of white chocolate made with partially hydrogenated oils.)

1/3 C. Sugar

3 large Egg Whites, at room temperature

Pinch Salt

1/4 tsp Vanilla extract

1 & 1/2 C. (3 sticks) unsalted Butter, softened and cut into cubes

Use the double boiler again to melt the white chocolate chips. Stir until completely melted and smooth. Remove the top part of the double boiler but leave the bottom with water simmering.

Put sugar, egg whites and salt in a heatproof bowl, (Double boiler or stainless-steel bowl) and set it over the simmering water. Whisk until the sugar dissolves and the mixture is very thin and warm, around 115°F .

Pour into a stand mixer with the whisk attachment. Mix on high until stiff peaks form. Reduce speed to low and mix until cooled, about 10 minutes.

Continue on low. Add the vanilla. Put in the butter cubes, one at a time, until blended. Add melted white chocolate slowly. Now, increase speed to medium and beat until buttercream is smooth and shiny.

Lovely!

Now bring that cake back out and crumb coat it.

That's just a fancy way of saying thinly ice the cake so the final icing job doesn't have any flecks of cake in it. It's more purdier! So be careful not to get crumbs from the spreader into the icing bowl.

After the crumb coat, refrigerate the cake to set that first layer of icing. Bring it back out and apply the final coat with the remaining Buttercream.

Minus what you snitched along the way. Don't worry. I won't tell.

All done! Ta-da!
The most Epically Awesome Chocolate Cake ever!

18

Pumpkin Cinnamon Rolls

I am so happy to have Robyn back to normal, I just keep smiling at her.

Like a creepy clown.

After we fill her in on what went down when she was in the depths of despair, and she has plenty of time to huff about how unfair it is that she missed so much, we face the bakery chaos like bosses. We clean until everything is shiny, lock it all up and collapse at a table with tons of paper and pencils.

Everyone except my parents and Bubby, that is.

They go for a drive. Bubby can't stay awake in a moving vehicle for more than thirty minutes, so this is a win-win. My parents can be lovey-dovey without scarring anyone and the rest of us can get stuff done.

They are pretty much impossible right now.

Anyway, the rest of us are making a plan of attack. The bake-off is only one day away and Jojo still isn't happy with any of the recipes we've tried.

We need something epic.

Something awesome.

Something epically awesome.

But what?

We each take a cookbook and pour over the contents, trying to find something that fits that description I just made up in my head. I am the sorry sop who gets the book without pictures. Why the butter bombs do people make cookbooks without pictures? How am I supposed to decide I want to eat something if I can't see what it looks like? Without a picture it's just a bunch of words.

And words do not look delicious.

I mush my cheek against my palm and flip pages, letting my eyes glaze over.

What is something we can make that will knock the socks off those restaurant people?

What is something that will keep those judges eating and eating so they are way too stuffed to try anyone else's food?

What is something Jake would never think to bake?

I have zero answers to those questions, but I wish I did. I'd love to be the one who finds the recipe that saves the bakery. I can tell Robyn feels the same way because she's flipping through books at hyper speed, tossing one after the other on the floor next to her.

"Chocolate. Chocolate is good." Jojo mumbles as she turns pages with the tips of her fingers. "People love chocolate. Souffle? Too finicky. Cupcakes? Boring. Almond bark, delicious, but not baked." She sighs and gives me a teeny smile. "Tomorrow is Thanksgiving. You guys traveled all the way here to spend it with us and here we are, stressing about a stupid bake-off. Maybe we should pull out?"

"No!" Robyn, Penny, and I say in unison without looking up from our books.

"We're in this now; we're gonna win it," Robyn adds.

GG smiles. "No matter what happens we are fine, but we are not fine because we give up. Keep fighting, Jolynn, we are not giver-up-pers."

I cover my giggles; I don't know if that's what GG meant to say, but I like it. We are not giver-uppers. We will find the most amazing recipe in the world!

I'm pretty sure.

"What about cinnamon rolls?" I turn to another boring page without looking at it. "Marissa and Mom told us cinnamon rolls fix everything."

"Cinnamon rolls!" Jojo's bright eyes slowly dim in front of me like someone slides her light switch down. "Oh, but Great Buns will do those. Besides, every Hermione Homemaker can make good cinnamon rolls."

"Not everyone." Robyn doesn't stop turning pages long enough to look up, she keeps flipping as she talks. "That's not a bad idea."

Jojo pushes her cookbook away and leans back to gaze at the ceiling. "What is fantastic? Everything I think of is so commonplace. We need something-"

"Epically awesome!" I supply.

Jojo laughs, closing her eyes. "That's the words. Epically awesome. So, what is epically awesome?"

GG tucks a lock of hair behind her ear. "We could always make something with-"

"Don't say pumpkin!" Jojo peeks one eye open.

GG laughs. "But pumpkin is this time of year! It is delicious. Everyone in town loves the pumpkin."

"True." Jojo closes her eyes again. "But everyone around here knows all our pumpkin recipes. They are amazing, but not epically awesome."

I don't think the look on GG's face agrees with Jojo's words, but I'm not going to point it out to them. All my brain powers are needed to solve this dilemma.

What can we make?

What.

What.

What?

"Did you find anything, Penny?" Robyn asks without tearing her eyes away from the flipping pages. I'm going to go back through the books she's discarding; there's no way she's seeing everything.

Penny, unlike Robyn, hasn't turned a single page in a really long time. "No."

"What are you looking at?" I abandon my lame choice to peek over Penny's shoulder. "What is that?"

Penny lifts the book so I can see the cover. I don't recognize the place, but it's a cookbook for some bakery in Washington. "Sorry, I got distracted, this page talks about unlikely combinations."

"What does that mean?" I wonder.

"Oh, you know." Jojo's eyes flutter open. "Like maple and bacon, fig and goat cheese, apple and cheddar cheese, things people didn't normally like to put together."

"Oh." I lose interest. I don't know anything about weird combinations. But I do know that I can't bring myself to look at the book of ultimate boringness in my lap for one more second. I let it drop to the pile on the floor and reach for one with pictures.

But my hand freezes in the air, hovering like a UFO over the Nevada desert.

"You okay, honey?" Jojo asks.

I turn slowly, working my mouth so it's ready to unleash the bestest idea in the whole entire world. "I know what we should make!"

Robyn sits up. "What?"

"No." I shake my head, slapping both palms on the table. "You don't understand, I thought of the perfect thing! It popped in my head just now, like lightning in my brain!"

"Well, what is it?" Jojo's eyes light up.

Robyn puts a hand on Jojo's arm. "Cat just does this, give her some suspense."

"Suspense?"

Robyn nods and puts both hands on her cheeks, her mouth drops open to a perfect oval. Penny drops to her knees, clasping her hands to me, with pleading eyes. GG claps the back of her hand over her forehead, draping her body across the back of her chair.

A slow smile spreads across Jojo's face. With a horrible Southern accent, she flutters her eyes. "Oh, Cat, you must tell us your idea, or I shall..." Then she falls to the floor in a swoon.

I grin as I look at each of them, hanging on my every word. Now, they are ready. "Why don't we make pumpkin cinnamon rolls!" I raise both hands in the air and wait for the applause.

It comes.

Very slowly and doesn't sound a bit like the thunderous clamoring I imagine.

So, actually, all that's just in my head, but it is enough.

"Pumpkin cinnamon rolls?" Jojo says, like she's trying the taste of the words in her mouth.

"What are those?" Penny drops to her bottom and stares up at me.

Robyn wrinkles her nose. "Have we had them before?"

"I love it! I love the pumpkin!" GG claps.

I knew GG would be on board.

"No, I haven't had them before, but I think that's what makes this idea so epically awesome. Let's make up our own recipe! Like Penny's book, we'll take things that don't normally go together and create a thing! I think it will work!"

GG hops to her feet, pretty spry for someone with white hair. "Let us try now!"

Jojo rises more slowly. "Would we put pumpkin in the dough? Or in the filling?"

"We try both!" GG disappears in the second it takes the rest of us to follow her through the kitchen doors.

I'm so excited they take my idea seriously; I dance like Penny across the tile. This is it! I can feel it! These pumpkin cinnamon rolls are going to win us the thing!

"What smells so good?" Mom's voice comes through the door just an instant before the rest of her does.

I meet her and Dad to grab their hands and drag them to the table. "Come try, one of these, and one of these." I hand them a pumpkin roll from each tray. They are still warm, the caramel drips onto my hand, but I don't mind cleaning up that mess. I suck on the side of my palm while Mom and Dad take their bites.

"Oh wow!" Dad looks at the roll in his hand like he wonders if he can fit the whole thing in his mouth at once. "This is fantastic!"

"What is it?" Mom asks, holding out her roll to exchange with Dad. He looks sad to hand his over but is quickly mollified when he tries the roll Mom had.

"Pumpkin cinnamon rolls!" I still want to throw a parade and dance on the tables. The excitement hasn't worn off at all in the last two hours. Having ideas is the funnest. "Which one do you like best?"

"They are both so good." Mom licks a bit of caramel from her bottom lip. "But I'm a sucker for cream cheese. I like that one best."

Dad trades back with Mom and holds up the roll he tried originally, the caramel one with pecans. "I like this one."

I look over my shoulder at the others. Penny makes tick marks on a piece of notebook paper.

"Where does that put us?" Jojo asks, stirring caramel sauce on the stove so it doesn't congeal while we wait for the next batch of rolls to come out.

"Cream Cheese wins." Penny bites the lid of the pen.

"No!!" I slump into my chair. I really, really want to make the caramel rolls. I think they are epically awesome enough to win the bake-off. There has to be something else I can do. Someone else that can vote. The perfect solution comes out of nowhere like a smack to the bottom. "No! We haven't asked Bubby yet!"

"Bubby!" Robyn swoops in on him as he slips into the kitchen, blinking sleepily. His blanket is curled over his shoulder, hiding his thumb so he can't easily get to it.

He's trying to quit.

Robyn scoops him up and brings him to the table, giggling and squirming from her tickles. She pulls off a bit of each roll and hands it to Bubby. "Which one do you like best?"

I watch him, holding my breath.

He grabs both and shoves them in his mouth, swallowing without chewing. "Yummy. Can I have more?"

Probably we should have known better than to leave the fate of the bake-off in my six-year-old brother's sticky fingers. Robyn has a lot more patience than I do. She tears off another piece and hands it to Bubby.

"Do you like this one?"

He chews with his mouth open. "Yes! Yummy!"

Robyn gives him some of the other. "How about this one?"

Bubby chomps it down, noisily. "Yes! Yummy!"

I sigh, dropping my head to my hands.

Robyn, again, demonstrates her super patient powers. "Don't you like one of them, just a teensy bit more than the other? I'm glad you think they are both yummy, but is one of them yummier?"

Bubby points. "That one."

I groan.

Because now we are tied. I guess I didn't think that through very well.

Penny ice skates across the tile so I can see her list. "That means you, Bubby, me, and Dad like the caramel pecan rolls with the pumpkin in the filling, and Robyn, GG, Mom, and Jojo like the cream cheese icing rolls with the pumpkin in the dough." She chews the top of the pen some more. How are we going to break the tie?"

"I'll change my vote." Robyn lifts one hand. "I really thought they were both fantastic."

I roll my eyes; that is so Robyn!

"Did you hear that?" Penny looks around.

"What?"

"It's the doorbell." GG hurries to the back door, the service door. But the bakery has been closed for hours. Who comes to the service door after hours?

Jojo reads my thoughts. "It's probably the dairy delivery; sometimes they're late." But then she freezes in place like someone zapped her.

That's because we hear a cheery male voice greet GG.

Jake.

GG's eyes are starry as she leads him to the table. "Now you can save the day! Tell us which you like best."

"GG!" Jojo hisses, pulling her aside. "You can't do that! Did you forget what these are for? He shouldn't be here." She looks at him. "What are you doing here?"

An easy grin curls Jake's mouth. "Well now, definitely not spying on your bakery in outlandish disguise."

That's true. He's wearing his small-town dude uniform of jeans and a plaid shirt.

Jojo glares at him. "Nice. Why are you here then?"

"I forgot to leave the invoice this morning."

"Sure you did." Jojo crosses her arms.

I'm totally with her; he's full of custard. He's totally spying on us with the invoice as an excuse.

Except that, for realsies, *We* didn't even know what we were baking up until a few hours ago, so there's no way Jake would have known we were working on the bake-off now.

Unless he has the place bugged.

I eyeball him.

I wouldn't put it past him.

Jake moves towards the table with a nudge from GG, but Jojo steps in his way. "You can't try these."

"He would break the tie," Robyn says, reluctantly.

Jojo gives her a gremlin face. I wonder if those things are genetic, cause Penny does one that looks just like this one's identical twin. Robyn examines her cuticles, her long hair falling over her face.

"Jolynn, dear, it can't possibly hurt to share with our friend Jake."
Jojo snorts.

My mom and dad watch the whole thing with amused eyes, but I totally have Jojo's back. Why doesn't anyone else seem to notice what a revolting person Jake is?

Jake gives Jojo a look that I can't even define. "What is the big deal, Jo? Why don't you want me to taste your creation? Think it's not good enough for me?"

Jojo steps forward just a tad, making Jake step back or breath in all her exhales. "No. That's not it. Not even close, smart guy. I'll tell you, so you don't imagine you're better than us, or something equally ridiculous. We are practicing for the bake-off and invented the most amazing thing in the whole world. What do you think about that?"

"Oh, so many things." Jake's eyes dance.

Without any warning, Jojo flies forward. Both palms wham into Jake's chest. He flails backward, his arms all over the place. GG tries to catch him, but he falls on his behind, *hard*.

Robyn reaches out a hand but doesn't move forward. My mom gasps. Jake sits there for a moment, looking surprised.

Then his face gets really, really sad.

The downturn of his mouth and the way his shoulders sag does something weird to my belly.

GG sends Jojo a few thousand tuts in rapid fire as she struggles to help Jake to his feet. We all just watch, like we're on McGonagall's chess board and moving will cost us the game.

Jake leans heavily on GG's shoulder until he gets his feet working again. "Thanks."

Jojo watches with her arms clutched to her chest, as Jake sweeps the back of his jeans and stretches out one of his knees. Finally, he meets her eyes. "Never a dull moment, Jojo, thanks for the fun time. I'd better be on my way."

"Yeah, you'd better," Jojo spits out, but there's something in her eyes that looks the way my belly feels.

Jake brushes off the back of his jeans. "I know the way out. Thanks, GG." But before he makes it to the door, he turns slowly, extending his arm toward Jojo. "I just have to ask this. I probably should keep it to myself, but I have to know. Jolynn, why do you hate me so much?"

His question echoes in the room in the most awkward way possible. It's like when someone sings a solo and their voice cracks. You want to give them support and sympathy with your eyes but looking at them is super embarrassing.

It was bad enough that he spoke at all, now he just keeps on going.

"I don't get it. I'm a super likeable guy. I can't think of anyone that doesn't like me. Except you." His eyes flick down to me. "And you."

Don't bring me into this, buddy.

"I'm not saying that to blow my own bugle." Jake reaches out a hand. "I just don't get it. I wish I knew what I did to make you hate me. All I can think is that time I stole your Kit Kat in the cafeteria in third grade. That's what I got. If I thought that was the reason, I'd buy you a Sam's Club box of the huge grand-daddy bars to make up for it." He tries to smile, but can't get it to stick.

"We don't have a Sam's Club." Jojo purses her lips together.

And that makes Jake roll his eyes. "I will drive to Flagstaff, or pick them up at Costco next time I visit my folks in the valley. See that, I'm willing to go the distance for peace."

I fold my arms, trying to keep everything rigid so I don't crack. Jojo is pretty stoic, too, her shoulders back, feet rooted to the floor. We aren't going to give in, even if what Jake said was kind of cool.

Or would have been if it wasn't him who said it.

Jojo shakes her head, completely stone faced. "You're ridiculous."

"Is that why you hate me?"

Jojo lifts her arms. "What makes you think I hate you?"

Why did she bother asking him that? Even I could come up with a decent list of answers to that question.

"Give me a break, Jo." Jake shakes his head. "I might sound like it, but I ain't stupid."

"No?" Jojo lifts an eyebrow. "Then you can figure it out yourself, smart guy."

Jake sighs. "Tell me straight, please."

That please is a little heart wrenching. At first, I think Jojo isn't affected, then she cracks, just a slight softening in the eyes. Maybe I imagined it though, her voice is hard as overcooked caramel.

"You deliver to our bakery for years and years, gleaning secrets, and then you open your own bakery to compete with us, and you wonder why I hate you?"

"Secrets?" Jake laughs without humor. "What are you even talking about? You know GG gives copies of her recipe cards out to everyone that comes in here! I'll eat my boots if fifty percent of the population of Arizona don't have one. But, you notice, people still buy from you, because there's no denying you girls do it better."

"You think we're better?" Jojo presses her lips together.

Jake shrugs one shoulder. "I never made a secret of that."

"Then why did you open your bakery? Why did you apply for this bake-off?" Jojo's voice no longer sounds accusing, it sounds pleading.

Maybe even a little hurt. "Why are you always making things so dang difficult?"

Jake tosses his hands in the air. "I swear, woman, you make me want to swear. I told you a thousand times, the bakery is Nathan's place. You think I'd come up with a name like Diet Starts Monday? No way. I'd name the place Jake's Bakes because it rhymes. Nathan volun-told me to head up this Arizona branch of *his* bakery. He put in the application for the bake-off. That's it. And, if you gave me a speck of attention, you'd notice I don't sell nothing that's on your menu. I ain't trying to compete with you! John Wayne knows I would have been happy to keep delivering flour. That dang mill keeps me busier than I want to be already."

"Wait." Robyn raises her hand like we're in school.

"Yes, Robyn?" Jojo calls on her.

Robyn points at Jake. "What about when we were at your bakery, and you said all that stuff about Jojo? You told us you were serious competition and stuff!"

Jake runs his hands through his hair and groans. "You gotta be... Seriously, ain't you girls ever heard of joking?"

"You were joking? You seemed pretty worked up."

"Joking." Jake shakes his head. "Just playing. Messing around. I'm not trying to compete at all. In fact, I'd love to join forces."

Jojo's shoulders come away from her ears, just a little. "Are you for real?"

"Do you think I'd lie?" Jake kneads his way around the brim of his hat. "I only ever wanted to be friends with you, ever since grade school. Could we do that? Maybe? What do you say to a truce?" Jake shoves his hat under one armpit and extends his hand, waiting for Jojo to take it.

She steps forward, one of her hands inching toward Jake, the other clasped across her belly. My heart pounds as their fingers get closer and closer to one another. I want to call out; I can see what's coming like I have a crystal ball in front of me.

Sure enough, just as their fingertips brush together, Jojo's cheeks puff out. "Excuse me." She chokes, barely making it to the sink before she totally throws up.

Pumpkin Cinnamon Rolls

Remember those cinnamon rolls from Bake Believe? We're gonna make them again, with some important changes. Get ready!

1 TBSP active dry yeast, not instant!
1 C. Hot to the touch tap water
1 TBSP Sugar
Combine and let the yeast do its thing for about 10 minutes.

2 C. Whole Milk
1/2 C. Butter
Combine and warm in the microwave until the butter is melted. Let cool until it's warm to the touch but doesn't burn your finger. Very important, friends! If it burns you, it will kill the yeast, remember?

2 Eggs
1/4 C. Sugar
1/2 TBSP Salt
Combine and beat until foamy.

4-6 C. All-purpose Flour
Place all these mixtures into the bowl of a super awesome stand mixer that is made for dough. No names mentioned but it knows who it is. Turn onto low and slowly add the flour.

This next bit is very important!
You might not use 4 cups or 6 cups. It totally and completely depends! Add it slowly until the dough is slightly sticky to the touch but not shiny and not slimy.
Never ever slimy!

Remove to a large, greased bowl to rise for 1 hour.

Filling:
1 can (29 oz) Pumpkin Puree
1 TBSP Pumpkin Pie Spice
1 TBSP Cinnamon
1 Egg
1 C. packed Brown Sugar
Mix the filling ingredients until all combined.

Turn the dough out on a floured surface, thick enough that you could write your name in it, and gently roll the dough out until it's a pretty uniform rectangle. Spread the filling mixture to the edges.

Starting at the long edge, roll the dough slowly over itself. If it is sticky, throw some flour at it and keep rolling. Pinch the edges to keep it together. Slice the unsightly end pieces off to bake into a mini loaf, and then slice the pretty swirls about an inch to an inch and a half thick. Place each slice onto a greased baking sheet, leaving plenty of room for them to rise.

Because they will.

Let sit, covered with a towel, for 30 minutes. This is a good time to heat the oven to 375° degrees. Bake each sheet for about 13-17 minutes. They should be golden brown. Remove immediately to a cooling rack.

Didjaknow that bread sweats? Totally does, if you leave the rolls on the hot sheet, it will make the dough soggy. Yum, right?

No. That's a big no.

Remove immediately and cool to the touch.

Now what?

Now, you cast your vote. Caramel or Cream cheese?

I think we're ready to give caramel sauce a whirl. After that chocolate cake, we can do anything, right?

Caramel Sauce:
3/4 C. Buttermilk

1 tsp light Corn Syrup
1/4 C. Butter
3/4 C. Sugar
1/2 tsp Baking Soda
1 tsp Vanilla extract

Mix all ingredients except vanilla in a super huge pot. Don't look at me weird, I know it's only like 1 cup of liquid, but the baking soda gives it lofty ideas, so trust me on this one. You don't want to be cleaning caramel off of your stove top.

Ain't nobody got time for that.

Heat to boiling, reduce heat and simmer until it becomes a rich, deep caramel color, you know what I'm talking about. About 10-20 minutes.

Remove from heat, stir in vanilla. keeps in the refrigerator for 1 month but I seriously doubt it will last that long.

Drizzle some over the Pumpkin cinnamon rolls along with some chopped pecans! Yum!

Or you can totally cream cheese frost them. Equally delicious and amazing!

Frosting:

1 pkg Cream Cheese
1 tsp Vanilla extract
1/4 C. Milk
Powdered Sugar

Mix all the ingredients, then add powdered sugar (2-4 cups) until it is thick but spreadable, creamy, and so beautiful you want to cry. You can admit it if you do, we are all friends here.

19

Cinnamon Buttermilk Bread

"Well." Robyn bumps my knee with hers. "That was epic."

"Yeah, but not awesome." I lean back on my elbows to look at the huge expanse of clear sky overhead. The concrete stair I'm sitting on seeps cold through my jeans, but I don't care, my head is stuffed full of troubling thoughts.

"Interesting though," Robyn says, glancing at me as she twirls a strand of hair. "Don't you think?"

I lean over and start messing with my shoelaces. The last thing in the universe I want to do is rehash the last forty-five minutes. I'd rather watch Liam drink sardine milk. "Can you believe we only have two full days before we head home?"

"And tomorrow is Thanksgiving." Robyn says, absently.

"What the what?" I bolt upright. "We haven't cooked anything for Thanksgiving! I totally forgot all about it, what with the bakery war and bake-off and scavenger hunt..."

I'm completely appalled.

I just spaced a National Holiday.

"Oh, don't worry about it." Robyn waves one hand. "GG does an exchange with one of her friends, they bring us Thanksgiving dinner and we supply their pies."

"That's cool." I relax back down. "But it seems kind of unfair. Isn't dinner way more work than pies?"

Robyn shrugs. "We make really good pies. I guess they think it's worth it. You know, I was thinking…"

Oh no! I know what she's thinking, and I think she should keep it to herself.

Unfortunately, I don't have a mute button that works on Robyn.

"You know how Jojo threw up on Jake? Doesn't that remind you…?"

I lean forward, my elbows on my knees, looking at the ground. There's a little beetle crawling down the steps. It falls onto it's back and stays there, waving six thin legs in the air. I look for a stick and use it to gently turn the beetle over. It sways in place while it gets oriented and then scurries away.

What is this insect thinking? It's cold outside. Shouldn't it be hibernating or something?

"Cat!" Robyn pulls my arm until I look at her. "Do you remember that day we went to the mall right before school started?"

She talks like that was a thousand years ago instead of a couple months. Plus, also, it was the most embarrassing day of my whole entire life, thank you very much.

So yeah, I remember.

"Cat!" She shakes me.

I pull my arm away, "Yes, okay? Yes, I remember." I'm hoping my tone is enough to change the subject, but Robyn doesn't get the memo.

"Don't you think it's interesting Jojo threw up on Jake, and you threw up on—"

"Look, a shooting star!" I point.

Robyn swats my arm. "Don't you think it's interesting?"

"Make a wish!"

"*Cat!*"

I stick my nose in the air. "I think it's gross to talk about bodily functions."

"Since when?" Robyn snorts.

"Since now." I sniff. "I am not going to talk about this anymore."

There's silence for a couple minutes.

Long enough that I start to think I won.

I should have known better. I mean, this is Robyn.

"I think it's related."

"What?"

"The puking thing. I think it's all connected."

I let out a short laugh. "That gluten done rot your brain." My small-town accent isn't as good as Jake's, but I'm still proud of it.

"No really, listen." She holds up two fingers. "Jake has a brother named Nathan that owns this bakery, Diet Starts Monday." She pulls one of her fingers down. "Just like the one in Boise."

I stare at the empty space where her fingers once were. "So?"

"Nathan."

"I heard you. I still don't get what you're saying."

Robyn runs her hands through her hair. "Cat! A common nickname for Nathan is Nate. If Nathan is Jake's brother and he has a son named Nate, and they live in Boise..."

Oh.

Now I get what she's saying.

But I still refuse to talk about it.

"Nate." Robyn snaps her fingers a bazillion times in the most obnoxious way possible. "Nate at the mall. You know..."

I cover her mouth. "Don't say it."

Her jaw stops moving, so I free her from bondage. I should have just let her talk; her eyes are saying more than her mouth would ever be able to.

I slump into the stairs. The edge jabs my back, but I don't move around anymore. Trying to find a comfortable spot on concrete stairs, as cold as well-diggers toes, is pretty much impossible in the first place.

Trying to do it with troubling thoughts is pointless.

"Cat?"

"Hm?"

"Something super weird is going on around here."

I pick up the stick I used to help the beetle and trail designs through the dirt next to me. My silence doesn't deter Robyn a tiny little bit.

"Something super weird. At first, I thought it was pretty incredible that we have this ability to bake feelings. Super cool. And I still think so, except now, I think there's more to it. Like, I don't even know, something bigger than this or all of us." She waves her hands around the empty air.

I add a cherry to the top of the cupcake I etched in the dirt.

"I've been thinking about the clues. So, there was the graveyard or the gravestone. Then there's the thermometer that is a replica of the family bakery in France. So, Evie and the bakery, and then a moon clock and wishes..."

"I don't know why you think any of that has to do with Jake or Nate. GG made the hunt for us to learn about *our* family."

"Then why did GG make a clue in Jake's bakery? I think Jake's family is somehow tied into all of this. Which means Nate is too."

"Oh gross." I lean forward, hugging my arms.

"It makes sense." Robyn clasps her hands over her knees.

"Whatever. That's a whole lot of what ifs. We don't even know for sure if that clock is a clue." I completely ignore the fact that I was the one who insisted it was. "Or if Nate is related to Jake."

Robyn ignores me. "What does it all mean? What connects the dots of Evie, Jake, the moon, wishes, and the bakery?"

I poke some sprinkles in the icing, jabbing the stick harder than I needed to. All of Robyn's words swirl around me like that experiment where you cover your finger with oil and stick it in water full of pepper. The pepper can't touch you. But then, something she says sticks.

Not only sticks, it blows my mind.

I drop the stick.

"I just remembered something," I say in a hushed voice.

It takes Robyn a few minutes to pull her mind to the present. "Yeah?"

"I remembered a story I heard."

Robyn's eyes narrow. "Are you trying to get me off topic 'cause you don't want to talk about Nate anymore?"

I don't blame her for being suspicious, but I still give her my most offended look. "No, listen, it's about wishes and the moon."

"Tell me then." She pulls her knees in and cradles them with her arms.

It's impossible for me to remember the story word for word, it was a while ago and a lot has happened since then. So, I'm going to wing it. I rub my hands together, both for warmth and because I'm getting excited.

Embellishing facts in this case isn't lying, it's storytelling.

"It's a French Folktale about the Harvest moon. It's a time of great feasting and merry making. People prepare for the moment the orangey red orb rises from the earth, like an eye that sees and blesses their harvest for the winter."

Robyn smooshes her cheek into her hand. "Your French accent needs work."

I stick my tongue out and drop the accent. "Anyways, hard work is rewarded, cause it's like a proverb or something. At the moment the full moon reaches the highest point in the sky and the stars begin to appear; one lucky person can get a wish granted."

Robyn raises one eyebrow. "Wait a second, you told me this already, remember? Around Halloween, I caught you doing that weird dance in your backyard, and you told me you were trying to get a wish, then we both jumped three times on the trampoline, touched our toes together, closed our eyes and wished for something."

Okay, I totally forgot about that. Also, I made most of that up. I was embarrassed Robyn caught me acting like a loon and so I told her it was the French wish making ritual to make it seem cooler. It's a good thing she can't see my face right now, I do not blush pretty.

"And it didn't even work." Robyn scratches her chin. "I'm still waiting for world peace."

I clear my throat. "Maybe we missed a step. Anyway, the important thing here is that the people all believed this folktale thing. And it worked for them."

"How do you know?"

I hesitate. Actually, I don't know it worked for them, but it must have, or it wouldn't be a story that people keep sharing.

Right?

"I just know it did."

"Hm." Robyn grunts. "So who grants these wishes exactly?"

I shush her with a wave of my hand, why is she so skeptical? Isn't it more fun to believe it might be true? "Did you hear the part where wishes *do* come true?"

"Yeah, but who grants them?"

I look around for inspiration. "The magic Full Moon Fairy."

"Whatever." She rolls her eyes. "So, what you're saying is, these people believe if someone wishes under the full moon at the right time—"

"And with all of the sincereness of their heart." These words pop into my head like someone put them there, in a French accent way more authentic than mine.

"Okay, with all their heart, then their wish will come true?"

"That's how I heard it."

"What does that have to do with our family and the bakery…?" Robyn stops talking and grips my arm.

Does she sense it, too?

Something shimmers in the air between us, a feeling I don't know how to describe. It is powerful though, reverberating all through my soul.

Then, as if someone has a string attached to our heads, Robyn and I tip our heads to look at the twinkling stars. There is no moon tonight, but I feel like it's there anyway, watching us back.

"Do you think wishes *really* come true?" Robyn asks in an awed voice.

"If you asked me that question a few months ago I would have laughed my socks off at you for asking. But now… Yes, I think I believe in everything now."

"Me too." Robyn tips her head back and squints at the sky. "I think I believe in everything, too."

My eyes pop open before the clock on my nightstand has a chance to beep. It's funny how quick the human body can adjust to new things. Like this early wake-up schedule I've established here. I just hope I also adjust back to a normal sleep schedule when we get home. I do not want to wake up before the crack of dawn once there isn't a bakery to bake in.

That would be the worst.

"How did you sleep?" Robyn asks, this time it doesn't surprise me a bit that she's awake. She was still staring at the ceiling and murmuring to herself when I drifted off last night. The hazards of that detective brain, she can't rest until the mystery is solved.

"All right." I yawn and pull on a pair of jeans I snatched from my overflowing suitcase. I don't know if they are clean or not, but I don't really care. There aren't any green bio-hazard fumes coming off of them, so I think I'm good. "How about you?"

"I don't think I slept at all." Robyn swings her legs over the side of her bed. "My mind is like a tornado. Can I come bake with you?"

"You don't want to try and sleep more?"

Robyn shakes her head; I can barely see the movement in the dark room. "I want to move around, stop thinking. This dark room is like a breeding ground for more and more thoughts. I'm running out of places to put them!"

I giggle as I slip on a long sleeve shirt. I think it's my middle school sweatshirt, but I'm not totally positive. "Do this!" I tip my head to the side and shake like I have water in my ear.

Robyn tosses her pillow at me. "I wish that worked; I need a pensive like Dumbledore!"

"Yeah, have you noticed we keep referencing Harry Potter? Like, more than usual?"

Robyn stands up to stretch her arms to the ceiling. With a groan, she lets them fall to her sides and swing there. "Maybe because we listened to the audiobooks on the drive here. That's like a hundred billion minutes of Harry Potter in our heads."

"Exaggerator." I toss her pillow back.

"Learned from the best." She flips the pillow over her shoulder; it rolls off onto the floor on the other side.

Penny peeks her head into the room. "Are you guys awake?"

"Yep."

"Oh good." Penny slips through the crack she made in the door and fumbles with her hands out until she finds Robyn's bed. She perches on the corner.

"Since we're all awake, we can turn on the lights." Robyn laughs.

"Just leave it. We're about to go downstairs anyway." I fumble through the stuff on the vanity table until I find my hairbrush. Or maybe Robyn's? It doesn't matter, we use each other's stuff all the time.

"I was thinking about the clue, the one about wishing."

"We were just talking about that," Robyn says, even though we barely brought the subject up.

"Oh?" Penny stretches her legs in a way that looks inhuman. "I was thinking about all the things people can make wishes on. Obviously, there's lucky clovers, right? Wishing wells, lucky pennies, eyelashes—"

"What?" Robyn interrupts.

"Eyelashes, you know?" She taps her cheek; it must be getting lighter in here because I don't have to super squint to see her. "If one falls on your cheek you get to make a wish."

"I never heard of that." Robyn sounds incredulous. "I wonder if it works? I'd pull them all out right now if that means we figure out what's going on around here."

"I wouldn't risk it," I flip the top of my hair up into a messy bun. The bottom is still too short to stay put, but I'm fine with that. I can't think about growing out my hair without getting overcome by the smell of rotten strawberries.

Yeah, still too soon.

"But I think I figured it out," Penny says, bouncing a little to get our attention back on her. "Have you guys been out back?"

"Uh-huh."

"There's a wishing well. I noticed it when we first got here, but that was before we started looking for clues, so I don't know if it's anything. What do you think?"

I turn a circle so fast I get kind of dizzy and have to steady myself on the vanity chair. When the woozy clears, I skip to Penny and squeeze her face. "You are the bestest little sister in the whole wide universe!"

"Yeah?" Her poochy cheeks try to smile through my hands.

"Yeah." I let go of her face and pat her head twice. "Let's go check it out as soon as we're done helping GG."

"With what?"

"Baking, of course!"

"But it's Thanksgiving..."

Robyn wraps an arm around Penny's shoulder. "There is no rest for the bake horse," she says in a solemn voice.

"Is the bakery open?"

I shake my head. "But we have to make a bu—I mean, *boatload* of pies for GG's friend. Plus, Jojo told me it's tradition to have French toast made from cinnamon buttermilk bread."

"Yes!" Robyn fist pumps. "I forgot about that, let's go, let's go, let's go!"

"Oh." Penny's smile wavers. "Can I come?"

"Of course!" Robyn loops her hand through Penny's arms. "We are practically the three musketeers now. Three clues solving, costume wearing, sassy musketeers."

I open the door for the two of them to pass through, then latch onto Robyn's other arm, "We should have a theme song."

Robyn groans.

"Well," I huff, "then at least a catch phrase." I deepen my voice to sound like the dude who does all movie previews. "Three girls, one desire,"

"Stop!" Robyn shakes her head. "I can't handle this much cheese first thing in the morning!"

Penny giggles.

I let go of Robyn so we can get down the steep stairs without falling to our dooms. I jump the last few and land with an enthusiastic ta-da.

"You are so weird." Robyn brushes by me, swinging my arm back in line with hers.

We have to separate again to get through the kitchen doors, and then it's just awkward to re-hook. But I keep thinking, as I help GG crack eggs for breakfast cinnamon bread, that Robyn is my cousin, Penny is my sister, and sometimes they both make me bonkers. But despite all of their shortcomings, and despite all of mine, we are really real friends now.

All three of us.

And that feels pretty awesome.

Cinnamon Buttermilk Bread

Batter:
1/4 C. Butter, softened
1 C. Sugar
2 Eggs
1 tsp Vanilla extract
2 C. all-purpose Flour
1 tsp Baking Powder
1/2 tsp Baking Soda
1/2 tsp Salt
1 C. Buttermilk

Sugar Layer:
1/4 C. Sugar
1 TBSP Cinnamon

You can eat this right away, spread with butter, or wait a couple days for it to dry out and make French toast. Either way, your taste buds will thank you!

In a stand mixer, beat butter until light and fluffy. This is fun to watch, by the way.

Transformation!

Gradually, add 1 cup sugar. Add eggs one at a time, beating after each addition until everything is combined all happy.

Stir in the vanilla.

Combine flour, baking powder, baking soda, and salt in a separate bowl. It means more dishes but makes it so the dry stuff is all even steven.

And everybody loves even steven.

Add the dry stuff to the creamed mixture alternately with buttermilk. Like, one hand dry, one hand buttermilk, mixer on. Some dry, some buttermilk, some dry, some buttermilk, until both are all in.

Mix just until moistened. Transfer half of the batter to a greased bread pan.

Combine cinnamon and sugar. Sprinkle ¾ over batter. Top with remaining batter and sprinkle remaining cinnamon sugar.

Layers!

Bake at 350° for 40-50 minutes or until a toothpick inserted comes out clean.

Cool for 10 minutes before removing from pan to wire rack to cool the rest of the way.

French Silk Pie

After we finish making breakfast, there is only time to inhale it before GG starts in on the pies.

I melt the chocolate, which I think is the best job in the whole world, while Robyn savors her cinnamon French toast and Penny cracks more eggs into a huge bowl. GG does the pie crusts, because she says they need special handling.

Pie crust is finicky, apparently.

I love how we make food sound like it's human.

Jojo, on the other hand, is a bouncy mess, running from one place to another without really doing anything and my parents, well, they are fired.

After accidentally putting flour into the whipping cream, instead of powdered sugar, because they still can't keep their eyes off each other, GG sent them on a bunch of random errands. I know they are random; GG totally doesn't need nutmeg; I saw a whole huge container of it in the pantry. She sends Bubby along with them to keep them focused.

You know you're in a bad place when a kindergartner is put in charge of you.

GG saves the day again by getting Jojo to fold a huge pile of cardboard pie boxes. This rhythmic chore seems to do the trick. Jojo's eyes aren't swirling like a hypnotized cartoon character anymore.

We work steadily for a long, exhausting time, but then the result is a line of beautiful pies. It makes my soul satisfied to see them.

"One more thing." GG adjusts the neck strap of her apron with a tug, then opens the utensil drawer.

Penny, who had just collapsed into a chair, sits back up, trying to look perky.

GG pulls out five forks and passes them around. "We must taste to make sure they are not poisonous."

Oh, yes!

I take a fork and reach for one of the French silk pies. After inhaling the fumes of chocolatey goodness forever all day, I can't wait to dig in!

"Should we get plates?" Robyn wrinkles her nose at me.

Jojo pauses with a forkful of apple pie almost to her mouth. "No way. Just make sure we're all snatching from the same pies. That way we leave some unscathed for the Slades."

My first bite of French silk pie explodes on my taste buds.

"Oh my gosh," I say thickly, then I quit talking so I can keep shoveling. So good. It's so good.

"Can I try the French silk?" Penny asks.

I want to tell her no way and crouch under a table like Gollum with my own, my pie, my precious, but I muster willpower from somewhere and hand it over. My eyes follow each bite Penny takes until she makes a face and turns her back on me.

I sigh.

"It's good, yes?" GG twinkles at me. "Try the lemon; you like it too, I think."

I take a bite, but it tastes lame. Out of curiosity, I try a bite of every other pie. They all taste lame.

What the heck!

"Oh no!" I drop my fork. "I think I'm cursed or something! The pies don't even taste good."

Jojo's eyebrows furrow. "What do you mean? Did we forget the sugar? I did that with the pumpkin pies a few years ago. It was awful."

I take deep breaths, my hand over my heart to steady myself. "I tried a bite of every single pie after I ate the French silk and they hardly taste good at all. I mean, they taste dim...or something."

Jojo places a hand on each of my shoulders. "Breathe, hon, in and out, you're gonna be fine."

"How do you know?" I wail, I'm pretty sure an ancient family curse just swept through here and stole my taste buds. I can't live without my taste buds. They are uber important.

"Listen, focus on me, Cat. You say you ate the French silk pie first?"

"What?"

She repeats her question slowly.

"Oh, yeah, I ate the French silk first."

Jojo laughs so hard she leans into me. "Babe, you are not broken. Here's the thing." She holds out her hands to command everyone's attention. "Rule Number One: never start with the French silk pie. Never!"

"What?" I ask again.

"It's so good," Jojo says, "it makes everything else taste less good. Eat the others first. Enjoy them. French silk has to come last. Also, that keeps you from eating the whole pie yourself, when you fill up on the other pies first. Not that I would know, of course."

She pulls me in for a tight hug and then starts loading the untouched pies into her baking box masterpieces. "The Slades will be here soon. Let's get the place cleaned up so we can chill for the rest of the day."

I sit down, my knees still knocking together. Good news. My minor freak out seems to have snapped Jojo out of hers. I guess I can be grateful for that. Like, taking one for the team.

Or something.

"You have this figured out GG." Dad pushes back from the table to make room for his protruding belly. It might be illegal, how much food he just put away. "That was excellent! We need to find someone in Boise that we can trade pies for dinner."

"Lovely idea." Mom wipes her mouth with a napkin. "Except I don't make pies."

"Well, Penny and Cat do. They rocked it, put them to work!" Jojo points her fork at us.

GG smiles. "Or, come back to visit us every year."

Now that sounds like the winner to me. I take a second helping of mashed potatoes and gravy, even though I'm pretty full. Not only is it practically a rule to stuff myself on Thanksgiving, but I'm not eating any dessert. I already had my fill of pie for one day.

The picking and chewing gradually slows to a stop, so Jojo brings out the pie. I decide to clear plates and load the massive dishwasher. It only takes me about three minutes because I hardly have to rinse at all, the thing is so powerful it could slap the flower pattern right off the dishes. I really gotta talk to Mom about getting one of these industrial things at home.

When I get back to my seat, I feel the turkey sleepiness set in. My cheek finds its way to Robyn's shoulder, and I watch with half a gaze at the game of MASH she and Penny start on a napkin.

"Two billion." I point, then cover my jaw-cracking yawn.

"That's the kids column." Robyn looks at me.

I nod.

Robyn shakes her head, but writes it in. "You know, if Penny chooses this one and it comes true, she's going to call you to babysit all two billion of those nieces and nephews."

"No way." I yawn, again. "She's going to call Cousin Robyn, the sucker."

Robyn bumps me off her shoulder with a flick to my nose.

"Hey!" I sit up, rubbing the spot until it stops stinging.

"What am I thinking?" Jojo jumps to her feet. "We can't sit here. We have to work on these pumpkin rolls, ladies. I want to practice making them over and over until they are perfect."

"Jolynn," GG tuts, "it is the holiday."

"Yeah, and the bake-off is tomorrow. Seven am. We still haven't decided which kind we like best. We have no time to lose," She claps her hands, "Come on people. The whole future of our bakery depends on how perfect these rolls are."

"But no pressure." Penny giggles under her breath.

I roll myself off the chair to set a good example. I'm not quite upright, but it'll do for now.

Mom and Dad get up, too.

"We're game," Dad says. "Put us to work."

Jojo's smile is a trifle forced, but she recovers quickly. "Yes! Thank you! Let's go!"

We troop into the kitchen, following Jojo like the Pied Piper. I really hope our story turns out better than it did for the kids in that town. Winning this bake-off would be the perfect happy ending. All my sleepiness disappears as these zealous thoughts set in. I'm sure we can do it, save the bakery, and win the day!

Jojo starts barking orders the minute we're all in the kitchen. Most of us look like our eyes were replaced by bowling balls. I didn't know we just joined the Marines.

GG laughs. "Jolynn, relax my child. We work hard for you, but no perfection. Mama always said perfection will kill creation only every time. Let's not kill our bakery today."

Jojo puts her hands on her hips. "Okay fine, no perfection, but hard work, okay? As close to perfect as we can get!"

"Also, fun!" GG reaches for the flour container and tosses some in the air. It settles in her hair and on her shoulders as she reaches for the radio remote to turn on some sassy country music.

Robyn bobs her head.

I tap my feet.

Penny twirls across the kitchen.

My parents tango.

Cringe.

GG tries out a dab - yes, she did do that - and Jojo finally smiles.

"And fun," she concedes. "Let's have some fun making contract winning pumpkin rolls." She swings into a Travolta worthy disco pose.

"That is my girl." GG smiles. "Now, let's get to work."

We become pumpkin roll machines, each person falling into a task. We get so good at it; we could make them in our sleep. In fact, I'm positive Penny dozed off for a moment, but since she's in charge of monitoring Mr. Bojangles, I don't think it was a big deal.

Really, he does most of the work.

"It's ready." Penny pushes the lever to zero so Jojo can scoop out dough. Jojo takes it to an abandoned countertop and starts working her magic. I watch out of the corner of my eye. This is the first time Jojo has really baked since we got here. She hums and sways as she rolls and sprinkles. It's kind of beautiful.

I rub the corner of my eye and get back to measuring and mixing.

The sweet smell of pumpkin fills the air in no time at all. We reach a good stopping place, so Jojo calls us away from our tasks to try out all the rolls. We take one pumpkin one from every batch and try those first.

Not only are they delicious, but I also notice a distinct difference in the texture from when we did the first batch, to the last batch. The dough gets airier and fluffier. I don't know exactly what we did differently, but it totally rocks! I guess Marissa was right when she told me it's not just the ingredients, it's what you do with them that matters.

Although, I still think butter is a very big deal.

"These turned out so good! We nailed it!" Jojo twirls around and around, grabbing Penny to join her. "We have a chance here ladies, we're going to win this thing!"

"And even if we don't," GG's musical voice reminds us, "we are proud we made a new roll."

"Hurray!" Penny throws a handful of napkins in the air.

"How are we going to serve them to the restaurant people?" I wonder. "We never did break the tie."

Jojo pulls me into a hug and squeezes my eyeballs out. "We'll do both! Caramel pecan on some, cream cheese frosting on the others. That will help us stand out, see, we accommodate all palates!"

I have no idea what she just said, but I nod my head and grin like I get it.

"What are we going to do with all of these extra rolls?" Robyn looks at the overflowing table and counter tops. "Should we box them up for the food bank too?"

"Some, yes." GG nods. "The others, we'll deliver to friends. Bridget and Drew can do that, I think."

Jojo shakes her head. "Your faith is astounding, Grammy; they will be too busy smooching, and read all the addresses wrong."

"I resemble that!" Dad flips a towel at Jojo's back.

"It's fair." Mom takes his hand.

I bend over to hide my smile and pick up all the napkins from Penny's celebration. Seriously, I just swept the floor. Kids these days.

"Are you okay dividing these up?" Jojo asks.

GG nods. "Of course, I have all this help,"

"Great!" Jojo claps her hands. "Let's set aside a dozen of the most pretty for tomorrow. I want to call the restaurant and go over the details for the bake-off."

Jojo pulls her cell phone out of her pocket and steps out the back door. I hope she moves away from the trash cans because I noticed the other night that they are getting super stinky.

I put myself in charge of assembling more bakery boxes for GG and Robyn to fill. Penny helps me. Once we get the hang of it, we start a friendly competition to see who can do them the fastest. By friendly, I mean I get several paper cuts and accidentally on purpose knock Penny's elbow to throw her off so I can get my stack done faster.

She gives me an evil glare of sisterly death.

I smile sweetly in return.

We all turn when the back door opens. Jojo bounces in with a grin. "We're all set! We meet at the high school auditorium tomorrow. Seven sharp! I totally can't wait!"

French Silk Pie

Filling:
1/2 C. Sugar
2 Eggs
1 & 1/2 C. semi-sweet Chocolate Chips
1 tsp Vanilla extract
1 C. Heavy Whipping Cream

Topping:
Chocolate curls or shavings - run a potato peeler over the side of a room temperature plain chocolate candy bar!
2 C. Heavy Whipping Cream whipped with 2 TBSP Powdered Sugar

1 baked Pie shell

Combine sugar and eggs in a saucepan over medium heat until liquified and smooth. Continue stirring until they thicken up and reach 160°F.

Remove the whole pan from the heat and stir in chocolate and vanilla. It will take a few minutes for all of the chocolate to melt into velvety goodness.

Let cool all the way while you beat the whipping cream. I do this separately from the topping cream cause it's easier to keep track of. Fold the whipping cream into the chocolate mixture and pour into the prepared crust.

Refrigerate for one hour.

Now beat the cream for the topping with powdered sugar. Cover and refrigerate until pie is set, about an hour, and ready for topping. Spread with whipped cream. Put chocolate curls and/or shavings on top to make it look pretty.

(The difference between a shaving and a curl seems to be how cold the chocolate bar you're using is. The warmer the curlier, the colder the shavier.

Serve right away or keep in the fridge for up to 3 days.

Pshaw, it'll be gone way before then!

21

Bake Off

I sleep in the next morning, GG's orders. She's closing the bakery for the day so we can focus on the bake-off. She said everyone will understand.

And by sleep in, I mean I wake up all bright-eyed at five in the morning.

But that's just enough time to shower, get dressed, and do my hair. I wish I'd brought something bakery professional to wear, but all I have is jeans. At least my shirt has a churro on it.

When Robyn and I walk into the kitchen, it is so still it's eerie. Jojo and GG linger over steaming cups of tea, Mom and Dad still make goo-goo eyes at each other, and Penny stands over the stacks of bakery boxes like a bodyguard. I sort of thought everyone would be headless chickens up in here, but it's so calm.

I guess the hard work is done.

Robyn and I each grab a slice each of leftover cinnamon bread and join the adults at the table.

"Tell me again how this bake-off works?" Robyn tears off a piece of her bread but doesn't eat it.

Jojo sets her cup down with a series of tinkling. I didn't notice until now that her hands are shaking. "It's simple really, we meet at the high school, set up our table and wait for the restaurant owners and chefs to come around and try our rolls. Easy peasy."

"Are we going to decorate the table?" Penny asks.

Jojo freezes, her eyes wide. "Oh! I meant to, I planned… Shoot! I completely forgot about that. What are we going to do? Blaze will have a great display; our rolls are going to look lame on the empty white table all alone!"

"Sometimes less is more," my mom offers.

The corners of Jojo's mouth turn down. "Sometimes more is more."

"We'll take care of it." I'm as surprised as the rest to discover those words came from me. I don't know the first thing about decorating a bake-off table, but I know we can figure it out. I'm pretty sure Robyn, Penny and I can do anything!

"Yes!" Penny fist pumps.

Robyn nods. "We got this Jojo, don't worry."

"But you need supplies…"

"Drew and I will run them to the store."

"It's six-o-clock in the morning." Jojo's voice is dazed.

Dad stands up, his keys jangling from his hands. "There's a Wal-Mart, right? Those are always open."

GG smiles. "Yes, the Wal-Mart is right next to the hospital."

"Got it!" Dad gestures to get us all to follow him.

Once we are settled in the car and Dad has us pointed in the right direction, Mom turns around in her seat,

"All right, girls, what's the plan?"

Nothing.

Silence.

Crickets.

"You probably want a tablecloth." Mom encourages us with her eyes.

"And decorations," Dad adds.

"Pick a color scheme, so everything coordinates."

"Pink!" I blurt. "Pink, for sure."

Mom nods. "While normally I am in favor of pink, it's Fall, and the rolls are pumpkin."

"Orange, maybe?" Robyn says.

Ew.

"What do you think, Penny?" Mom smiles at my gremlin face then turns to my sister.

"Um." She shoots sidelong glances at Robyn and me. "Whatever you guys decide is fine with me."

I point my finger at her. "Do you have an idea?"

"Not if you guys do." Penny bites her lip.

I elbow Robyn. "Then, we got nothing. Zip. Zilch."

"*Nada.*"

Penny's eyes narrow just a little. "Are you sure?"

"Positive." I nod once. "If you don't help us, we will fail dismally."

And without further ado, Penny talks our ears off the whole rest of the drive and doesn't stop until we're in the party section of Wal-Mart.

Know what else?

Her ideas are fantastic!

"Hey, Kitty Cat," Mom pulls me aside while Dad helps Robyn and Penny unload the cart at checkout. "I just have to say thank you for how you've been treating your little sister this week. It makes me so happy to see the two of you get along like this."

"Penny's cool, Mom."

Mom laughs. "I know that! I'm just glad you know that now, too.".

I snuggle into Mom's side as she wraps her arm around me.

"How do you think we're doing?" Her voice is muffled into my hair. "With our deal to be good for anything? Do you think we're surviving?"

I twist my neck to look at her. "I wish you'd told me sooner why you hate baking."

Mom sighs. "I wish I had too. In fact, I wish I'd done a lot of things differently. I wish I'd been wiser; I wish Jojo and I hadn't fought; I wish I hadn't quit baking; I wish I'd brought you back here before now; I wish I realized sooner that family is the most important thing..."

"Fruit kabobs, that's a lot of wishes!"

"And a lot of regrets." Mom sighs again.

I twist one of my bracelets around my wrist, "You know you can let all that go now, right? Jojo doesn't think baking emotions is a big deal, she totally tried to do it too."

"Yeah." Mom looks over her shoulder to see how the others are doing. We bought a ton of stuff; they are still loading it onto the belt. "I think that's my fault, actually; I set a horrible example for her."

I know we don't have much time before we have to go, but I can't ignore an opening like that. "What did you guys fight about exactly?"

Mom gives me a long look. "I'm surprised you took so long to ask; I was starting to think I might not ever have to tell you about it."

"Ha!" I point at her.

She mimics, right back at me, so amazingly that it's like looking in a mirror.

An older, taller mirror with glasses, but whatever.

I giggle. "Will you tell me what happened, Mommy Mom Mom? I really want to know."

She looks over her shoulder again. "They're almost done."

"*Please.*"

Mom brushes a lock of hair out of my face and tucks it behind my ear. "Okay, okay, I'll tell you."

I cheer inside, but don't make a peep. I don't want to distract her.

"Jojo helped me make that cake for your dad, but she didn't know I was putting feelings into it. Back then, she felt really strongly about only baking happy, so when she found out, she was the maddest I have ever seen her. I avoided her for as long as I could, but she wrote me a note"—Mom pauses to take a long breath—"It stung. That girl is good with words. But the thing that stung most was that everything she said about me was true."

"Bridge!" Dad calls to us, his arms full of bags.

"Go on, we'll be right behind you!" Mom waves, then leans toward me to whisper. "I was angry. More than that though, I was ashamed of what I had done. Horrified. And it was too late to change anything. Your dad and I got married right after graduation, moved away and never came back."

"And you never even talked to Jojo again?"

Mom threads her arm through mine and steers us toward the exit, taking small steps. "Never. I called GG every once in a while, and you know your Granny Penny came to visit sometimes, but I couldn't with Jojo. It's funny, the anger wore off quickly, but the fear and shame hung on tight. I couldn't face her."

I hug her arm, squeezing it like I can wring out all the sad feelings. "But it's okay now? You and Jojo...all of it...right?"

Mom's smile is a little wavery. "Yes. ma'am, it is okay now. I guess all we needed to do was see each other to realize the past is the past."

"Too bad we didn't try that sooner." I move to take my mom's hand and swing it as we walk into the cool morning air.

"It is too bad." Mom sounds sad again but tries to perk herself up. "Anyway, thank you so much for including your sister this week. You are becoming the person I wish I had been at your age."

I let those words warm me up. I'm going to carry them with me this whole long day, like a good luck charm. This is all going to work out, I know it.

"What do you think?" Penny stands back to survey her word with a critical eye.

The table is all white and silvery with some kind of paper stuff that makes the top look like an iced over lake. She made pine trees out of baby pinecones and somehow constructed a raccoon over a tiny fire roasting marshmallow. Our rolls are arranged on two white cake pedestals, with the rest under the table where we can cut more samples. These on top are just for show.

It's beautiful.

I put my arm around Penny and squeeze her guts out. I have no words.

"We're ready." Jojo adjusts her white baking jacket and steps behind the table. Her straight back and smile make her seem so professional, like a real baker.

I mean, I know she's a real baker, but now she looks like it.

"We're going to walk around." Mom takes Dad's hand. "I'm too antsy to stand here and wait."

"We'll go, too!" Penny takes Bubby's hand, just in time to pull him away from the rolls on the pedestals.

Robyn bounces from one foot to the other. "I can't stand the suspense either. I'll go with you."

"Me, too." GG takes Robyn's hand so she will stop wringing her own.

"Are you all leaving me?" Jojo's eyes get wide, transforming her from professional to five years old.

I shake my head. "I'll stay."

Jojo's smile makes it obvious I made the right decision. We watch the others leave and I don't know about Jojo, but my heart is racing.

"Are you ready for this?" I whisper.

"Ready as I'll ever be."

"What happens if we lose?"

Jojo's voice shakes. "Then we lose."

"That's it?"

"Listen." Jojo looks at me, her brown eyes so much like mine it's kind of creepy. "We worked our heinies off and made a dang good product. If they don't like it, their loss. We will be fine."

"But what if Jake wins?" I say the thing that has really been bothering me this whole time.

"Then Jake wins."

"But—"

"We will be fine." Jojo squeezes my hand tighter. "They're coming,"

We put smiles on our faces and make polite talk with the judges. They each try each one of our pumpkin cinnamon rolls. I totally can't tell if they like them, other than the fact that they are chewing and swallowing instead of gagging and spewing.

Right about now I start wishing for that gauge thing on the side of our neck that tells people what we're feeling. I'd trade it showing all my secrets, even the embarrassing ones, to know what those judges are thinking right now.

They thank us and walk away, making notes on their clipboards.

Jojo lets out a huge gust of air and leans against the wall. "I'm so glad that's over. I totally have to use the bathroom. You okay if I step out for a minute?"

"I'm good," I say absently. My attention is fixed on the judges.

At the next table.

Jake's table.

His decorations aren't as good as ours, but then, no one's are. When I scoped out the competition earlier, I determined that this thing comes down to us and Jake. That might not have been the case if Blaze actually showed up, but he called in sick and it looks like an off day for the cinnamon rolls at Great Buns.

But whatever it is Jake's serving, some kind of hand pie or turnover thing, looks amazing.

I already know he's a good baker. If we lose this thing, it will be to him. And I can't stand the thought of that.

My heart sinks as I watch the judges' faces light up. One asks for seconds. They chat with Jake for way longer than they did with us.

Crap.

As the judges turn to leave, Jake catches my eye. His satisfied smile slowly disappears, like someone pulls it down with string. His eyes move from the judges' backs to my face, to his table. He reaches forward and snags one of the judges by the elbow.

They all lean in close for whisper time.

What I wouldn't give to be a button on one of their jackets.

That is, if buttons could hear and talk and process important information.

Jojo comes back just as the judges reach their microphone. She grabs my hand in a vice grip.

"We want to thank you all for coming. There is no doubt in any of our minds that the White Mountains are brimming with baking talent. Unfortunately, we can only choose one of you, so, the winner is..."

Jojo hisses a sharp breath inward.

I close my eyes.

"L'Amour Bakin'."

Applause breaks the silence. My eyes flutter open. Everything seems to be moving in slow motion.

Wait, what?

"We did it!" Jojo squeezes my shoulders, taking me up and down with her. "We did it!!" She rushes to the judges to shake their hands and say thank you about a bazillion times.

I can't stop looking at Jake. He claps the hardest and the loudest, a huge grin on his face. I know I should be excited. I know I should be thrilled. But I'm not, something squeezes my insides like a lemon juicer.

"You okay, Cat?" Robyn puts a hand on my shoulder.

I didn't see my family come back into the room. I try to smile. "Sure, isn't this great?"

Her head drops to the side as she watches me with narrowed eyes.

The judges start to leave, everything is winding down, while I'm still frozen in place. My brain moves like thick chocolate fudge.

Penny takes a bunch of pictures of our table with mom's phone. As the room clears out, and the excitement fizzles, Jojo finally notices Jake. Her lips curl into an evil grin.

Uh-oh.

I want to do something to stop her, but I can't. I just stand and watch like a nincompoop.

"So, Jake, did you notice we won?" Jojo cups her hands to shout, her words bounce back from the ceiling like fairy bells.

Evil ones.

Jake tips his hat. "Yes, ma'am. Congratulations, Jojo, you deserve it."

She lowers her arms; her face hardens as she stalks over to his table. "Now it's obvious who has the best bakery in the White Mountains. This is proof."

"I never doubted it." Jake lowers his hand to hook a thumb on his belt loop.

Her mouth works, but no words come out for a while. Finally, she blurts out, "Yeah, well, now you'll never forget it!" She tosses her sassy head and takes long strides away from Jake.

When she gets closer to Robyn and me, she flings her arms out. "You guys, we did it! Let's celebrate!"

They all carry the boxes of decorations and leftover rolls away, laughing and talking. The clamor bounces off the walls and swirls around my head, pounding like trays of macarons on the counter.

It takes, like, forever for the noise to fade away, and then it leaves me with a weird buzzing in my brain.

Also, the world's most ginormous headache.

"Cat?"

I shake my head at Robyn without responding and walk to Jake. When he looks up, his shoulders tense.

"Howdy, girls."

"What did you do?" My whisper is hoarse.

"Pardon?"

"What did you say to the judges?"

"Now, Cat, I believe that's between me and the judges."

"I know you did something... What was it?"

Jake tips his hat again, just for me this time. "Congratulations on your victory; the best bakery has won. Excuse me." He squeezes by and disappears.

I rub the goosebumps on my arms, but none of them go away.

"Come on." Robyn pulls me after her but doesn't ask me anymore questions.

I'm super grateful; I don't have any answers.

Back at the bakery, we order way too much pizza and eat way too much ice cream while we sit around the kitchen reliving every part of the bake-off.

Eventually, everyone leaves to do other things. Even Robyn goes to take a nap.

Soon, it's just Jojo and I. She stands up and stretches her arms high over her head.

"I feel like I've lost a zillion pounds." She grins. "Now that it's over, that bake-off thing was kind of fun, huh?"

"Yeah."

"Yeah. Well, I'm going to give Debbie a call. I'll be right back."

"Who's Debbie?" I gnaw the crust of my pizza just for something to do. It's all stale, kind of like chewing on deliciously seasoned tree bark.

"The restaurant owner. Now that we've won, I can start coordinating details with her. Man, I feel so much better! what are you going to do, Cat?"

"Finish my pizza, I guess."

She's already walking away with her phone out. I pull mine out, too, looking at it. It's my turn to email Tobey, but I can't think of anything to say. Just like GG told me the other day, if I say anything, I will say too much. I mean, how can I sum up the last few days into a breezy email?

I can't; it's impossible.

Ugh.

This emotional baking business is exhausting.

I clear my place at the table, wiping crumbs, and then take my dish to the sink. As I rinse it off, I hear a shuffle behind me.

"Jojo?"

She walks back into the kitchen. Well, walk is a relative term. She drags back into the kitchen with slumped shoulders and sagging eyebrows.

I drop my dish with a clatter. "What's wrong?"

Jojo holds out her phone like it will tell me what happened. It doesn't. I don't care how cool technology is, it still can't do stuff like that.

Her eyes stop on me. "I just got off the phone with Debbie."

"Yeah?"

"Well,"—Jojo leans into the counter—"she told me she's happy to have our business."

"That's good news?" I can't help but add the question mark; Jojo doesn't make it look like good news.

"She also said the judges were leaning toward choosing Jake until he withdrew his name and his bakery from the competition."

"Jake?" That tingly feeling I had at the bake-off starts up again. "Why did he do that?"

"She didn't know." Jojo tucks her phone in her back pocket. "She didn't tell me anything else, but I'm going over there to talk to him."

"Right now?"

Jojo twists her pinkie ring around her finger. "I have to. If I don't go right now, I'll lose my moxie. Will you go with me?"

"Absolutely."

I shoot a quick text to my mom to explain, then leave with Jojo. We walk in silence, both of us burdened by our own thoughts. I'm surprised a few minutes later when we stop in front of a small brown house. I guess I didn't realize Jake lives so close to us.

But then, maybe everything is close in a small town.

Jojo lets go of my hand at the door and stops to take some deep cleansing breaths. I wish there was time to bake her calm cookies, but she's going to have to do this one on her own.

With me for back up obviously.

Jojo knocks, moving from side to side while we wait. I really hope he's home, this much nervous energy with no way to resolve it might erupt into sprinkles before our eyes.

Luckily, Jake answers the door right away. When he sees us, a weird look comes over his face for just a second, before he masks it with a pleasant smile. "Well, howdy, ladies. What can I do for you today? I'm just on my way to dinner with the fam."

Jojo stutters. "Are you going to Phoenix right now?"

"No." Jake leans on the door jamb. "They came here. We're having a family dinner at the bakery."

"Oh." Jojo just stands there.

It is seriously awkward.

Jake finally breaks the silence with a throat clearing. "Did you need something?"

Jojo isn't quite capable of speech yet, and I'm not much better, but I do manage to croak out. "We wanted to say thank you."

"For what?" Jake looks so blank I start to wonder if we are confused, and he didn't drop the competition for us. If that's the case, this is about to get all uncomfortable up in here.

I mean, more than it already is.

Right when I'm about to deploy my ninja vanish distraction technique, Jojo finally finds her voice. "Debbie, she told me about the judges and the bake-off..."

Jake shifts to his other foot and runs his thumb along the side of the door without looking at us.

Jojo steps forward. "Did you drop out, Jake? Did you really do that?"

He tugs on the collar of his shirt. "Debbie wasn't supposed to say nothing."

"But then, you did?"

His ears get red, sending splotches down his neck. "Yes."

"Why?"

Another unbearable pause makes me squirmy. It takes Jake a long time to meet Jojo's eyes. When he does, his whole stance softens. "Because I know this account is important to you. I wanted you to have it."

Jojo looks at him, as though searching for something he isn't telling her. After a minute she groans. "That was really, really nice of you, Jake. I don't deserve it; I was so awful to you. I am so sorry."

He ducks his head. I swear, if he says 'aw shucks', I'm going to run away screaming, but even as I think this, another thought worms its way in.

What Jake did for Jojo, that was way cool.

Maybe he isn't such a horrible person?

Jojo reaches her hand closer to Jake, moving very slowly. He lifts his own hand and touches the tips of her fingers lightly. I suck in a sharp breath. Yeah, we all know what happened last time they tried to shake hands.

Jojo swallows hard and places her palm against Jake's, then wraps her fingers around his hand. After a moment, she looks up. "Thank you."

Jake's eyes glisten, he squeezes her hand, his knuckle turning light pink. "You're most welcome, Jojo."

And then the world explodes.

<h1 style="text-align:center">22</h1>

Pretzel Bites

J ust kidding.

That doesn't happen.

I kind of think it should, because Jake and Jojo shaking hands is pretty epic.

And awesome.

But the world doesn't actually explode.

They just smile at each other for longer than is comfortable for the teen observing, that would be me, then we leave.

Jojo looks up at the sky and takes a deep breath. "Thanks for going with me, girl." She puts an arm around me and pulls me close.

"No prob, bob." I skip over a crack in the sidewalk so I don't break my mother's back.

"Look, that cloud looks like a star." Jojo points. "We should make a wish."

"I don't think it works like that." I squint at the cloud.

Also, I think it looks more like a platypus.

Jojo laughs. "Hey, we never pass up a perfectly good wish!"

We stop walking and close our eyes to make a wish. I don't know about her, but I really wish for nothing. Seriously. Right now, at this moment, I feel like I have everything in the world.

Wait!

"Jojo!" I clap my hand over my forehead, blinking my eyes. Going from closed eyes to bright sun is not good. I still see blotches in the corners.

"What is it?"

"I just thought of something super important. We're leaving tomorrow and we haven't turned in our clues! We haven't heard the story of Evie and the bakery!"

Jojo smiles, ruefully, "There has been a lot going on."

"Yeah, but what if we don't find out everything about everything before we leave? What if we never find out why we are a bunch of weirdos?" My heart speeds up. "We have to get back to the bakery right now! I did not come all this way for nothing!"

I grab her hand and pull her like a tow truck towards the bakery. When the cute, old building is finally in sight, I bolt the rest of the way. GG better be done with her nap! I am completely patient-less.

Luck is with me, she's in the kitchen.

Baking.

Of course.

"GG! I think we found all your clues; will you tell us everything now?"

"Oh my! You startled me." She places a hand over her heart. "What's that?"

"We figured out the clues, and we're leaving tomorrow, and I have to know everything!"

GG laughs. "Well then, you shall. Jolynn, be a dear and gather the family so I only have to say this story one time? I believe everyone will want to hear."

"On it."

GG flips a hunk of dough into a humongous bowl. "That can rest while we visit." She washes her hands and walks to the table with a towel.

I sit next to GG.

She dries her hands and folds the towel neatly in front of her. "Do you enjoy the hunt of the scavenger?"

"Yes." I nod. "It was way fun. Thank you for doing it for me."

"My pleasure. Tell me the clues you find."

Even without Robyn's notebook of power, I remember everything. "The bakery thermometer, Evie's grave, the moon clock at Jake's, and the last one with something about wishes. Penny thinks it's the wishing well in the backyard."

"Well done, you! You find them all." GG rests her elbow on my shoulder as she runs her fingers through my hair, front to back, in a gentle rhythm.

A herd of elephants' thumps into the kitchen. My troop of favoritest people in the whole entire world. Their voices hush as they find seats around GG. No one says a word, every pair of eyes fix on GG, waiting.

She smiles at us all. "Hello, my dear family."

A round of hellos and a squeaky howdy from Bubby answer her. GG sends him a wink before going on. She also starts brushing my hair with her fingers again. It's totally making me sleepy, but I fight the heavy eyelids, there is no way I'm missing this.

"The girls worked so hard this week to find clues for me to tell you this story. About my mama. I never tell this story to any soul." GG's eyes find their way to Jojo. "She asked me to keep to myself until the time is right, and today, I think it is right. But please, do not tell this to anyone. Few will believe you and even less will understand."

This sounds like the perfect place for a solid round of dun dun duns. I realize I'm holding my breath and let it go slowly. Passing out would be super inconvenient right now.

"As you all know, our family has the gift, a way to bake happy so that others can be happy too. What you do not know, I think, is how this came to be. That is what I will tell you today."

"Finally!" Robyn squeals, then covers her mouth with her hands. "Sorry, I will be quiet now." She keeps her hands there in case her excitement makes more words leak out.

GG chuckles, a low, soothing sound, and resumes combing through my hair. "Evie Grace, my mama, lived long ago in a small village in France. Her papa owned a bakery that became more popular as his daughter became more beautiful. There is no better way to bring in the customer man than delicious food and a pretty face." GG taps the side of her nose.

"Here-here," my dad says, lifting his and Mom's hands.

I exchange eye rolls with Penny.

For reals, how long is this going to last?

"You see!" GG now points at my parents, nudging me with a wink. "Though, for a young girl, this much attention is not so good. My mama, she taught me when I was very young to bask in such attention, but do not inhale. It finds the way straight to your head."

GG mimes her head inflating to show us what a bloated ego can do. Bubby gets the giggles so bad, Jojo pulls him in her lap and smothers him with kisses until he stops.

"She knows this because, when she was only fourteen, there were many of the men vying for her hand. And she let it go to her head."

I'm not sure what vying means, but if it has anything to do with getting married at that age, I'm out. That is disgusting.

GG laughs at mine and Robyn's faces. "It is a different time you see. What is common then is not for now. And even though it is, how do you say it? Acceptable to marry so young, my grand papa did not think anyone good enough for his baby girl. None of the suitors were accepted, but still they came. By the time Evie was sixteen, she had almost every young man in the village desperately in love with her."

Desperately?

I wonder if that's the same as madly.

"Mama, she was just happy to do the flirting. She loved the attention, not so much the men."

I suddenly get the squirms.

GG places a hand on my shoulder, her eyes full of love. "She just loved the people. Sometimes, she did not know she was flirting. She just loved the people, attention, and fun."

It's like I'm sitting on a porcupine. I know GG's not talking about me, but it totally feels like she's talking about me! Until I got this super crush on Tobey a few months ago, I just really liked the flirting too. Sometimes I even played with guys' feelings. I didn't really realize what I was doing, I just thought it was fun.

Now, I think I'm the worst.

Suddenly, I don't feel so good.

"One of the customers who came most to the bakery was the son of the local miller, a young man named Nathaniel. I say young, but to Evie, he was so old." GG's eyes crinkle. "Twenty-six is ancient to eighteen. This Nathaniel loved her so much he could not convince himself to stay away, though he was poor and not so handsome as others. Mama told me he thought she was in love with him. Why else would she smile the way she smiled at him? Love can make us blind, and he only saw what he wanted to see. He thought she must love him as he loved her.

GG shakes her head. "After a year of penny buns and profiteroles, he convinced himself to ask for her hand."

"Why did he want her hand?" Bubby wrinkles his face. "That's gross."

"It means he wanted her hand in marriage, he wanted to marry her," Jojo explains.

Bubby makes a worse face. "That's grosser."

GG smiles. "In those days, a young man went to the father of the woman to ask for her hand. But Nathaniel traveled much, all over the province, delivering the flour, and he had modern ideas. He wanted to ask her himself, in a romantical way. He decided to wait until the Harvest Moon Celebration. When Mama stepped outside away from the fires, Nathaniel was there waiting.

Without any warning, overcome by her beauty, he fell to his knees and begged for her to be his wife."

"Ew!" Bubby squeaks.

Robyn, Penny, and I shush him.

"Mama had no idea he felt this way. She told him no, she would not marry him. Nathaniel asked again. Again, she said no. She did not love him, and she yearned for love in the marriage.

"She tried to explain this to Nathaniel, but he did understand. He said she can grow to love him if she wants. She did not agree. Where a heart full of anticipation once was, Nathaniel's heart grew cold. Then hot. Love morphed into anger and he said many things he couldn't take away.

"Mama's temper flared, the two hissed horrible things to each other until they ran out of breath. Then, Nathaniel stormed away. Mama wanted nothing more than to go in her room and cry until the pain was gone, but there was much to do at the bakery. With an air of dejection, she served customers, who missed her smiles, and cleaned without seeing what she did. When her family went to bed, she took a long walk into the woods.

"On the bridge, over the stream, Mama paused. Nathaniel poisoned this night for her. She did not know she could be so unkind. It hurt her heart to think of it. But she also blamed him. Who was this miller's boy to ask to marry her? He was old, so very old. She never gave him a reason to think she would like to marry him.

"What was she to do now? She could not go about her normal days. She could not accept the flour delivery as though nothing happened. And even more troubling was the thought that maybe all the men in the village believed as Nathaniel did, that she loved them and wanted to marry them.

"The harvest moon peeked into the corner of the river where she was. Mama watched the reflection as it rose over the lake, getting more and more agitated. Why did Nathaniel speak? Why could he not keep his feelings to himself? Why did he not think of her, instead of asking for what only he wanted. Why?

"And then, in a burst of feeling, raised her voice to the sky and wished he understood how she felt. She slumped down to the bridge and there she stayed until her father found her and carried her home.

"In the morning, she woke, ready to believe all that happened the night before was a horrible dream. With a cheery heart, she baked bread while her mama rolled the dough for pastry. The day went on, customers came and went. She noticed, those who eat her bread are happy. Very cheerful and friendly. But she thinks no more of it, people in her village are happy people.

"Not many days later, Mama's darling dog was found dead in the yard. She raised Chien from a puppy. Her heart was broken. When Mama baked buns that morning she noticed the change. Those who ate the buns, left with their feet dragging, their faces full of sorrow. Those who came happy, left feeling the sorrow she felt.

"This was when she knew something happened, something changed. She tested her theory in simple ways and discovered that what she felt when she baked, was what others felt when they ate.

"She knew just what to do! This was a blessing! She baked lace cookies full of forgiveness, but when she took them to the mill, she learned

Nathaniel left France, not to return. At this moment, she saw she could not fix what happened. It almost broke her heart all over again. This is when she vowed to spend her life baking for others to be happy. Never again did she experiment, only happy feelings for her. This is what she taught me, so I do not bake if I'm not happy. I know what this can do. I teach my Penelope to only bake when happy, but she does not listen." GG shakes her head.

"Wait, what?" Jojo looks up. "Mom bakes?"

"When she was younger. But she, like Cat, has too many strong feelings—it never went well for her. Instead of only baking happy, she chose not to bake at all."

"So..." I have a sinking feeling I'm trying to keep afloat. "Then, everyone can do what I do. All of us can bake strong emotions." I shouldn't feel so devastated, but really, I thought I was special. I kind of liked that thought.

GG holds up a finger. "Not all. You see. I tried to bake a different emotion. I was curious. But nothing happened. I can only bake to make others happy."

"I wonder if that's the same for me?" Jojo says. "When I tried to do something else, it didn't work."

"How many times have you tried to bake other than happy?" Robyn asks, her detective mode flaring up.

Jojo shrugs. "Just the one time, for Jake. But, like I said, it didn't work. So, maybe I can only bake happy?"

"That's how it works for Marissa," Mom says.

I don't have a chance to ask my question, Robyn does it for me. "Why is it different for Cat, then?"

GG purses her lips to hide a smile, but I can see it in her eyes. "My dear child, I say what I say with all the love in my heart. It is only my thought, I believe those with nature so much like Mama, will bake the emotions like her."

"The nature..."

I don't get it.

Robyn's eyes light up, she too tries to hide a smile but is super unsuccessful. "Are you saying the reason Cat bakes so powerfully is 'cause she's a super big flirt like Evie?"

"Hey!" I sit up, pushing my seat back without meaning to.

That's not what it means, is it?

GG places a hand on my back. "I would say again, those with the people-loving, fun-filled nature of my mama are those who can bake most like her."

My mom groans, her head dropping into her palm.

Dad squeezes her shoulders. "It's okay honey, you're married now. Your raging flirt days are behind you."

She slaps at his hands, and I think maybe their second honeymoon is over.

I wrinkle my face, wishing for a comeback to defend myself and my mom. "Well, that explains why you can't do it," I hurl at Robyn.

I have terrible aim, apparently, because she crosses her arms and sits back with a satisfied smile. "Yes, it does."

My whole brain comes together, working to think of something I can say that will wipe that stupid smile off Robyn's face. Not that I want her to feel bad about not baking emotions, I just don't want *her* to make *me* feel bad about being able to do it.

And, also, I sort of hoped the reason I can do what I do would be something cooler. I mean, for realsies, I bake strong emotions because I like to flirt with boys?

What's that about?

Although maybe I should be grateful. Maybe I would rather be a raging flirt if it means I have the ability to bake emotions.

Maybe.

I don't know yet.

GG claps her hands and I come out of my thoughts long enough to realize the whole family is chattering to one another, filling the kitchen with echoes of voices both interested and upset.

"This is a lot to take in." GG rests her sympathetic eyes on me.

"A lot." Jojo nods.

"What say we fill our bellies with pretzel bites to help us think this through?"

Timed to perfection, the oven timer beeps.

Pretzel Bites

Dough:
4 & 1/2 C. Flour
1 tsp Salt
1 tsp Sugar
2 TBSP Yeast
2 C. hot tap Water

Dip-Dip:
1 C. very hot Water
1/4 C. Baking Soda

In a stand mixer, pour in tap water, sugar and yeast. Give the mixture a little spin and let it rest for 10 minutes to foam up.

Add flour, a little bit at a time to form a soft, smooth dough that cleans up the sides and bottom of the bowl. This means it's ready and is awesome because it also practically did the dishes for you.

Knead in the mixer or, if you're a rockstar, by hand, for 4-5 minutes until the dough is soft and stretchy.

Cover and rise for an hour.

Preheat the oven to 500°F. Whoa nelly, that's hot! It's okay, I promise it will all work out! This high heat makes the pretzels super brown on the outside and soft on the inside.

Super cool, yeah?

No, actually it's super hot.

Line two cookie sheets with parchment paper.

Dump the dough onto your counter, after you sprinkle flour all over it, and cut the dough into four strips. Then cut each strip into 8 pieces.

Bites, see?

Whisk the dip-dip ingredients together until the baking soda dissolves.

Dip each pretzel bite in the baking soda mix. Dip-dip! Get it? Shake each one before you put it on the parchment paper to get rid of extra water.

Rest for 10 minutes or so.

That was a lot of work!

Now, bake the pretzels for 7-8 minutes until golden brown.

When they come out of the oven, brush them with melted butter and sprinkle with coarse salt. You don't have to do this part, but believe me, you want to!

You do!

23

Baking Right

Cat Anderson (kittycat14@email.com)   November 26ᵗʰ, 7:36 a.m.

To: Tobey

Dear Tobey,

I'm sorry I didn't write back forever and a day and a half! Things got straight up kooky dukes here. I'll have to tell you about it when I see you at school on Monday. I took a bunch of pictures of all the things that I baked so I can make you drool over each one. Aren't you lucky?

Don't you think this break went by soooooooooo fast?

I hope you had a good Thanksgiving, though! I totally did, mostly because I discovered French silk pie. I think you would love it!

So, we did go scope out the bakery competition, I'll tell you all about that and the bake-off. It did not go the way I expected. It's a long story.

I'm sorry Conner ate your cinnamon roll. That kid really loves to steal your stuff! But the good news is, we invented pumpkin cinnamon rolls for the bake-off. I'll make them for you and you can tell me which kind you like better!

I can't wait to come home!

But I'm also sad to leave.

I'm not telling Robyn, because I gave her a super hard time about all her goodbyes, but I want to do the same thing. In the last week, I've put down some roots in this bakery, pulling them up is going to sting a little.

I especially want to spend a minute or two with Mr. Bojangles. After all these mornings together, I really think we have something.

But when I get downstairs, narrowly missing my mom, I can hear GG moving around in the kitchen. I'm not quite ready to see her yet, so I run my hand along the top of the cash register and then down the counter. When I reach the end, I see sticky notes.

Perfect!

I scribble a note to the family, zip up my hoodie and slip out the back door so I don't have to worry about the bell on the front. My feet know exactly where to go, so I let them lead me, while I hug my arms to my chest to keep out the chill. Even with the sun out, it's still cold enough to make clouds with my breath.

About halfway up the hill to end all hills, I finally beat the chill and have to unzip my jacket. As I pass thousands of trees, I laugh to myself about that first day when we came here, and Robyn said Evie was next to a tree. I go straight to her grave.

I remember the bench.

Under the tree.

The sun winks off the corner of her gravestone as I plop into the stiff, frosty grass. I squint at the words etched into the stone and trace each one with my finger.

"We're going home today." I say quietly. There's no one around, so I'm not all that concerned about looking like a loony. But, even if there was a boatload of people milling all over the place, I would still talk to Evie.

I've come a long way, baby.

"I'm going to miss the bakery. Even the getting up early part. I'm glad you brought it here, from France. This place is pretty great, and I love the bakery. Maybe I'll come back and work with Jojo when I'm done with school. If I do, I promise I'll bring you fresh flowers every day."

I brush leaves away from her headstone. My hand stops, hovering above the encroaching grass. I gaze at the words that disappear into it and without making the decision, my fingers pull at the grass. It's really stuck on there, but I don't stop, even though my fingers ache with cold.

After one last, mighty yank, I clear all the grass away. I knew there were more words, I could feel it when we were here before. But what they say means something different to me now then it would have then. So maybe it's a good thing I didn't see them until today.

Maybe everything happens for a really good reason.

I wipe the last of the dirt out of the way and whisper Evie's words out loud.

"I will bake things right again."

My voice catches on the last word, tears come from nowhere and splatter the words. "Oh Evie, I'm sorry. I'm so sorry. I wish you could have resolved things with Nathaniel. I wish you could have left with peace. But you know what? It's okay, cause I'm going to bake things right again for you. From now on, I'm not going to bake for selfish reasons. I'll do everything I can to be like you. I'll bake people happy and serve and stop giving Robyn such a hard time when she volunteers us for stuff. Keep an eye on me Evie. I'm going to finish what you started."

"You know, they have a term for people who talk to themselves."

I scramble to my feet, wiping my eyes with the sleeve of my hoodie.

On the path behind me, is Jake.

"I wasn't talking to myself." I sniff.

"No?" He lifts an eyebrow.

"No, I was talking to my great-great-great-great-great-great grammy Evie Grace." I'm super flustered, so I think I went a little overboard on the greats.

A smile tickles Jake's cheeks. "You didn't let me finish. Do you want to know what the term is?"

"Sure, okay." I hug my arms together to keep out the chilly morning wind.

Jake shifts the flowers he's holding from one hand to the other. "I was going to say, those who talk to themselves, in graveyards especially, are considered very...wise."

What?

I shake my head. "That's not a thing; you made that up."

"Maybe, but only so I feel better when I do it."

"Who are you visiting?" I look around as if his ancestor is going to leap out and show himself to me.

"My daddy." Jake gestures to a spot just down from where we stand.

"Oh." I suddenly don't know what to do with my hands. It's one thing to visit the grave of a great great great, it's another thing altogether to visit the grave of your dad. "I'm sorry."

"It's okay." Jake shrugs. "I spent a lot of years with him, working at the mill. We're good. It's the way of the world, right? Anyway, I like to keep his flowers fresh, have a little chat every day. Keeps me grounded."

"That's really nice." I give Jake a smile in return. "And you know what else is really nice?"

"Hm?"

"Backing out of the restaurant bake-off for Jojo. That was really nice."

A grin bursts across Jake's face. "Well, I'm a pretty nice guy, you know."

I roll my eyes. "Sure. The nicest guys are the ones that tell you all about it themselves."

"Exactly, Ms. Cat," He adjusts his hat as the sun makes new shadows. "I was happy to do it. *L'Amour Bakin'* is great, and Jojo, well, I'm glad she can stop all that worrying."

"Me too." It was super fun to see Jojo dance around the kitchen and bake again. "We're leaving today. I mean, in an hour or so."

"Are you?" Jake frowns theatrically. "Well, that's too bad. Just when we were beginning to get along."

I roll my eyes again, this time with gusto. "Whatever. You'll be nice to Jojo though, right? I'm going to miss her." My voice chokes on the last words. I have to change the subject or I'm going to start bawling all over again, right here in front Jake.

Great lasting memory.

"Is all your family here, in Arizona?" I blurt. It is the only thing I can think to say while I'm willing the tears to dissolve before they can roll down my cheeks.

Jake scratches his cheek. "No. My mama and sisters live in the Valley, but my grand-daddy lives in Idaho, near my brother."

"Your brother?" I chew on the words for a minute. I feel like there's something important about that, something Robyn and I were talking about. But it's as slippery as Bubby when he spilled a huge bottle of olive oil over his head.

"Yeah, my big brother lives in Boise."

An alarm goes off in the back of my mind. Like my morning clock when I forget to hit snooze. "I live in Boise." I say slowly, thoughts hovering in my mind.

"Yeah? I think I might have heard that. Nathan has a boy that's probably your age."

"Nathan?"

Jake chuckles. "I'd ask if you know him, but then you'll think I'm one of those small-town guys who assumes everyone lives in a place where you know all your neighbors by first, last, and middle name."

I swallow around the thing suddenly stuck in my throat. "Yeah, that would be supes embarrassing. What's your nephew's name?"

"Ah now, he got wrangled with the family name, that makes him the fourth. But we all call him Nate."

The name sits in the air and then explodes in my mind. "Nate?" I squeak. My heart pounds. "Nate Miller?"

"That's the one." He jabs the flowers at me. "So, then you must know him, yeah?"

Do I know him? That's a question and a half.

My stomach squirms with the last memory of him. Well, the last real memory. Ever since that day at the mall, I've done my best not to create any more lasting memories with him in them.

Lucky for me, he's been avoiding me just as hard.

Things click into place in my mind, like that moment at the end of a long puzzle where your fingers find pieces without you even looking at them, and they mostly all fit. My heart rises to marathon running levels.

"You alright there, Cat?"

I nod, but it takes all my effort. "I am. Sorry. I think I better get going; they'll be wondering what's taking me so long. Thanks again, Jake. It was really nice talking to you."

"The pleasure is mine." He extends his hand and I take it. Not only would it be super rude to refuse it, but I have to see if anything happens. My stomach ties in knots, the excited kind, not the nervous or disgusted kind this time.

I grip his hand and pump it twice.

"You take care of yourself, Cat, and if you see that knucklehead nephew of mine, you tell him Uncle Jake says to be nice to you." Jake tips his hat with one hand.

"Thanks again, Jake. Bye."

My brain buzzes like I just took up beekeeping. I'm surprised I got any words to come out just now, and even more surprised I can walk away without stumbling over my own feet. At the gate, I pause to look back at Jake, switching out the flowers of his dad's gravestone.

The one Robyn, Penny, and I saw that first day in the graveyard.

The one with all the chrysanthemums.

The one for Nathaniel Maurice Miller.

Acknowledgments

Thank you Publishing Team! As always, it is a pleasure to work with all of you!

Danke to my wondermous family, marveloso ward family, and fantastical friends, who give me a boost when it's needed most. Love your guts!

Merci to Hazel and Rachel, the bestest recipe tryer-outers in the world! Your help is as appreciated as all the encouragement you give me along the way!

Gracias to my Inklettes -Melissa and Jackee - for hanging in there with my randomness and inspiring me to keep going. Yay for Writing Wednesday!

And a huge Shout-out to you beautiful people who read Bake Believe and came back for more! I can't tell you in words how much I appreciate you. If I could, I would make you all ooey-gooey cinnamon rolls!

Bake Happy, my people!

About the Author

Cori Cooper lives in the magical Arizona Mountains, which she's pretty convinced is the setting for all the fairy tales.

Besides writing stories, she adores hanging out with her family, camping, playing board games, sewing, painting, and baking, baking, baking. Like Cat's family, she's positive Cinnamon Rolls fix everything.

Connect with Cori

Instagram, Bookbub, Goodreads, and www.coristories.com

If you liked this book, be sure to check out the others!

The Bake Believe Trilogy
Bake Believe – Bake Off – Bake Happy

The Senior Year at Cromer High Series
*Sage Advice – The Importance of Being Roxie – The Perfect Girl for Kai –
Gavin to the Rescue*

*Ways to Improve Baily
A Tale of Two Crushes
One Quarter Villain
Tears into Gold
Drama, Drama, Drama
Merry's Christmas*